MASSACRE!

As they hid behind the rock, Fanny Kelly held the five-year old Mary, shushing her to keep quiet. She looked at the carnage around her with horror. All the soldiers, and all the men, women and children of the wagon train were dead. Suddenly, she saw a soldier on horseback, galloping toward her. It was Fergus Kelly! Somehow her husband had escaped, and, as the Oglala Sioux were now preoccupied with picking through the wreckage of the wagon, there was a chance she would make it to freedom.

Fanny stepped out from behind the rock, pulling Mary with her. If she could put Mary on the horse, at least the girl would be safe.

"Fergus, stop!" she called out, desperately trying to flag her husband down. "Stop! Take Mary!"

"Get the hell out of my way!" Fergus shouted in a fear-crazed voice. He slapped the reins across the horse's neck and plunged his spurs into its flanks.

Fanny realized that he wasn't going to stop, and she realized, also, that he was going to run down Mary!

"Mary!" she screamed to the little girl as she stood, frozen in terror. Fanny saw the blood spurting from the animal's heaving flanks where the spurs had dug into the flesh, as the horse bore down on the little girl.

"Mary!"

WOMEN WHO WON THE WEST

Lost Lady of Laramie

Lee Davis Willoughby

A DELL/JAMES A. BRYANS BOOK

Published by
Dell Publishing Co., Inc.
1 Dag Hammarskjold Plaza
New York, New York 10017

Dell ® TM 681510, Dell Publishing Co., Inc.

ISBN: 0-440-05034-0

Printed in the United States of America
First printing—May 1982

1

Sergeant Resaca was reading *Harper's Weekly*, sitting in a chair, leaning it back against the wall of the Sutler's store. He chuckled.

"Here, listen to this," he said to Amos Beardsley, the Sutler clerk. He cleared his throat before he read aloud. "This here is from *Humors Of The Day*. 'My notion of a wife at forty,' says this feller, 'is that a man should be able to change her, like a bank-note, for two twenties'." Sergeant Resaca laughed aloud. "Do you get it?" he asked. Change one forty year old woman fer two twenty year old women?"

"I get it," Amos said. He was wiping the counter with a cloth, and he looked through the door of the store, out across the sun-baked quadrangle of Fort Laramie. In the distance, a rifle platoon

5

was listlessly going through its drills, and the barking orders of their platoon sergeant could barely be heard. Beyond the drilling platoon, a dozen or so wagons sat by the far wall, and the members of the small wagon train milled around, the men checking on the loading and the equipment, the women tending to pots suspended over fires, as they prepared the evening meal. Amos saw a beautiful young woman coming toward the store. She was medium in height, very slender, with hair as tawny as a mountain lion's coat in spring. Her eyes were deep, deep blue, and in certain light, they were almost violet. The woman's name was Fanny Kelly, and she was the young wife of Lieutenant Fergus Kelly. Amos, who had been at Fort Laramie since 1859, made a point of appreciating beautiful women, and he was convinced that Fanny was the most beautiful woman ever to grace the post.

"Well, what do you think about it?" Sergeant Resaca wanted to know. "Don't you think it would be a good idea?"

"I'd settle for just one twenty year old, if she looked like the one about to come through the door here," Amos said.

Sergeant Resaca leaned forward so the front two legs of his chair were once again on the floor. "That'll be Lt. Kelly's wife, I reckon," he said. He folded the *Harper's Weekly* shut. "She'll be wantin' her magazine."

"She's entitled to it, she paid her subscription," Amos said.

The door opened and Fanny stepped inside, then smiled at the two men. She fanned herself. "My, how pleasantly cool it is in here, compared to outside," she said.

"Surely you haven't forgotten last winter ma'am?" Sergeant Resaca asked. "It was colder'n blue hell then, and the snow was that deep you couldn't even walk."

"I know, but it's hard to even imagine snow on a day such as this, isn't it?" Fanny asked.

"You'll be wantin' your magazine, ma'am?" Sergeant Resaca said, handing it toward her.

"You may finish reading it if you wish, Sergeant. I know how anxious you and the others out here are to keep up with the war. What is happening?"

Sergeant Resaca opened the magazine to the double truck page at the center. "Here's one of Waud's drawin's, ma'am, of General Barlow chargin' the Secesh at Cold Harbor."

Fanny looked at the large, two page drawing. In the center of the picture soldiers from the North and South were engaged in mortal combat, with flags flying and smoke curling up from the ends of the rifles. In the foreground, and all around, men were lying on the ground, dead and dying. The picture was so realistically done that Fanny could almost hear the rattle of musketry, the shouts of challenge, the cries of pain and fear. She shivered.

"I suppose we don't really know how fortunate we are to be safe here, while the war is still going on back there," Fanny said.

"Fortunate, ma'am?" Sergeant Resaca said forcefully. "You consider it good fortune to be stuck out here at God's end of the world while all the honor and fame is going to those who are finding glory on the battlefield?"

"What glory is there for this poor man?" Fanny asked, pointing to a soldier in the drawing who was on his back, feet akimbo and arms stiffened in death. A rifle with a bayonet pierced his heart, and though Fanny was reasonably certain that the rifle would not really have been left sticking from him, it added a certain gruesomeness to the scene.

"Better to die in battle, than of boredom," Sergeant Resaca said. Then he smiled. "At least we'll be getting a change of scenery when we go to Green River tomorrow, though, eh, Mrs. Kelly?" He smiled broadly.

"You are going then, Mrs. Kelly?" Amos asked.

"Yes. My husband will be establishing a small post at Green River to guard the settlers. I'm rather looking forward to the excitement of the journey, and to spending time with the friends I've made among the members of the wagon train."

"Your husband is certain that it is safe, I suppose, or you wouldn't be going along," Amos said.

The expression on Fanny's face darkened just a bit. "Mr. Beardsley, have you some reason to suspect that the trip may *not* be safe?"

"Oh, no, Mrs. Kelly, of course not," Amos said quickly. "I didn't mean to alarm you. I'm sure it is safe, and I am sure you will enjoy yourself."

"I know I will," Fanny said. She smiled. "I shall especially look forward to traveling with little Mary. She is such a lovely child."

Mary Davis was a five year old girl with long blonde hair and wide, blue eyes. She was the youngest member of the wagon train party, and during her brief stay at Ft. Laramie, she had captured everyone's heart. She had free run of the post, sometimes wandering through the enlisted men's barracks, and other times going into the homes of the officers and their wives. On the evening parade the day before, she had ridden in the saddle with Colonel Albertson, the Post Commander, as he reviewed the troops.

"She is a delightful little girl," Amos said. "The post will not be the same with her gone. And now, Mrs. Kelly, what can I do for you?"

"I was told that you recently received a shipment of ribbons. I wonder if you might have violet ribbon? According to *Harper's*, that is the *couleur de predilection* for the summer."

"It so happens that I do have," Amos said, going to his material and notions shelf. He found a spool of violet ribbon and took it down. "Here it is," he said, handing it to her. "It is a lovely color, Mrs. Kelly. It very nearly matches your eyes."

Fanny blushed and looked down. Her lashes, long and tawny, closed over her eyes as gracefully as if they were fans, held by the daintiest hands.

"I'm sorry, Mrs. Kelly," Amos said. "I meant no disrespect."

"No disrespect taken, Mr. Beardsley," Fanny said easily. She laid a coin on the counter. "Thank you very much." Then she added, pointedly, "for the ribbon."

"Mrs. Kelly, I'll bring the magazine by tonight," Sergeant Resaca promised.

"No need to, Sergeant," Fanny said. "Just bring it with you tomorrow. I may find time to read it during the long journey." She left, tossing a good day over her shoulder as she stepped back out into the sun.

Fanny may have blushed at the comment Amos made, but the embarrassment she felt was more than compensated for by the pleasure the compliment gave her. Fanny seldom received compliments from her husband, no matter how hard she tried to please him. Even if she did something as innocent as make an attempt to make their drab quarters look more attractive, she was accused of being frivolous. It was because she was so starved for recognition from Fergus, that she welcomed it from others when it was offered.

Fanny had only been married to Lieutenant Kelly for nine months. She had been a close friend of Elizabeth Bacon, and when that socially prominent young woman married the dashing young General George Custer, Fanny was one of Libby's bridesmaids. Fergus Kelly was a West Point classmate of Custer's, though Fergus was still only a Lieutenant while Custer had risen to the rank of General. Despite that, Custer still considered Fergus a friend, and Lieutenant Kelly had been a member of Custer's wedding party. That was how Fanny and Kelly met.

The excitement and romance of the six weeks of preparing for the Custer wedding, the obvious happiness and love Libby and Custer felt for each other, and the handsome young Lieutenant Kelly in his dashing uniform, soon so seduced Fanny with its glamor, that her senses were befuddled. Fergus Kelly proposed marriage to her, and she accepted, marrying him in the same Catholic church in which she had been christened as a baby.

But the marriage began to go sour almost from the beginning. When the excitement of the occasion wore off, Lieutenant Kelly found himself with a wife he didn't really want. He considered her excess baggage, and he began to treat her as such.

Fanny tried to preserve the excitement which had led to their marriage in the first place, but she was only one person, and it took both of them if love was to be kindled in this relationship. Fergus Kelly did nothing to sustain the flame, and now, the embers were growing cold.

There had been a time, shortly after they were married when the excitement and passion was still fresh, that the marriage might have worked. Fanny thought she was in love, and she eagerly went to him at night in their marriage bed. There, she discovered that she had a healthy appetite for lovemaking. But alas, even that proved to have an adverse effect, because Fanny's enthusiastic response to him only antagonized Fergus Kelly.

"No decent woman really enjoys this," he told her in disgust one night when he perceived that Fanny *was* enjoying it. From that time on, Lieutenant Kelly was always a little wary of his wife, and he watched her as if she suffered from some terrible social disease which could, at any moment, drive her to an act of insanity.

As a Catholic, divorce was out of the question, so there was nothing Fanny could do but bear with the life she had made for herself. And yet, despite her sour marriage and Fergus Kelly's foul disposition, Fanny Kelly was not a bitter woman. She could have easily succumbed to the travails of an unhappy marriage, but she didn't. She was a vivacious woman who genuinely enjoyed life and liked people. She was quick to smile, and slow to complain, and Lieutenant Kelly, of all who knew her, was the only one who did not recognize what a true gem Fanny was.

Fanny walked across the quadrangle, passed the drilling soldiers, and over to the wagons. Sarah, Mary's mother, and Mary were at the fire, and a couple of other women were sitting in the shade of the wagons, doing needlepoint. She noticed the wheel off one of the wagons, and Matt Parker, the wagonmaster, was overseeing the greasing of the wheel hub.

Matt looked up as Fanny approached the wagons, and he touched the brim of his hat in greeting, then looked back toward his work. Their eyes met, just for an instant, then each looked away from the other . . . but not before Fanny felt a flash of heat, and a degree of guilt over the brief encounter. In fact, Fanny had nothing to feel guilty over, she and Matt had never spoken one word to each other in private, had never exchanged a glance longer than a moment, and yet, there was something about him which affected her. Matt Parker was unmarried, but Fanny was a married woman, and thus had no right to be affected by him.

"Oh, Aunt Fanny, isn't it exciting?" Mary squealed in delight as Fanny approached the camp Though Fanny was not related to the girl, she had taken to calling her Aunt. "We are leaving in the morning!"

"Yes, I know," Fanny said.

"Are you still going to ride in the wagon with me?" Mary asked.

"Of course I am," Fanny said. "Haven't we

planned it? Why, we'll be just like the three musk-eteers; Sarah, Mary and Fanny."

"The three what?" Mary asked, confused by Fan-ny's comment.

Fanny laughed. "Never mind, it's just a story."

"Oh, a story! Will you tell it? Please?"

"Not now, dear," Sarah said. "Let her save it for when we are on the trail."

"Promise you'll tell it then?"

"I promise," Fanny said. "Sarah, look what I bought." She showed the woman her spool of rib-bon.

"Oh, how beautiful!" Sarah said, reaching for it. "Why, see how it matches your eyes! I can't wait to see it on the dress you are making. Lieutenant Kelly will be so pleased to see you in such a lovely thing."

"Yes," Fanny said. "I'm sure he will." She care-fully avoided letting anything in her voice show what she really believed would be Fergus's re-action, for she believed that any problem she had with Fergus was of a most personal nature.

"Will you and the Lieutenant be taking supper with us tonight?"

"No," Fanny said. "We must dine with the Post Commander and his wife."

"Of course you must," Sarah said. "I wasn't thinking." She smiled. "Anyway, we shall have many meals together on the trail. I am so happy that Colonel Albertson is sending a military detail to Green River, for that means we shall be neigh-bors."

"So am I," Fanny said. "It will be great fun."

"Come on," Mary said. "Let me show you where you will ride."

"She's seen where she will ride, dear," Sarah said. "Many times. You've shown her every time she's come over, ever since you learned she would be going with us."

"But I want to show her again," Mary insisted.

"And I should like to see it again," Fanny laughed, and Sarah, shaking her head and smiling at the antics of her daughter, went back to her cooking as Mary, tugging Fanny by the hand, led her to the wagon which would be Fanny's home for the next month.

Fanny spoke to the others as she passed them, then, she followed Mary along the back side of the wagons, between the wagons and the wall of the fort, until they reached the last one.

"You'll ride right here," Mary said. "Daddy will be on a horse, Mama will ride there, and I'll ride in the middle. You will be sitting there, right next to me. Isn't that wonderful?"

"Yes, it is wonderful," Fanny agreed.

"And sometimes, when I get tired, I'll just climb in the back and lie down, like this," she said, and she started to climb the wheel to demonstrate.

"Here, let me help you," a man's voice said, and strong hands lifted Mary up and put her on the wagon.

"Thanks, Mr. Parker," Mary said. "Watch, this is where I'll go when I get tired." Mary disappeared into the wagon.

Fanny looked at Matt Parker. He was a man of the plains, strong, and handsome, with steel-gray eyes, and hair the color of straw in the sun. He was lean, and rawboned, and he moved with the grace of a cat. There was about him a sense of suppressed energy, as if beneath his slow, graceful movements, there lurked the potential for an explosion. This was physically, the closest Fanny had ever been to Matt Parker, and she could feel her skin tingling at the proximity, as if she were wearing one of those electric belts for good health she saw so frequently advertised on the back pages of *Harper's*.

"Mary seems pleased that you are going," Matt said.

"Yes," Fanny replied.

"I'm pleased too," Matt said.

Before Fanny could respond to the comment, Mary's head reappeared. "Did you see me?" she asked. "Did you see where I will go when I get tired?"

"Yes, dear, that's a fine place," Fanny said. "You'd better get down now, I must be getting back. Your father will be hungry, and your mother will want you to help her with supper."

"All right," Mary said. She held her arms out to be helped down and both Fanny and Matt reached for her. They bumped into each other, and Fanny felt her skin burn where it contacted Matt. She moved away, quickly, and let Matt swing the girl back down to the ground.

The evening cannon boomed then, and Mary squealed and laughed, and put her hands over her ears.

"Goodness, is it retreat already?" Fanny said. "I had better get back."

"Uh, uh," Matt said, smiling.

"I beg your pardon?"

"No one can move until the flag is lowered, Mrs. Kelly. You are an officer's wife. You should know that as well as anyone."

"Oh, yes, of course," Fanny said. Her cheeks were burning with embarrassment now, because Matt was right. After the evening cannon, the bugler played retreat, during which time the flag was lowered. The entire garrison was turned out in formation, and they stood at attention, presenting arms, as the flag was lowered. Those soldiers who were not in formation by virtue of a detail or a guard duty, would turn to face the flag and salute, while the music was being played. All civilians on the fort, from the laundresses on soapsuds row, to the children and wives of the soldiers, to the Sutler clerk and the visitors, in this case the members of the wagon train, turned toward the flag and stood in respectful silence until the ceremony was over. The entire ceremony took about four minutes, therefore, for four minutes, Fanny was standing so close to Matt that she could reach out and touch him. When the last note faded into a dying echo, she started for her quarters, moving so quickly as to almost run. She could feel Matt's eyes on her, and the sensation was both thrilling and terrifying.

When Fanny pushed the door of their small house open, she saw her husband standing over the chifferobe, pouring water into a wash basin. His shirt was off and his yellow galluses hung down to each side of his blue trousers, forming a yellow loop with the broad, yellow stripe down the sides of his legs. His pants were stuffed into high, polished boots.

"Where were you during retreat?" Fergus asked. He sat the pitcher down, then began stropping his razor.

"I bought a spool of violet ribbon," Fanny replied. "I was showing it to Mrs. Davis."

Fergus soaped his face, then reached around with one hand to draw his skin taut, while with the other he pulled the razor through the lather. "You'll have time enough to visit with her during the trip," he said. "We are to dine with Colonel and Mrs. Albertson tonight, or have you forgotten?"

"No, I haven't forgotten," Fanny said. "I'll be ready."

"See that you are," Fergus said. He dipped his razor in the water, then raised it back to his face. "I've just learned that someone is going to be promoted to captain next month, and the Colonel will have the final word on who receives it."

"Do you think it will be you?" Fanny asked. She slipped her dress off over her head, then selected the dress she wanted to wear to the dinner.

"And why *shouldn't* it be me?" Fergus asked, snapping the question at her as if she had challenged him. "After all, if that . . . that . . . boy genius, Custer, can make General, then I can certainly make captain. We were in the same class at West Point, and I ranked higher than he did at graduation. But he was chosen to fight in the war while I was forced to come out here." Fergus studied his face in the mirror. He had a square jawline, with a beard so heavy that it required him to shave twice a day. His hair was dark and curly, and he had dark eyebrows over brown eyes. "Custer's rank is only a brevet rank," Fergus went on. "When this war is over, he will be cut back down to size, and if he reverted to captain, then I shall rank over him by virtue of seniority." Fergus chuckled. "Then we shall see what a genius he is." He turned toward Fanny. "Don't wear that dress," he said.

"But it's a new dress I just finished making," Fanny said.

"I want you to wear the red dress."

"No," Fanny said. "I wore it to the Sutler's Dance, remember? Colonel Albertson stared at me all night."

"He liked the dress," Fergus said. "He told me so."

"He didn't like the dress," Fanny said. "He liked where the dress left off. I felt as if his eyes were burning my bosom. I was never so uncomfortable in my life. That dress is too low cut for my taste. I don't care whether the Colonel likes it or not, I won't wear it."

"Being nice to the Colonel might make all the difference in the world as to who gets promoted now," Fergus said.

"Fergus, I will not play the infidel with Colonel Albertson for you."

"I'm not asking you to," Fergus said. "All I'm asking you to do is to make a good impression on him. Be nice to him, that's all."

"You can't be nice to a lecherous old reprobate like Colonel Albertson. I feel sorry for his wife. Why she stays with him, I'll never know. And you, Fergus, I can't believe I am hearing you say this. You are always so concerned that I be the proper lady. You even protested when I went riding last week."

"You were wearing pants, and you rode astride," Fergus said. "Of course I protested, as would any husband who is concerned about his wife's reputation. But you are misunderstanding everything. What you wear in the discreet company of a private dinner, and what you wear on the parade grounds, are two different things. Now, I want you to wear the red dress, and I want you to be nice to the Colonel."

"How nice?" Fanny asked. She didn't like the way the conversation was going, and she was purposely baiting him.

"I want you to be very nice," Fergus said. "Everything is considered when a promotion is at stake. Everything, do you understand? It's not only a man's performance of duty, but other things as well. It is important that the Colonel like you. That's why everything has to be just right."

"And if the Colonel insists upon staring, I am to grant him an eye-ful?"

"You are an attractive woman, Fanny. I would think you would enjoy the appreciative stares of a man."

"What makes you think I would enjoy the lustful gaze of a lecher?" Fanny replied.

"Because I know the kind of woman you really are," Fergus said flatly. "Your true nature is known to me, and has been known to me since the day we were married. You are the type of woman who takes indecent pleasure in pursuits of the flesh."

"Fergus, that isn't fair," Fanny said, stung by his remark. "You are my husband! If I respond to you, it is because . . ."

"It is because you are a woman given to prurient behavior," Fergus said, interrupting her. He laughed, a small, evil laugh. "Do you think I flatter myself that you love me, my dear? I know that your heart is as empty of love for me, as mine is for you. The pleasure you take from me in our nuptial bed, you could take from any man. *Any* man. Now, I'm merely giving you the opportunity to use your wantonness to our advantage. I insist that you wear the red dress, and I will not discuss this matter any further."

"Very well," Fanny said. "I shall wear that dress, and I shall put myself on display for the Colonel. But remember, Fergus, you asked me to do this."

Fanny stepped behind the dressing screen to put on the dress, but before she did so, her anger moved her to an act of impetuousness. She peered over the top of the dressing screen to see if Fergus was watching, and when she saw that he was not, She removed her camisole. When she slipped the dress down over her head a moment later, she pulled it over bare breasts. The neck of the dress was cut so low that the tops of her breasts were clearly visible. Without the restriction of the camisole, more of her breasts were visible, and indeed, if she put her arms together and leaned forward, a careful observer would be treated to a glimpse even of her nipples. Fergus wanted her to be nice to the Colonel, she thought. Well, if she were any nicer, she would be stark naked.　　　　　⌡§

2

Though Fanny had dressed in foolish bravado, now that she was actually in Colonel and Mrs. Albertson's quarters, she felt extremely self-conscious, and, on the pretext of being cold, asked Mrs. Albertson for a shawl that she might put around her shoulders.

"I don't doubt that you are cold, child," Mrs. Albertson said with a disapproving glance at Fanny's dress. She gave Fanny a shawl to wear. Fanny kept the shawl around her shoulders for the whole of the meal, and even when Colonel Albertson made some remark about the heat of the evening, the shawl stayed in place.

After the meal, they adjourned to the parlor where Fanny admired Mrs. Albertson's quilt work, while the men talked.

Colonel Albertson lit his pipe and drew several puffs from it before he spoke. The smoke encircled his head like a wreath, and filled the room with its pungent, but pleasant aroma.

"I'm telling you, this war could be ended in one month," he said, pulling the pipe from his mouth and using the stem of it as a pointer to underscore his words. "One month, and that's a fact."

"But the war is going so well on all fronts, surely it will end within another month or so anyway," Fergus suggested.

"No," Colonel Albertson said. He sucked on his pipe again. "No, it's going to go on, and on for months, maybe even a couple more years. But if Sam Grant would do what I told him to do . . . why he could wind this business up in no time."

"Do you know General Grant very well, sir?"

Albertson chuckled. "I thought I did. But the Sam Grant I knew was a failure in everything he tried to do. His military career was less than brilliant, he failed at farming, he failed at running a store. How he came to be Lincoln's most important General, I don't know. I guess it is just because so many others have failed, that it came Grant's time to try. Who knows, maybe everyone in the army will get an opportunity to be its General. That is, those who are back east. I don't imagine any of us will get that chance."

"You said you had a plan for ending the war, sir. What is it?" Fergus asked.

"Why it's amazingly simple," Albertson said. "I would merely arm every Negro in the south. Every man, woman and child of color would be given a gun and told to turn it against their white masters."

"But . . . . why, that's a brilliant plan, sir," Fergus said. "I'm amazed that no one has thought of it before."

"How would the Negroes know who their enemies are?" Fanny asked. Fergus fixed Fanny with a disapproving stare, for in general, women didn't speak during these times, and specifically, one didn't find fault with the suggestion of a commanding officer when that officer held your promotion in his hands.

"That's a foolish comment," Fergus said.

"No, it's a most astute observation," Colonel Albertson said, holding out his hand to stifle Fergus's protest. "Your wife is intelligent, as well as beautiful, and she does have a point. The only drawback in my plan is the fact that the Negro, with only minimal, animal-like intelligence, has no way of determining who are his friends and who are his enemies. He would most likely be moved to kill all whites, without distinction."

"But . . . . surely, you've thought of a way to handle it?" Fergus suggested.

"I believe I have," Colonel Albertson said. "For some time, this very tendency would work to our advantage. The fact that the Negro would go on a rampage against all whites, would terrify the Southerners. Soon, they would be forced to sue for peace."

"Who would they sue for peace?" Fanny asked. "Your plan makes no account for leadership among the Negroes. Who would speak for them?"

"No one," Colonel Albertson said. "That's the beauty of it, don't you see? They would not be able to sue for peace with the Negroes, because the Negroes are totally unorganized, and have no spokesman with whom negotiations could be conducted. The South would have to come to us and beg for peace."

"But, once we have armed the Negroes, could we then disarm them?" Fanny asked.

"No, my dear, we could not," Colonel Albertson said. He removed the pipe, and smiling, used it again as a means to underscore the point he was about to make. "But what we could do is to ally ourselves with the white southerners, and, together, crush the revolution by exterminating all the Negroes."

"You mean you would first solicit the support of the Negroes, then you would ally yourself with your enemies to make war against our friends?" Fanny asked.

"Well, my dear, enemies and friends are all a matter of politics, are they not?" Colonel Albertson said. "Those who live in the South are our enemies today, but tomorrow, they will be our friends. The Negroes, however, will always be Negroes, today, tomorrow, and forever. And I didn't say make war against, I said exterminate. I would kill them all."

"Yes," Fergus said. "Colonel, there is more brilliance to your plan than meets the eye at first glance. Not only would your plan end the war quickly, but, in the long run, it would eliminate the problem which divided our country in the first place. If there were no Negroes, there would be no Negro problem."

"Precisely," Colonel Albertson said. "A case in point, is the Indian situation back east. Do you think there is any possibility of an Indian attack on New York, Boston, or Philadelphia?"

Fergus laughed. "I hardly think so."

"There is no problem now," Colonel Albertson said. "But two hundred years ago, that was a definite possibility. For then, what is now New York, Boston and Philadelphia, belonged to the Indians. Those Indians were all killed, or, forced to move out. The way I see it, what was successful there, will be successful everywhere. The Negroes should all be killed, or run out, and whatever Indians remain out here should also be killed, or run out."

"But, aren't most of the Indians out here at peace now?" Fanny asked.

"My dear, peace, for an Indian, is merely an opportunity to plan more devilment against the whites. If President Lincoln had any real courage, he would take the mightiest army ever gathered, and use it to ensure peace in this country for all time to come. Eliminate the Negroes and the Indians, I say, and we will enter a millenium of peace."

"I whole-heartedly agree," Fergus said. "And I would deem it an honor, sir, if I could be a part of the holy crusade against the Indians."

"I don't agree at all," Fanny protested. "I think the Negroes and the Indians are the victims of whites, not the oppressors. All this land belonged to the Indian, long before the white man came, and it is we who have disturbed the peace. And the Negroes who are in this country were brought here, in chains, from their own homes, so they could be slaves to the white man."

"Yes, but that is merely the order of things," Colonel Albertson explained. "Consider this. Before the Indians came to this land, it was inhabited by lower orders of animals, was it not? The buffalo, for example. And does the Indian not kill the buffalo for his own use? It is part of God's plan, that the Indian, who is a higher life form than the buffalo, have rights over the buffalo. And, as we are a higher life form than the Indian, it is part of God's plan that we should have rights over the Indian. Of course, this same analogy also extends to the Negro. The Negro was brought here as a beast of burden, like the horse. If a horse goes bad, it is a man's right to eliminate that horse. If many horses went bad, then it would be just as natural to eliminate all of them. The Indian and the Negro are like the buffalo and the horse. They are, in the natural order of things, lower than the white man, and whatever disposition is made of those creatures is right, simply because we choose to do it. That is the law of nature."

"Do you anticipate your plan being adopted?" Fergus asked.

"In so far as the Negroes? No," Colonel Albertson said. "The noble purpose of this war was to free the slaves, or, so our people were told. That provided the rallying cry needed to ensure popular support. I do not believe the people could be so easily changed from the concept of freeing the slaves as a noble cause, to the idea of killing them off as an even more noble cause. The Negro question and the slave issue are too much a part of the fabric of everyday life." Albertson removed his pipe and pointed with it again. "Ah, but the Indian, now. The Indian is still a terrifying creature to the people. They have supported a program of extermination in the past, and I've no doubt but that they will continue to support it in the future."

"Colonel Albertson, I can't believe you mean to systematically *kill* all Indians." Fanny said. "How can you discuss the murder of human beings in such a cold-hearted way?"

"My dear, you must keep things in proper perspective," Colonel Albertson said. "We are now engaged in a great Civil War, in which human beings are being killed every day. I'm talking about white, Christian, English speaking human beings. Our very brothers, and cousins are killing each other, for what they consider a greater good. I am a professional soldier, and this war is being conducted by people of my kind. It is a terrible thing, but it is a thing which has happened many times throughout history. Now, if I, as a soldier, can contemplate killling my brother and cousin, for a greater good, why is it more difficult to consider killing Indians for a greater good? Indians, after all, are not the same as us."

"They are human beings," Fanny protested.

"No," Fergus said, quickly. "They are not human beings. I agree entirely with Colonel Albertson's ideas, and you would too, if you had occasion to come in contact with the Indians."

"I've seen Indians at the trading post," Fanny said.

"My dear, those are tame Indians," Colonel Albertson suggested. "Consider if you will, what it would be like if you were, for some reason, forced to live with the Indians."

"Really, dear, is this conversation necessary?" Mrs. Albertson asked with a shudder. "No decent, Christian woman would ever have to consider such a thing, for it just wouldn't be done."

"Indians are known to set a tremendous store by white women," Colonel Albertson said. "I would imagine a woman as comely as Mrs. Kelly would be of particular value to them."

"Please!" Mrs. Albertson said. "I've told you I don't wish to discuss this. You know about poor Ella Cummings, and how it disturbs me to think of it."

"Of course, my dear," Colonel Albertson said. "I'm sorry, I don't mean to upset you with unpleasant memories. But Mrs. Cummings' case just proves my point."

"Mrs. Cummings?"

Colonel Albertson got up and walked over to the fireplace where he began cleaning the bowl of his pipe, scattering the ashes in the cold fireplace. "Yes," he said. "It's a truly tragic case. Ella Cummings was traveling with her husband and young baby in a wagon, bound for Fort Bridger. There had been no reported trouble with the Indians, but the Indians set upon their wagon none-the-less. Mr. Cummings was scalped by the Indians and left for dead. They started for Mrs. Cummings and she . . . ." Colonel Albertson examined the bowl of his pipe for a long moment before he put it on the mantle, and completed his sentence. "She did the only proper thing she could do under the circumstances. She killed her baby, then she turned the gun on herself. Her husband recovered from his wound, but not from the loss of his wife and child. He has never been the same since."

"You mean . . . . you mean she committed suicide?" Fanny asked.

"Dear, under those circumstances, there is no church on earth which would consider such an act suicide," Mrs. Albertson put in. "Not even the Roman Church. Indeed, it would be a greater act of Christian faith to take your own life under such circumstances, than to . . . . to submit to the animal lusts of those savages."

"I don't know if I could do that," Fanny said. "Commit suicide, I mean."

"Of course you could do it," Fergus said. "It would either be that or become the concubine of some Indian."

"And of course, once a white woman is stained in such a way, she may as well stay with the Indians for the rest of her life," Mrs. Albertson said. "Surely, no such woman would be welcomed back in proper society, nor should she be."

Colonel Albertson smiled. "Well, this is certainly an unpleasant subject of conversation to carry on on the eve of departure for these folks. I'm sorry it got onto this subject my dear. I wouldn't want you to be frightened, for of course, the business with Mrs. Cummings happened seven years ago. There has been little trouble since then, and I certainly don't anticipate any trouble now. If I did, I would send a much larger escort than the ten men your husband is taking with him."

"I would welcome some trouble," Fergus put in. "It would give me an opportunity to put into practice some of your ideas of handling the Indian situation."

"My theory of Indian relations is well known out here," Colonel Albertson said. "And that, more than anything else, has acted as a deterrent against any Indian mischievousness. They know full well what my reaction would be, should they attempt anything. I know you may hope for some action, but I see little likelihood of anything occurring. You may rest assured that your journey and the establishment of a new fort will be routine."

"Well, I for one, am glad of that," Fanny said, smiling in relief. "Not only for myself, but for the others in the party as well. Particularly little Mary. She is such a sweet child, I would die if I thought she was in any kind of danger."

"She is a darling little thing," Mrs. Albertson said. "And you are so good to her, it makes me wonder why you have no children of your own yet."

"Well, we've hardly been married long enough," Fanny said.

"And, I should like to be a bit higher in rank before we start our family," Fergus put in.

"Oh, I think if you were to start now, you would be a Captain by the time the child came along," Colonel Albertson said.

"Do you really think so, sir?" Fergus asked, leaping quickly at the inference.

"Yes," Colonel Albertson said. "I really think so, and after all, I should be in position to know, shouldn't I?" He laughed at his own joke. "So you

can see, Lieutenant, there is really no need for
you to put off having a family any longer. You
can start right away."

As Colonel Albertson spoke the last line, he
stared directly at Fanny, and his eyes grew deep
and hungry. The intensity of his stare made Fanny
extremely uncomfortable, then she realized that she
had allowed the shawl to slip down from her shoulders, so that she was exposing to him, all she had
promised to expose, during her moment of foolish
bravado behind the dressing screen. She looked
down in quick embarrassment, and readjusted the
shawl.

As the light seemed to come on in Colonel Albertson's eyes, it went off in Mrs. Albertson's eyes.
Fanny realized that the Colonel's wife was just as
aware as she, of the Colonel's lustful interest in
her, and though she bore her hurt in silence, she
was hurt nevertheless. Fanny made an extra effort
to be friendly with her, commenting at length about
the quilts the older lady had made during her
years on the frontier, but the damage had been
done. Mrs. Albertson said very little for the rest
of the evening, and Fanny felt guilty for being the
cause, albeit unwillingly. She was glad when Fergus finally stood and begged permission to leave,
using the excuse of getting an early start in the
morning.

Colonel Albertson walked to the front porch
with them, though Mrs. Albertson, saying she had
to put her quilts away, bade them goodnight from
the living room. Albertson stood out on the porch
for a moment longer, talking to Fergus, ostensibly
about the new post, but, Fanny could see that in

the moonlight his eyes continued to stare at her breasts, now more exposed without the shawl. Finally, mercifully, they said goodnight for one last time and they walked back across the moonlit quadrangle to their own quarters.

"Did you hear what the Colonel said?" Fergus asked as they walked across the hard-packed dirt, which was now giving back some of the heat of the day. "He said I would soon be a Captain! That means I'm going to get the next promotion! I know it!" Fergus was trying to speak softly, but he was so excited that he was hard pressed to keep his voice down.

"I'm very glad for you," Fanny said.

"Ten o'clock, and all is well at Post Number One!" a sing-song voice called out from the distant darkness of the stockade wall.

"Ten o'clock, and all is well at Post Number Two!" another voice called.

"Ten o'clock, and all is well at Post Number Three!"

The call for Post Number Four was so close as to startle Fanny, and she saw the soldier standing near the Post's only cannon, under the flagpole, cupping his hand around his mouth as he gave his call.

That call was repeated by Post Number Five, and so on, until finally Post Number Eight, the final Post, gave his call and it was as far-off and plaintive as the first call had been.

Fanny looked around at Fort Laramie. She had once read the history of the post in the Commandant's Log, and she knew that it had originally been erected in 1834 as a trading post, then, was taken over by the Army in 1849, to protect the trail for the gold rush to California.

The structures of the post were built around a parade ground, 200 feet long, by 150 feet wide. The long sides lay north and south alongside the river. The post was surrounded by log palisades, plastered with mud, and standing at least twelve feet high. The north end had the main gate, wide enough to allow the wagons and gun caissons through. The post stockade, post hospital, and post headquarters, were also at the north end. The enlisted men's quarters and soapsuds row were along the western side, the stables and the parking area for wagons along the eastern side, and the officers' quarters were along the south side. The Commander's quarters were adjacent to the headquarters building on the north side, thus the necessity for Fanny and Fergus to walk across the wide, quadrangle to return to their own quarters.

The moon was floating high and silver, so bright that the stars immediately around it were dimmed by its brilliance. The fort was bathed in silver and black, moon glow and shadow.

The fire, by which Sarah had prepared supper for the members of the wagon party, had burned down, and now was but a soft, orange glow. Fanny looked toward it, and saw that many were still around the fire, sitting on the ground, talking quietly among themselves. Tomorrow she would be a part of that group, and she felt a renewed sense of excitement. Whatever concern Colonel Albertson might have put in her head about Indians was gone now, pushed away by the anticipation of the journey.

From a nearby barracks, she heard a soldier's ballad, then, she heard the mournful sound of taps, played by the post bugler, sending the official signal to all the troops that it was time to go to bed. Of all the military rituals, the playing of taps was the one which most affected Fanny, and she never heard it without feeling a slight chill.

Fergus saw Fanny shiver, and he misunderstood the reason.

"I don't blame you for being cold," he said. "Dressed as you are."

"You chose this dress," Fanny said.

"I didn't tell you to wear nothing under it," Fergus said. "But it was a good idea, the Colonel was pleased with it. I could tell. Couldn't you?"

"Yes," Fanny said flatly. "I could tell."

Fergus rubbed his hands together. "A captaincy," he said. "And my own post. I shall name the post Fort Kelly."

The lights began going out in the enlisted men's barracks, and the ballad the men were singing died as the post began to settle down for the night.

Suddenly a man seemed to materialize from the shadows in front of them, and his unexpected appearance startled Fanny. She gasped, and jumped back in fright.

"I'm sorry, Mrs. Kelly, if I frightened you," the man said. It was Matt Parker. "I just wanted a word with your husband."

"Yes, Parker, what is it?" Fergus asked.

"Lieutenant Kelly, I was talking with Sergeant Resaca tonight, and he said that you intended to head straight for the North Platte River, bypassing Fort Halleck."

"That's right," Fergus said. "It'll save us nearly a week of travel."

"But Lieutenant, the Indians have recognized the white man's right to travel the Overland Trail to Elk Mountain. We could go that way without a military escort. The way you propose is going to make us cut right through their holy ground."

"Don't worry about it Parker. You do have an escort."

"If you'll pardon me, Lieutenant, you will have only ten men."

"Ten members of the U. S. 6th Mounted Infantry," Fergus said proudly. "We will be more than sufficient to provide for your safety. Hell, man, I'm taking my wife with me. Do you think I would take her if I thought it unsafe?"

"I don't know," Parker said. "Maybe you just don't know what you are doing, Lieutenant."

"Mr. Parker," Fergus said coldly. "May I remind you that you and your party are here at the sufferance of the U. S. Army? You are here with our permission, and you will travel with our permission, and you will travel only over those routes we authorize for you to travel. You will go the way I have planned, or you will not go at all."

"You are a fool, Kelly," Parker said, and, something about the tone of his voice caused Fanny to feel another chill. But this wasn't the same kind of chill she had felt with the playing of taps. This was the kind of chill her father used to say meant that "Someone was walking on her grave."

3

THE FIRST PINK fingers of dawn painted the Eastern sky as the wagon train pulled out of Fort Laramie. Fanny turned in her seat and looked back toward the place which had been her home for the last few months. How barren, how lonesome it looked now, standing all alone on the prairie. And yet, she was now bound for an even more lonely existence.

"Don't worry, my dear," Sarah said, reaching over to pat Fanny's hand, reassuringly. "We won't have time to be lonely where we are going."

Fanny was startled, because Sarah's comment was as if she had read Fanny's mind. Sarah laughed. "You are wondering how I knew what you were thinking, aren't you? It isn't so mysterious. I imagine we all are thinking about how far away from civilization we will be."

"Doesn't it frighten you a little?" Fanny asked. "The idea of being so lonely, I mean."

"No," Sarah said. "I have my family with me, Will and Mary. And what more company could a woman want? But of course, you know that. You have your young Lieutenant."

"Yes," Fanny said. "Of course."

Fanny tried to get comfortable on the hard, board seat of the wagon, but that wasn't possible. Sarah was driving the wagon, and Sarah's husband, Will, was riding at the point alongside Matt Parker. Just behind Matt and Will, Fergus rode at the head of his small band of soldiers.

Mary, who had been so excited about riding with Fanny, was now back in the wagon, sound asleep.

"Bless her heart," Fanny said, looking toward the young, sleeping girl. "Look how peaceful she is."

Sarah laughed. "She must have asked me a dozen times to be sure and wake her when we started. I tried, but she just couldn't stay awake."

"She's better off sleeping. She will have enough riding in a wagon before this trip is finished," Fanny said.

"I imagine we all will," Sarah said.

"It's a shame the railroad doesn't come out this far," Fanny observed.

Sarah laughed. "If it did, we wouldn't be here. The attraction this place holds for Will is in the elbow room he can find."

"He should have plenty of that," Fanny said. By now the sun was a full disc up over the eastern horizon behind them, and the vastness of the land before them was vividly evident. The plains stretched out in folds of hills, one after another; as each ridge was crested, another was exposed, and beyond that, another still. The dusty grass gave off a pungent smell when crushed by the horses' hooves and wagons' wheels.

The golden light of morning soon gave way to the white brightness of day, and the heat began to build up, until Fanny could see it rising from the ground in shimmering waves. Mary woke up, was excited for a while over the prospect of actually being under way, then, even her spirit began to wilt under the ceaseless sun.

The wagon train pushed hard all day, and by nightfall they had covered twenty-five miles. Matt found a good campsite beside a fast-flowing stream of water and the horses were unhitched, watered, then secured inside a hasty remuda. The wagons were formed in a circle, and the members of the wagon train set up their camp just inside.

"You are going to fix beans?" Fanny asked. "But won't that take a long time?"

"Not if you're smart," Sarah explained. "You see, I sealed them in this pot to soak before we left this morning. Now they are all swelled up, plump and tender, and ready to cook."

"I'm going to have to learn a few tricks like that," Fanny said.

"I'll tell you a good trick for washing clothes," Matt said. He was sitting nearby, drinking a cup of coffee.

"*You* know a trick for washing clothes?" Fanny asked, surprised by Matt's comment.

"Sure," Matt replied easily. "I don't have a wife to wash my clothes for me, and I do wear clean clothes occasionally."

"All right, let's hear it," Fanny asked.

"It's simple," Matt said. "All you need is a good, tight bag which will hold water. Put water and soap in the bag, put in your dirty clothes, and tie the bag to the saddle of your horse. The movement of the horse during the day will keep the water moving around, and at the end of the day your clothes are clean. All you need do is wring them out and lay them out on the ground to dry in the night air. The next morning you have clean clothes. He smiled. "Sometimes they are a little damp. It is best if you can let them dry in the sun."

"Why, thank you, Mr. Parker," Sarah said. "I do believe that is a fine idea. It should work in a wagon as well as on a horse, shouldn't it?"

"If you get enough motion in the wagon to agitate the water, it should work fine," Matt suggested.

Sarah and Fanny both laughed. "I'd say there is enough movement and bouncing, wouldn't you?" Sarah said.

"Yes, I guess there would be at that," Matt said, smiling in amusement at Sarah and Fanny's reaction.

"What kind of bag do you use that will hold water?"

"I use the lining of a buffalo stomach," Matt said. "But you could use a washtub, just as you normally use. You could just set it in the floor of the wagon."

"Yes," Sarah said. "I suppose I could at that.

Thank you, Mr. Parker. I imagine your little trick will save me some time."

Will and Fergus came into the camp then. Fergus had posted the guards, and Will, who was responsible for the animals of the wagon train, had been seeing to the horses. Will sniffed the air.

"It's already beginning to smell good," he said. "Or else I am already very hungry."

"It is said that hunger is the best chef," Matt said. He chuckled. "When I cook for myself, I must say that hunger is always the most effective spice."

"I can't believe that, Mr. Parker," Fanny said. "After your hint on how to wash clothes, I'll bet you are equally at home as a cook."

Fergus was pouring himself a cup of coffee, and he looked up and laughed. "A hint on how to wash clothes?" he said.

"Yes," Sarah replied. She didn't catch the mocking inflection in Fergus' voice, and she was anxious to sing the praises of their wagonmaster. "Mr. Parker has a most ingenious way of keeping his clothes clean. He puts them in a . . . ."

"I have a better way of doing it," Fergus interrupted. "It's called letting a woman do what is a woman's work."

"Suppose there are no women?" Matt asked, remaining unruffled by Fergus' barbed comment. "Does the woman's work go undone?"

"I wouldn't know about that, Mr. Parker," Fergus said. "As an officer and a gentleman, I have never found myself in a situation which required me to demean myself in such a way. But of course, you, being a civilian, safely away from the war and any possible danger to your own person, wouldn't understand the significance of that fact."

"I wasn't always a civilian, Lieutenant Kelly," Matt said easily. He walked over to the fire and stirred it up, then tossed a couple of logs onto it. "I was in the army for a while."

"Which did you do, Mr. Parker?" Fergus asked. "Take your bounty, serve ninety days and then leave, or did you desert?"

"No," Matt said easily. "I resigned my commission."

"You resigned your commission? Are you trying to tell me you were an *officer*?"

"Yes," Matt said. "I was a Colonel of Cavalry on General Meade's staff."

"You fought with General Meade?" Will asked. "Yes."

"Were you at Gettysburg?"

"Yes," Matt said.

Will stared morosely into his cup for a moment. "My kid brother was killed at Gettysburg," he finally said. "He fought in the Sixth Ohio. I know there is little chance that you knew him, as many man as were engaged in that battle. His name was George. George Daniel Davis. He was a Sergeant."

"I'm sorry," Matt said. "I didn't know him. My own brother was killed at that battle as well. Martin Parker; a seventeen year old, head-strong young man who wouldn't listen to anyone, and who was, possibly the bravest young man I have ever known."

"Is that why you quit?" Fergus asked. "Because your brother was killed at Gettysburg?"

"Yes," Matt said. He was standing over the fire

now, staring into its dancing, orange and yellow flames. His eyes were reflecting the fire, but as Fanny looked into them, she saw much deeper than that. She saw his soul.

"That's what happens in war, Mr. Parker," Fergus said easily. "Men get killed. And everyone who gets killed is someone's son, husband, father, or brother. One can not have glory without paying the price."

"There is no such thing as glory in war, Lieutenant," Matt said. "And the price extracted from me was too dear."

"Do you think you are the only man who lost a brother in that battle?" Fergus mocked.

"No," Matt replied. "But you see, Lieutenant, my brother rode for J.E.B. Stuart. He was a Confederate, and . . . ."

"Oh, Mr. Parker, no," Fanny suddenly said. "Oh, I'm so sorry."

"Sorry? What are you talking about?" Fergus asked.

"Don't you understand?" Fanny said. "Mr. Parker had to kill his own brother."

Matt looked at Fanny in surprise and admiration for her perception.

"What? Is that true, Mr. Parker?" Will asked.

"Yes," Matt said tightly. He finished the coffee, then tossed the grounds onto the fire. "My headquarters were well behind the main line of battle. We had been in hard fighting throughout the day, and I had just returned to my camp when, from out of nowhere, a band of Confederate raiders burst upon us. There weren't more than thirty of them, what they were doing that far behind our lines I'll never know. Perhaps they were on a scouting patrol when they suddenly discovered themselves upon us. When we saw them, and realized the hopelessness of their situation, we called upon them to surrender. Instead, they chose to attempt to fight their way back to their own lines. They were hopelessly outnumbered and we made rather quick work of them. One of the riders saw my tent, and perceiving it to be the headquarters, he tried to make his sacrifice count for something. He rode toward me, brandishing his sword. Evidently he was out of ammunition by then. I saw him out of the corner of my eye, and I turned and fired. I saw the bullet hit him in the chest, and I saw the look of surprise and pain on his face. Then, I saw the other look. The look of forgiveness as we recognized each other at about the same time. When I realized what I had done, that I had shot my own brother, I threw my pistol down and ran to him, just as he was falling from his horse. I held him in my arms as he breathed his last, and do you know what was the last thing he said? His last words were: "Are you proud of me, Matt? Didn't I put up one hell of a fight?" Matt turned and walked away from the fire, then sat on a rock nearby. "There's your glory, Lieutenant Kelly. My own brother, whom I had just shot, lay dying in my arms, and he wanted to know if I was proud of him."

"You were merely doing your duty," Fergus said. "And as an officer, you should have realized that duty transcends all. You were wrong to resign your commission. In fact, I would even go so far as to say it was a cowardly thing to do."

"Fergus!" Fanny said sharply. "How can you say such a thing?"

"He can say such a thing, because he doesn't know what he is saying," Matt said. "And I make allowances for children and fools."

"That is the second time you have called me a fool, Parker," Fergis said in a menacing tone of voice. He started to move his hand toward his pistol. "See to it that you don't make that mistake again."

"Lieutenant, don't threaten me by moving your hand toward your pistol," Matt said easily. "Do you really think you could open the flap which covers your pistol, and still draw it, before I could draw mine? I wouldn't have to be very good to beat you under those circumstances, now would I?"

"Gentlemen, please!" Will Davis put in quickly. "Do you realize what you are doing here? I hired you, Mr. Parker, to lead us safely to Green River. And you, Lieutenant Kelly, have been assigned by the Army to see to our safety. But at the moment, it would appear that the greatest danger we face is your inability to get along with each other. Now I must insist that this animosity which has developed between the two of you be put aside until our train arrives safely at its destination."

"You are quite correct, Mr. Davis," Matt said. He stood up and bowed toward the ladies. It was really no more than a dip of his head, but it was so graciously done that it could have well been a sweeping bow in a court of Europe. "Ladies, if you will forgive me? And, Lieutenant, I am sorry if I have offended you."

Matt turned and walked away from the fire,

moving away from the bubble of light and into the shadows of the night.

"Well," Fergus said a moment later. "If Mr. Parker can control his arrogance, I can certainly keep my contempt for him in check. You need not worry about me breaking the peace."

"Thank you, Lieutenant," Will said. He looked at the faces of all who were gathered around the fire and saw that they had become strained by the tension of the moment. He smiled, and rubbed his hands together. "What do you say we have a hoedown after we eat?"

"Oh, yes!" Mary squealed, clapping her hands in delight. She had not fully understood what was going on between Fergus and Matt, but even she had felt the tension, and now she was happy because she knew that whatever it was, it could be swept away by the music and dancing of a hoedown.

After Fanny ate, she washed out her plate, then went back to the beanpot and filled it again.

"Eating on the trail does give one an appetite, doesn't it?" Will said, laughing, as he passed by with his fiddle, headed for the area which had been cleared for the hoedown.

"Yes, I suppose it does," Fanny replied. She put a couple of biscuits alongside the beans and bacon, then, on second thought, added another spoonful to the original portion.

"Here," Sarah said, handing a hot pepper to Fanny.

"What is this?" Fanny asked.

"He likes a hot pepper with his beans," Sarah said quietly. "You are taking these to Mr. Parker,

aren't you? You don't really expect me to believe
you are going to eat all that?"

Fanny looked around in quick embarrassment,
and was relieved to see that no one had overheard
Sarah, or in fact, was even paying attention to
them. They were all interested in the upcoming
hoedown.

"It's just that I feel guilty about Fergus baiting
him so," Fanny said. "He drove Mr. Parker away,
and I know Mr. Parker must be hungry."

"I understand, dear, you don't have to apologize
or explain," Sarah said. "You'll find him just beyond that large rock over there." She pointed to
a large boulder which was some fifty yards beyond
the circle of wagons.

Fanny looked around.

"Lieutenant Kelly is with the soldiers," Sarah
put in, and Fanny blushed, because once again
Sarah had, intuitively, perceived Fanny's thoughts.

"Thanks," Fanny said, without any effort to deny
that she was concerned about Fergus seeing her
going to Matt Parker.

The rock outcropping was much further from
the wagons than Fanny had realized, and about
halfway there, she began to have some misgivings
about her mission. Perhaps it was dangerous to be
this far away at night, in such unknown territory.
She quickened her gait, and was glad when she
reached the rocks a few moments later.

"Mr. Parker?" she called. There was no answer,
so she called again, a little louder. "Mr. Parker?"

There was still no answer, and now Fanny began to grow a little frightened. Nearby an owl
called, and though she had heard many owls in

her lifetime, this one startled her by its nearness, and the haunting sound of its call.

"Matt?" Fanny called. "Matt, are you here?"

"I'm here," Matt said. Matt laughed softly. "I wanted to see what you would do if I didn't answer right away. You called me Matt, so it was worth the wait."

"You, you should have made your presence known."

"I'm sorry, really I am," Matt said. "I didn't mean to frighten you. What brings you out here?"

"I thought you might be hungry," Fanny said. She showed him the plate.

Matt smiled broadly, and Fanny could see his teeth gleaming brightly in the moonlight. "Ah, you don't know how good that looks to me," he said. "I made such a show of leaving that I entirely forgot that I hadn't eaten yet. And I would have felt foolish going back." He reached for it. "And a hot pepper too? I swear, Fanny, you are being too good to me."

When Fanny heard Matt use her first name, she looked down in quick embarrassment. "I, I just thought you might be hungry, that's all," she mumbled again, then she turned to leave.

"Not so fast," Matt said. "You should be properly thanked for this."

Before Fanny realized what was about to happen, Matt reached for her, and grabbed her by the shoulders. "And there's only one way to thank a beautiful woman," he said.

"What?" Fanny asked in sudden alarm. "What are you doing?"

"I'm kissing you, Fanny, the way you need to be kissed," Matt said.

Matt pulled her to him, crushing her lips with his. His arms wound around her tightly, causing her body to mold against his. At first, Fanny struggled against Matt, both out of anger, and fear. But the harder she struggled, the more determined Matt became to hold her, until finally Fanny abandoned the struggle and let herself go limp in his arms.

The moment Fanny abandoned the struggle, a sweet, though forbidden pleasure began to overtake her. Matt's lips opened on hers and his tongue pushed into her mouth, thrilling Fanny with its insistent boldness, yet shocking her, because she was a married woman. Despite her surprise and indignation over Matt's total disregard for her marital status, she uttered a moan of passion. Her blood ran hot, diffusing her entire body with its heat.

Fanny was certain that they would be discovered at any moment, and she tried to resist the floodtide of pleasure she felt from the kiss, so she could gain the strength to break away from the kiss and walk away. But if Fanny was concerned, Matt was not, and he kissed her with slow, hot lips, taking his leisure as if only the two of them existed, and he had all the time in the world. He showed not the slightest nervousness, nor tension, nor uneasiness. When finally he broke off the kiss, he held her for a moment longer and looked at her with a slight smile of amusement on his face.

"Now," Matt said. "You've been kissed the way you should be kissed."

Fanny looked at him with her senses reeling. Finally, sanity returned and she realized with a start what she had done. Her cheeks flamed in embarrassment, and she felt a rush of anger. She slapped Matt.

"Who do you think you are?" she demanded. "I am a married woman! You can't just make love to me at your pleasure."

"My dear, we didn't make love," Matt said, still smiling that same, insolent smile of amusement. "We only kissed. Had we made love, it wouldn't have been just my pleasure, but your pleasure as well. You would enjoy it fully as much as I."

"You are an extremely vulgar and conceited man, sir," Fanny said. "And you have no right to take such liberties, either with my person, or my emotions."

"Someone needs to, Fanny," Matt said. "You are too spirited and too beautiful a girl to be married to a man who is as unappreciative of you as Fergus Kelly."

"Sir, you . . . . you assume a great deal," Fanny said. She turned then, and started back toward the wagons, walking with a quick, nervous stride. How dare he treat and talk to her in such a way? And yet, even as those angry thoughts were born in her mind, she found that the excitement he had engendered in her was many times greater than any displeasure over his actions.

Fanny walked back through the darkness toward the wavering yellow light of the campfire. She was less than halfway back, when a man suddenly appeared in the darkness. She gasped, and took a quick, frightened step, backward.

"Did I frighten you, my dear wife?" Fergus' voice asked sarcastically.

"Yes," Fanny said. She put her hand to the neck of her dress.

"Odd, isn't it, that a woman should be frightened by her own husband."

"You startled me, that's all," Fanny said. "I didn't see you in the dark, and it is an unnerving experience."

"Especially as you have just been doing something you shouldn't, eh, Fanny?" Fergus taunted.

"Doing something I shouldn't? Fergus, I have no idea what you are talking about."

"I'm talking about adultery," Fergus said. "You have been with Matt Parker, have you not?"

"No," Fanny said. "I mean, yes, I have been with him, but not in the way you say. I took him his dinner, that's all."

"How nice of you," Fergus said. "It must have been a most pleasant, or should I say, pleasurable, meeting.

"Fergus Kelly, how can you suggest such a thing?" Fanny asked, in a hurt tone.

"Oh, that's very good, my dear," Fergus said. "You had just the right amount of tremor in your voice. One might almost suspect that you are the injured party here, and not I."

4

"LISTEN," THE OLD CHIEF said, "and I will tell you the story of the Oglala Sioux."

Those who were around him, the men of the council, the warriors, and those who would be warriors, drew closer to hear his words. He was Ottawa, Chief of the Oglala Sioux, and he had the respect and admiration of everyone in his tribe. The women and the children grew quiet, not only because it was forbidden to make noise while stories were being told around the campfires, but because they knew it would be a good story, and it filled them with excitement to hear it.

"Once there was a young man," Ottawa said. He held up his finger and wagged it slowly back and forth. "He was not an Oglala, he was not a Hunkpapa, he was not a Minneconjou, he was not a

Sans Arcs, he was not a Santee. He was not even a Sioux."

"What was he, *unci*?" one of the children asked, using the word for grandfather.

"He was before," Ottawa said. "He was in the time of the beginning, before the winter-counts, when men could speak with the animals, and the spirits of the earth, fire, wind and water. Now the young man did not know this was unsuual, because he had always been able to do so and it seemed a natural thing for him to do. Then, one day as he stood watching an eagle fly, he thought that perhaps he would try and fly too, so he leaped into the air and he beat his arms like the wings of an eagle, but he could not fly and he fell to the ground . . . ker-whump."

Ottawa made the kerwhump sound in such a way as to amuse the children, and they all laughed.

"Foolish one, you cannot fly, the eagle taunted, and he soared through the air and laughed at the young man.

"Then the young man saw a coyote running swiftly, so swiftly across the plains, and he ran after the coyote, thinking to catch him, but he couldn't. 'Foolish one, did you think you could run as swiftly as I?' the coyote mocked.

"Then the young man saw a bear. The bear smelled honey in a comb which was high in a tree and the bear, with his great strength, pushed the tree over so he could have the honey. The young man was very impressed with the bear's great strength, so he, too, tried to push over a tree, but he could not. The bear, who was enjoying his honey, saw the young man, and he teased the young man, and called him a weakling, and told him he had no business trying to push over a mighty tree in the first place."

Ottawa shook his head sadly, and clucked his tongue.

"What did the young man do next, grandpa?"

"Oh, the young man felt very bad," Ottawa said. "He tore out his hair, and he gashed his face with rocks, and he cried out in anger and in despair. 'I cannot fly like the eagle,' the young man said. 'I cannot run as swiftly as the coyote, nor do I have the strength of the bear. Why am I on earth if I cannot do any of these things?'

"Suddenly, the young man heard a strange sounding voice, carried on the wind. 'Go—to—the—mountain', the voice said." Ottawa made his voice wail in a terrible sound and the smaller children were frightened. Some cried and others clutched the hands of their mothers tightly. The older children were frightened too, but they welcomed the fright because it made them feel brave to listen to the story without betraying their own fear.

"The young man climbed the mountain," Ottawa went on. "And as he climbed it, the voice in the wind continued to speak to him. 'You are a worm,' the voice in the wind said. 'You are a blade of grass. You are an ant, a mote of dust. You are nothing. You cannot fly, you cannot run swiftly, you have no strength. Climb to the top of the mountain.'

" 'Why should I climb to the top of the mountain?' the young man asked.

" 'You will know why when you get there,' the voice in the wind answered.

"The young man began to do as he was instructed, but he did so with a heavy heart. He believed that the voice instructed him to climb the mountain so he could jump off and kill himself. He was frightened and sad, but he felt that he must do what the voice told him to do."

"And did he climb to the top of the mountain and jump off, grandpa?"

Ottawa held up a finger, as if to caution the young questioner against impatience, then he went on with his story. "As the young man climbed a strange thing happened. The sun beat down upon him, and it made him very hot. As he grew hot, he began to sweat. When he sweat, all the poisonous thoughts passed from his body. He was no longer frightened, or confused, or ashamed. Only reason remained in his body, and with reason, the young man could think quite clearly. It is true, he thought, he could not fly like an eagle, but an eagle could not use his wings as hands. It is true, he could not run as swiftly as a coyote, but a coyote could not walk upright. It is true, he did not have the strength of the bear, but the bear could not make poems and music, nor dance to the rhythm of the drums. When the young man reached the top of the mountain he thought of all this, and he spread his arms wide and looked out over the valley, far below.

" 'Why don't you jump?' a woman's voice asked, and the young man looked around and there he saw *Ptesanwin.*"

"Buffalo Cow Woman!" one of the children said,

for Ptesanwin was the most sacred of all the legends of the Oglala.

"'No,' the young man said. 'I will not jump. I am not a worm, I am not a blade of grass, I am not an ant or a mote of dust. I am a man!'

"'Now,' Ptesanwin said. 'Now, your period of trial is over. Now you have the *woksapa*, the sacred wisdom, and from this day forth you will be the master over all the animals and over all the things of nature. You shall have a name and your name shall be called Oglala, and your people shall be many, and they will be mighty hunters and warriors.'

"'But wait,' the young man called. 'Wait, I have questions to ask. There are may things I do not know. How will I learn what is needed to know to be worthy of the fine name you have given me?'

"'I have given you the gift of *woksapa*, it is for you to acquire the way to use it.'

"'But how shall I do that?'

"'As you climbed the mountain you were puzzled,' Ptesanwin said. 'But you labored as you climbed, and as you labored, you began to sweat. As you sweat, you gained wisdom. Now, I tell you, when you wish to attain widom, you need only to build a sweat lodge. You will call the sweat lodge *Initi*, and when you wish to attain great *woksapa*, go into the *Initi* and it will come to you.'

"And that is why, even today, wise men use the *Initi*," Ottawa said. "The young man left the mountain and returned to the valley below. When he returned, he discovered that all the animals had been struck dumb as their punishment for mocking Oglala. The animals could no longer speak to him.

They couldn't even speak to each other, and every animal had to go for all time after that, unable even to speak to their own kind."

"Is that why men can speak to each other, but animals cannot speak?"

"Yes," Ottawa said. "For it was intended for man to rule over the animals."

"What happened to Oglala after that?" another child asked.

"Oglala took a wife and had many children, and the children took wives and had many children, and those children took wives and had many children. I am the child of one of those children, just as you are the children of my children. And that is the story of the Oglala Sioux."

After Ottawa finished his story, there were others who told stories as well. If the story was to be a story of bravery in battle, the one who spoke would walk over to the lodge pole and strike it with his coup stick, then everyone would know that he was going to tell a story of an enemy killed in battle. In such stories, the enemy warriors were always brave and skilled, because that made the warrior's own exploits all the more greater.

Not all of the stories were of enemies killed in battle. Some of the stories were of hunting exploits, and some told of things which had happened in the time of their father's father's father's, which had been handed down through the generations to be preserved as part of their history.

One man who had listened intently to many of the stories was Jumping Bear. Jumping Bear was the nephew of Ottawa, though, as his father had been killed in battle many years before, Ottawa was more a father than an uncle. Jumping Bear was a handsome man with a broad chest and powerful arms and strong legs. His eyes were clear and his teeth were good, and though he had been in many battles and had fought bravely, his face was unmarked by scars, and his nose was not disfigured by broken bones.

Jumping Bear had listened to all the stories, but he had listened with particular interest to the story told by Ottawa. Jumping Bear had heard it many times before, but this time it was especially significant to him, because he was troubled, and when he was troubled, he took comfort in the old things.

Ottawa had watched Jumping Bear all during the story telling time, and when the others left, and Jumping Bear himself got up to go, Ottawa called out to him, and patted the ground beside him, and invited Jumping Bear to sit near him.

"I told the story of Oglala for you, Jumping Bear," Ottawa said.

"For me, Uncle? Why would you tell the story for me?"

"Because you are troubled. I do not know why you are troubled. I thought perhaps the wisdom in the story might be of help to you."

"Yes, Uncle, I believe it will be," Jumping Bear said. "And I thank you for providing me with advice in such a way."

"What is it that troubles you?"

"I have had a strange dream," Jumping Bear said.

"Many men have strange dreams, and the dreams do not trouble them."

"But I have had the same dream for three nights in a row."

"Oh," Ottawa said. "Then that is reason for being troubled, for to dream the same dream three nights in a row is surely a sign. What is the dream?"

"In my dream, I see the wagons of the white man. The wagons are disturbing the ancient holy grounds, and one among them, a soldier chief, feels no sorrow for his sin. He is an evil man who wishes to kill all Indians."

"Ho, then clearly your dream is a warning," Ottawa said. "A sign of danger. But because it is a sign, we can stop the danger. We will attack the wagon train and kill this soldier chief."

"No," Jumping Bear said. "That was what I wanted to do, but a white horse with eyes the color of clouds at sunset, appeared before me, and the horse asked me not to kill all the white men."

"The horse spoke to you?"

"Yes," Jumping Bear said.

"Hmmm," Ottawa said. He had been eating a piece of meat, and now he wiped the grease off his hands by running his hands through his hair. "It is very powerful medicine when an animal speaks in a dream."

"But what does the medicine mean?"

"I don't know," Ottawa said. "But there is one way you can find the answer to the questions which puzzle you."

"Do you think I should go into the mountains and build a sweat lodge?" Jumping Bear asked. "Should I go into an *initi* to seek *woksapa*?"

"I think you must. For if you do not, the medi-

cine of the white horse with the strange eyes will
be lost."

"Thank you, uncle," Jumping Bear said. "I have
been puzzled about what I should do, but you
have helped me decide."

Jumping Bear stood up then, and he tossed a
pinch of the dirt upon which he was sitting into
the fire so that any of his soul which may have
escaped as he sat there, would be carried into the
heavens on the smoke of the fire, and not be
washed away and lost by the next rain. Tomorrow,
Jumping Bear would rise before the sun, and he
would go off by himself to seek whatever answers
would come to him in the sweat lodge.

One-Who-Waits was just beyond the tipi while
Jumping Bear and Ottawa were having their conversation, and he remained very quiet and strained
to hear what they were saying. One-Who-Waits
was also a nephew of Ottawa, but he was not a
favored nephew as was Jumping Bear, and One-
Who-Waits had spent most of his life jealous of
his more favored cousin. In fact, his very name
came from a lifetime of being selected second, and
now his entire personality had been twisted by
that fact. He wanted to change his name, but he
couldn't do it unless he committed a brave deed
which could earn that right for him. And now,
Jumping Bear may have just provided him with
the opportunity to commit that brave act. For if,
as Jumping Bear's dream implied, there was a
wagon train crossing the sacred ground of the
Sioux, then One-Who-Waits would lead a war par-

ty after it, and he would attack it, and kill everyone on the train.

One-Who-Waits smiled at the thought. He would be waiting no longer, for while Jumping Bear was sitting in the *initi*, One-Who-Waits would be leading men into battle. Now, he had only to go through the village and find warriors who would go with him.

If a white man had seen One-Who-Waits making preparations for the battle, he wouldn't have understood one thing that was going on. The white men had a compulsion for making chiefs of the Indians; war chiefs, council chiefs, high chiefs and sub-chiefs. Some soldiers had joked that all Indians were chiefs, and though they didn't realize it, they were much closer to the truth than they imagined. Indians had no elected chiefs, nor did a chief obtain his position by right of inheritance. The only criterion for being a chief was leadership. If one could get others to follow, he was a chief. If they would not follow, he was not a chief, and it was that simple. One-Who-Waits, by persuasion, promises, deals and threats, was able to convince over 100 warriors to agree to follow him in his planned attack on the wagon train the next morning, and therefore he was, by every definition of the term, a war chief.

Jumping Bear was not aware of the planned attack. He had gone immediately to sleep after his discussion with Ottawa, and now, with the position of the stars indicating that there were still three hours of darkness left, Jumping Bear got up and left the village, bound for the mountains where he would build the sacred *initi*.

One-Who-Waits was waiting again, this time for Jumping Bear to leave. He did not want to leave with his war party before Jumping Bear was gone because he was afraid that Jumping Bear would either talk the other warriors into abandoning the plan, or lead them himself. Therefore, when One-Who-Waits saw Jumping Bear's horse disappear over the far ridge, he smiled because it meant that he could put his plan into effect without fear of interference. Quickly, One-Who-Waits slipped through the village, entering the tipis and hogans of the warriors who had agreed to go with him, waking them with gentle nudges, cautioning them to quiet, then slipping out of their tipi to go into the next one. After a short time, all of his warriors were mounted in the center circle of the village, and One-Who-Waits sat on his horse before them. He held up a feathered lance, then let out a shout of pride and defiance, as he urged them on.

Now the whole village was awakened, and they came to the doors of their homes and looked out at One-Who-Waits who was brandishing the feathered lance of leadership. One-Who-Waits smiled proudly, and he felt a stirring of power in his heart, and he called out.

"Come, if you are brave and would defend our sacred ground against the invasion of the *Toka*! Come, join me if you are a warrior . . . . stay behind if you are a woman or child!"

One-Who-Waits' last, defiant challenge did just what he wanted it to do. It goaded others, those who would not have normally come, into joining the war party, simply because to stay home now would be considered cowardly. From the 100 who had originally agreed to ride with One-Who-Waits, the number had grown to well over two hundred. Two hundred who were ready to ride against the *Toka,* or enemy of the Oglala.

A horse blew, and stamped his foot, and the sound awakened Fanny. She had been asleep in the blankets on the ground beneath the Davis wagon. Fergus was in the blankets beside her, and she could hear his easy, steady breathing.

Fergus had come to her last night, after having accused her of committing adultery with Matt Parker. For some strange reason, which Fanny couldn't fathom, Fergus seemed randier last night than he had ever been before. It was as if he grew excited over the possibility of another man making love with his wife, and it drove him to the heights of animal passion.

Fanny, because she was a woman with a passionate nature, was able to enjoy the raw, physical pleasure of the episode, but underneath it all, there was a feeling of guilt which nagged at her. How could she enjoy the physical aspect of making love, when she knew that she didn't love her husband, and he didn't love her? And if Fergus was fantasizing last night that Matt Parker had made love to Fanny, Fanny was fantasizing that Fergis Kelly *was* Matt Parker. His embrace had been almost cruel in its demand for gratification, but Fanny didn't struggle against it. Instead she closed her eyes at the critical moment, feeling the tremors of desperate longing she had, not for him, but for Matt Parker, and with such thoughts, allowed her body to be consumed by the fire which blazed its rapture over her.

Now, lying on the blankets in the early morning hours, she thought of the night before, and she felt the heaviness of love-making still with her. She heard someone stirring nearby and she turned her head to see. It was Matt Parker, saddling his horse!

For one, wild moment, Fanny thought of getting out of her bed and going to him. No one else was awake yet, they could have several wonderful moments alone together to . . . . to . . . . to what? she asked herself. She closed her eyes and bit her lip, trying to fight back the wicked thoughts which preyed upon her mind.

Fanny lay that way for several minutes, then the sounds of the waking camp awakened Fergus, and he groaned once, then, with a sigh, sat up and ran his hand through his dark, curly hair. Fanny opened her eyes and looked at him. He was a handsome man, and it was that very handsomeness which had attracted her to him in the first place. But her grandmother used to tell her that beauty was only skin deep, and if that description ever fit anyone, she believed it fit her husband.

Fergus looked down at her, and for just a moment she saw a strange look cross his eyes. What was it? Hate? Disgust? The look made her blood run cold, and she shivered.

"I see you are still here," Fergus said.

"Where else would I be?" Fanny asked.

"I don't know. I rather thought that after I fell

5

-rimmed wheels rolled across the sun-
they picked up dirt, causing a rooster
o stream out behind them. The wood
ns was bleached white, and under the
off a familiar smell. Fanny sat on the
the wagon, looking out over the backs
which pulled them, concentrating on
gling lantern at the rear of the wagon
them. Because of the events of the
she had slept fitfully, and now, warm
e dozed as the wagon rolled along,
ly, across the broad plains of Wyo-

here was a creaking, snapping sound
on lurched so badly that Fanny wa
ssed out.

66

asleep last night, you might return to Parker's bed."

"Return? What do you mean, return?"

"Oh, yes," Fergus said. "I forgot. You, of course, are denying everything, aren't you? You've never been in his bed, you'll never be in his bed, and you don't want to be in his bed, I know."

Fanny bit her lip and looked away as tears began to well in her eyes. She said nothing to this latest remark, because in truth, she couldn't deny it. She had never been in Matt's bed, and she probably never would be. But last night, while her own husband was making love to her, it was her wish to be in Matt's bed which had brought her to the rapture she experienced. To that degree, she was guilty of Fergus' accusation; guilty as charged. She did *want* to be in Matt's bed.

"I must help Sarah with breakfast," Fanny said, pushing the covers to one side and getting out of bed. She reached for her shoes and pulled them on, feeling the cool dampness of them in the early morning darkness.

"Aunt Fanny," Mary called down from the wagon. "Aunt Fanny, are you awake?"

"Yes, dear, I'm awake," Fanny answered. "I'm just about to start breakfast. Do you want to help me?"

"Oh, yes," Mary said. She climbed down from the wagon, and, running her hand through her hair, walked over to join Fanny.

"Did you have a good night's sleep, dear?" Fanny asked.

"No," Mary said. "I had nightmares."

"Oh, nightmares? What kind?"

"I dreamed about Indians," Mary said. "It scared

me. Do you think
Fanny?"

"No dear, I do
all, that's why Lt.
to make sure som

"But dad said
going where we
ker said the Indi
we were here."

"Well, we'll ju
we don't do any
we?" Fanny said
pulling the little
I'm sure we ha
the statement as
for the little girl

As the stee
baked earth
tail of dust
of the wago
sun it gave
dried seat of
of the team
the unlit, da
in front of
night before,
and lazy, sh
ever so slow
ming.

Suddenly
and the wag
very nearly t

"Oh!" she gasped in a startled tone of voice. "What was that?"

"Whoa, horses," Sarah called, pulling back on the reins. The team stopped and the wagon sat there, listing sharply to the right.

"Mama, what is it?" Mary asked. "What is wrong?"

"I think we've broken an axle," Sarah said grimly. "Will! Mr. Parker!" she called.

The wagons in front of them, unaware that they had stopped, continued on at their same dogged pace, and they were slowly but surely pulling away.

"They are leaving us," Fanny said.

"Will!" Sarah called again, and Fanny and Mary added their own voices, so that Will Davis, on horseback near the first wagon, heard them, and he looked around.

"Matt," Will called. "Matt, stop the train!"

Matt Parker held his hand up, and the wagons stopped. Matt, Will and Fergus Kelly turned and rode back to the wagons.

"Oh, damn," Will said as he saw the broken axle. "I was afraid of this."

"You were *afraid* of it?" Fergus asked. "You mean you knew of the possibility of breaking an axle, but you came without changing it?"

"Lieutenant, since this train left St. Joseph, we have experienced two broken axles, three broken wheels, and a dozen broken spokes. When you are going across land without roads, you have to expect such a thing. I knew the axle was cracked, but we have only one spare remaining, and I thought it best to save it for as long as possible."

"Oh, you thought it best, did you?"

"I agree with him, Lieutenant," Matt said. "Cracked, there was every possibility that the axle could have made it all the way. It was important that we keep a spare for as long as we could."

"We'll have it changed in half a day," Will said.

Fergus twisted in his saddle and looked toward the other two wagons and his mounted soldiers. "No," he said. "No, it isn't going to cost me half a day. I'm going on."

"What?" Fanny gasped. "Fergus, what are you saying?"

"I have orders to establish a military post on the Green River as quickly as I can get there," Fergus said. "I'm not going to take the time to wait around for you to repair this wagon. You can just move to one of the other two wagons."

"No," Will said. "There isn't room for my belongings on the other wagons, and without my belongings, I couldn't make do in the new land. I'm going to repair this wagon."

"Then you can stay here and repair it without a military escort," Fergus said. "I'm going on ahead."

"Fergus, you can't do this," Fanny said.

"I'm in command here," Fergus said. "I can do anything I wish. Come along, Parker, get the train started again."

"No," Matt said. "I'm staying here with Will and Sarah Davis, to help repair their wagon."

"I'm staying too," Fanny said.

"Suit yourself," Fergus said easily. He turned his horse and started back toward the other two wagons. Some of the occupants of the other two wagons were now walking back to see what was going on. "It's all over, folks," Fergus said to them. "Get back in your wagons. We are going on."

"What about Will?" someone asked.

"Don't worry about me," Will said. "I'll catch up as soon as we've made the repair. We'll probably come rolling into the campsite sometime tonight, making such a commotion that I'll wake everyone up."

"I don't know," the man said. "It's not too safe for one wagon alone, out here. Maybe we'd better stay with you, and . . . ."

"No," Will interrupted. "Please, go on. Lieutenant Kelly intends to go on, and if you stay, you'll be without a military escort."

"What do you mean, go on? Isn't he supposed to protect us?"

"Only as a secondary duty," Fergus said. "My primary duty is to establish a military outpost on Green River. The fact that you are going that way just meant that I could provide you with an escort, but I'll not let anything come in the way of my primary duty."

"Please," Will said to the spokesman for the others. "Go on, now, and take my little Mary with you."

"No," Mary said. "I want to stay here with you, and mama, and Aunt Fanny."

Will sighed, and looked at the women. "That's another thing," he said. "I see no real reason why you women should stay here. Please go with the others."

"I'm staying with you," Sarah put in quickly. "But Fanny, if you would go, Mary could go with you."

"I don't want to go," Mary said. "I want to stay here."

Fanny realized then, that there was a very real danger to a wagon alone in hostile territory. And though she would have preferred to stay with them, she knew also that she owed an obligation to Sarah, to see to it that Mary was taken to safety. She smiled and reached for Mary.

"Come along, Mary," she said. "Let's go on ahead, so we can have supper waiting for them tonight."

"Will you eat supper with us tonight, Mr. Parker?" Mary asked the wagon master.

"You bet I will, honey," Matt said. "In fact, if you'd go on now, so we can get started, we might work so fast that we could catch up with you in time for me to gather the firewood. What do you say to that?"

"It would be good if you did that," Mary said. She, like the others, had climbed down from the wagon almost the moment it had stopped, and now she started toward one of the other wagons. "Let's go, Aunt Fanny. I want them to hurry so they can catch up with us."

"All right, dear," Fanny said. She looked toward Sarah, and she saw a look of suppressed fear in Sarah's eyes. Fear, and something else. She also saw a sadness, as if Sarah were reconciling herself to the fact that she may never see her child again.

"Sarah, I wish you would let me . . . ," Fanny started, but Sarah interrupted her.

"Don't worry, Fanny," she said. "We'll be all right. Please, go with the others now."

Fanny put her arm around Mary, then turned and started walking slowly toward the rest of the train.

"You can ride with my missus, Mrs. Kelly," one of the other men said. "Mary can ride in the back with my own two youngin's."

"Let's move 'em out!" Fergus called, holding his hand over his head and moving it around in a circle, then pointing forward.

Mary climbed into the wagon she would be riding in, and turned to look back toward Sarah, Will and Matt. Will and Matt were already starting on the wheel, while Sarah stood by, waiting to help in whatever way she could. Fanny thought she had never seen a braver woman than Sarah Davis.

One-Who-Waits gave the reins of his pony to another, then he climbed to the top of the hill. He knew the warrior's secret of lying down behind the crest of the hill so that he couldn't be seen against the skyline, so he lay down on his stomach, then sneaked up to the top and peered over. There, on the valley floor below him, he saw the enemy. It was obvious that the enemy had no idea they were in danger. It would be easy to count coups upon them.

One-Who-Waits smiled, then slithered back down the hill into the ravine where the others waited.

"Did you see them?"

"Yes," One-Who-Waits said. "They are on our sacred ground. The souls of our ancestors demand that we avenge them for this violation."

"When do we attack?"

"Now," One-Who-Waits said. He pointed down the ravine. "We will follow this around the side of the hill, and then we shall be upon them before they suspect our presence. I will lead you to a great victory."

One-Who-Waits leaped onto the back of his pony, then looked at the others. He felt pride in the size of the war party he was leading. Not for a long time, had there been such a magnificent war party from his village, and then it had been led by Ottawa. Jumping Bear had never led such a fine, large, group of men. He was so excited that he wanted to shout and whoop with joy, but he knew that to do such a thing would give away his presence to the white men, so he held the urge in check. Besides, there would be plenty of time for that tonight, around the council fire, when they celebrated his big victory. One-Who-Waits held his feathered lance over his head and using it, signalled the others to follow him.

"Can you move that rock, Mrs. Davis?" Matt asked. His voice was strained, because he and Will Davis were struggling at the end of a long pole. The pole had been placed under the front part of the wagon, and they had used it, like a lever, to lift the wagon. Now they were waiting for Sarah to slide a rock under the good part of the axle, so they could let the wagon down onto the rock, and still have the front of the wagon elevated. That way they could pull off the damaged part and replace it.

"There," Sarah said from beneath the wagon. She was in some danger at this point, because if Matt and Will lost their grip, or if the pole should slip, the wagon would fall on her. "I think I've got it now."

"Slide out from under there now," Will said, and his voice almost cracked under the strain.

Sarah rolled over, then crawled out and, with a mighty sigh of relief, Will and Matt set the wagon down on the rock.

"Whew," Will said, wiping the sweat from his forehead. "I'm glad that part is over."

"You and me both, brother," Matt said. He got down and crawled up under the wagon to begin pulling away the broken axle.

"Do you think . . . . ," Will started to say, but Matt held up his hand to stop him.

"Listen," Matt said.

"What is it?" Will asked, puzzled by Matt's strange behavior. "I don't hear anything."

"Listen," Matt said again.

All three were quiet for a moment, with only the sound of the ever-present prairie wind moaning its mournful wail. Then, Matt heard it again. The sound was so faint that it could barely be heard, but a momentary shift in the wind carried it to their ears.

"Thump, thump, thump." Three, flat, thumping sounds.

"What *is* that?" Sarah asked.

"I've heard that sound in a hundred battles," Matt said grimly. "That's the way gunfire sounds when it's far off."

"Oh, my God! Mary!" Sarah said, putting her hand to her mouth.

All of the wagons were in flames now, and men and women were falling, mortally wounded, all around Fanny. She clutched Mary to her, and they jumped from their burning wagon, and darted over to a clump of rocks, then hid behind them to watch.

The Indians had swept down on them, seemingly from nowhere, whooping and shouting as their horses galloped right through them. Fergus made a fundamental error by ordering his soldiers to dismount and return fire. That deprived them of their mobility, and they were so badly outnumbered, that mobility was an absolute necessity if they were to put up any kind of a battle at all. As it was, within a short time, most had been killed, and those who were left, broke, and ran in panic.

One-Who-Waits leaped over the rocks, and in and out of gulleys, shouting with joy as he pursued the fight. Soldiers fired at him, but it was as if he were impervious to their bullets. He leaped upon a burning wagon and looked at the battlefield, chortling in glee as the last soldier was put to the lance. Now all the soldiers, and all the men and women and children of the wagon train were dead. He would go to each of them and touch them with his coup stick, because, as the leader of this war party, he could count coup not only on those he killed, but on all who were killed. He began singing a victory song.

Behind her rock, Fanny held Mary against her skirt, shushing her to keep her quiet. She looked at the carnage before her with horror. Then, suddenly, she saw a soldier on horseback, galloping toward her. It was Fergus! Somehow he had escaped, and as all the Indians were now picking through the wreckage of the wagons, there was a chance he would make it.

"Mary, quickly," Fanny said to the little girl. "We must stop Lieutenant Kelly!"

Fanny stepped out from behind the rock, pulling Mary with her. If she could put Mary on the horse with Fergus, then at least the girl would be safe. Though she didn't realize it, Fanny's sense of responsibility to the little girl was so strong at that moment, that she wasn't even thinking of her own fate as she tried to flag her husband down.

"Fergus, stop!" she called. "Stop! Take Mary!"

"Get the hell out of my way!" Fergus called back in a fear-crazed voice. He slapped the reins of his horse across the animal's neck and plunged his spurs into the side. Despite everything going on around her at the moment, Fanny saw, out of the corner of her eye, blood spurting from the animal's side, where the spurs had dug into the flesh.

Fanny realized that Fergus wasn't going to stop, and she realized also, that he was going to run down Mary! "Mary!" she screamed, but it was too late. Fergus' horse ran over her, and one of the hooves caught the little girl in the head as she went down. She lay on the ground, deathly still, and quiet, with her eyes wide open. "Mary, no!"

Fanny screamed again, and she ran to the crumpled little body, and held her in her arms. The sound of the receding hoofbeats of her husband's fleeing horse pounded in her ears, and she cried, and held the little girl against her bosom.

"Little girl dead," a voice said from behind her, and Fanny gasped, then turned to look at half a dozen Indians who were standing there, watching her. In her grief over the child, she had forgotten for a moment that the Indians were even there.

"What are you going to do now?" Fanny asked. Perhaps it was shock; the shock of the attack, the shock of seeing all her friends killed, the shock of seeing her husband run away in cowardly panic, or the shock of holding her dear little Mary, dead in her arms, but whatever it was, it took away all her own fear. She asked the question not as a person in hysterics, but almost as a person who was disinterested in what the answer would be. If they told her they intended to kill her now, at this very moment, it would have meant nothing to her.

The Indians looked at each other in surprise. Never had they heard such a calm sounding voice from one who was about to die. The fact that it was a woman's voice made it all the more shocking to them. They began speaking to each other, and they spoke in their native language so Fanny could not understand what they were saying.

"She is a woman with powerful medicine. See, how she does not fear to die?"

"She fears death," One-Who-Waits said. "Did you see how she tried to make the Soldier-Who-Is-A-Coward stop for her?"

"No. She wanted Soldier-Who-Is-A-Coward to take the child."

"Soldier-Who-Is-A-Coward ran down the child. Perhaps she feels more anger for him than fear of us."

"She is afraid of me," One-Who-Waits said. "When I raise my coup stick to strike her, you will see fear in her eyes."

"No, I think not. I think Real Woman is without fear. Her medicine is strong."

One-Who-Waits did not like the way the conversation was going. He had led the battle, and he had won a great victory. His victory was great not only because many enemy had been killed, but because the soldier chief had run away. The others had named the soldier chief, Soldier-Who-Is-A-Coward, and to cause such a name of shame to be given to your enemy was as good as counting coup. But now, this woman who was his enemy, was being called Real Woman by the warriors. Real Woman was a name of respect. If she kept the name of respect, it would take away some of the glory of his victory. He could not let her keep the name, he must shame the name away from her.

"I will show you her medicine is not strong enough to overcome the fear of dying," One-Who-Waits said. "I will raise my war club over her head. If she shows fear, I will kill her. If she shows no fear, I will let her live."

"She will show no fear," one of the warriors said.

One-Who-Waits raised his war club, and he let out a menacing, blood-curdling yell.

Fanny was resigned to dying now, and the

strange, almost numbing calmness which had come over her before was still there. She was staring into the abyss and she didn't flinch.

"Show fear, woman," One-Who-Waits said in English. "Show fear, for I am about to kill you!"

The moment One-Who-Waits held the war club over her head, was the only thing left between Fanny and eternity. It was but a brief moment in the lives of those who were standing there watching, but it was a lifetime for Fanny, and she was composed to live it in dignity.

"Show fear!" One-Who-Waits shouted, and with that shout, Fanny realized that, ironically, the final victory was to be hers! She smiled at the thought.

"Aiyee," one of the warriors said in his own language. "Look at Real Woman, how she smiles in the teeth of death! Surely she has the greatest medicine!"

One-Who-Waits, frustrated by the turn of events, drew his war club back, and in anger, started to bring it crashing down on her head. But the warrior nearest him grabbed it, and wrenched it from his arm.

"No, One-Who-Waits," the warrior said. "She has bested you. She will live."

"Arrrrrrrrghhhhh," One-Who-Waits shouted in anger and frustration. Now, not only had his enemy been given a name of respect, but she had bested him, and made a fool of him as well.

"Come," the one who had taken One-Who-Waits' war club from him. "Follow me back to the village. We will take Real Woman before the council. Perhaps we can learn of her strong medicine."

A couple of the Indians took Fanny, gently, and led her to a horse, then helped her to mount. She realized then that, for some reason, she was going to be allowed to live. What she did not realize was that her action had caused One-Who-Waits to lose command of his war party. And she did not realize what a mortal enemy she had just made. &

6

RUNNING RABBIT sat on a rock overhang and peered out over the plains to the far south. Out there, somewhere, was the war party which had left with the sunrise early this morning. They had left without Running Rabbit, even though he had been mounted, ready to go.

Running Rabbit stayed behind, because he was "counted out" by One-Who-Waits, as being too young. It was no disgrace to be counted out for being too young, though one could also be counted out for having shown signs of cowardice, or untrustworthiness, or lack of enthusiasm for battle. When one was counted out for those reasons, it was a disgrace.

Running Rabbit did not really believe he was too young. He was convinced that if Jumping Bear had led the party instead of One-Who-Waits, he would have been allowed to go. It is just that Running Rabbit was Jumping Bear's good friend, and One-Who-Waits knew that, and counted him out because of that.

Behind Running Rabbit, was the village of the Oglala Sioux under the Chief Ottawa. This village they called *Miniwacipi*, which meant village of the sun water, so named for the sparkling sundance upon the swift, cold stream which tumbled through, providing the villagers with fresh water, and a source of fish.

Miniwacipi was a large village, with over three hundred tipis and hogans. It had two remudas, a herd of cattle and a herd of sheep. Many people lived in *Miniwacipi*, and now most of the women and girls were at the bank of the stream, washing clothes. Their laughter and conversation carried up the side of the mountain to Running Rabbit, and he made a scoffing sound at the idle gossip with which women occupied their time.

How glad Running Rabbit was to be a man, and not a woman! He had already been in on a buffalo hunt and could never be denied that right again, merely because of his age. Anyway, he wasn't that young. He had seen the count of twelve winters. He could have gone with the war party and pulled his own weight, he was certain of that.

Running Rabbit heard something from the plains then, a faint sound like the whisper of a distant wind, and when he looked back he saw a cloud of dust hanging over the horizon.

"They are back!" he said aloud. He turned, and

with a whoop of joy, started back down the mountain toward the village. He flew down the mountain, darting between the trees and rocks, and running through the stream, sending up a spray of silver water.

"Here, Running Rabbit, why do you run so? Has something frightened you?" a young girl asked, laughing at her own joke, and hoping Running Rabbit would take the bait of her teasing.

"I have no time for women or their foolishness," Running Rabbit said. "I must speak with Ottawa!"

Running Rabbit ran across the open ground, then through the tipis and hogans, to the largest hogan which was in the cleared circle in the center of the village. This hogan was decorated with furs and rugs, and three wives cooked around the fire, symbols of Ottawa's wealth and influence within the village.

"Ottawa, Ottawa!" Running Rabbit called.

"Here, watch where you run," one of Ottawa's younger wives called sharply. "If you kick dirt into the food, I will have your scalp."

"What is the disturbance?" Ottawa said, appearing in the doorway of his hogan. His eyes were puffy as if he had been asleep, but no one would dare suggest that a chief would nap in the middle of the day, so everyone carried on the deception that he was communing with the spirits which guide him.

"Ottawa, the war party," Running Rabbit said. "They are returning! They will be here soon."

"How do they ride?" Ottawa asked.

"In victory," Running Rabbit said.

Ottawa smiled broadly. "It is good that we will

have a victory to celebrate tonight, and not a defeat." He put his arm out toward Running Rabbit. "Come, we will go down to the stream and welcome them. Why is it that you did not go with them?"

"I was counted out," Running Rabbit said, disgustedly. "One-Who-Waits thought I was too young."

"Nonsense," Ottawa said. "When I had seen no more winter counts than you have seen, I was riding with war parties against the Crow and even against the whites. Is One-Who-Waits blind that he cannot see what a fine warrior you are?"

Running Rabbit beamed proudly at the words of Ottawa, and he went with the chief down to the side of the water, and stood there, waiting for the war party to reach them. The women, seeing the chief approach, knew by now that the war party was returning, so they took away their laundry and their washing utensils and waited, silently, with the other villagers who, in groups of four and five were also waiting. Bright, diamond-like jewels danced and sparkled from the surface of the stream, and the water sung to them as it flowed swiftly across the rocks, and through the twisting turns of its bed.

As the war party grew closer, one of the number broke ahead of the rest, and bending low over his horse to urge greater speed, he hurried until he was on the other side of the stream from the village. His horse stopped, then reared, and he had to hold on to the horse's mane, and pressed his knees tightly into the animal's side to stay on.

"We have won a great victory!" he called, and the people of the village cheered his announcement.

"We have killed all the *toka* but two. One ran away, and one was captured."

"And our warriors?" Ottawa called.

"None were harmed," the messenger said.

Again the village cheered, and before this cheer died in their throats, the war party was upon them, and they all saw the white woman who was the prisoner taken in the battle.

Fanny did not know why she had not been killed. Perhaps they would kill her here. She had mounted the horse which was brought for her, and she had ridden with the Indians back to their village, riding hard to keep up with them, blocking her mind to all thought, merely taking one moment after another to see what would happen next.

She saw all the women and the children of the village, gathered along the banks of the stream, staring at her with eyes open wide in curiosity and wonder. She vowed to herself that she would show them no more fear than she had shown the one who had raised his war club to her. She may be killed, but she would not die for their pleasure, of that she was certain!

The Indian who had threatened her with the war club, now came up to her and, gruffly, pulled her down from the horse. He and another Indian led her past the crowd, and into a tipi, where they pushed her roughly to the ground. Then they spread out her arms and legs and tied them with rawhide thongs to stakes which had been driven in the ground.

One of the Indians left, and the one who stayed

behind in the tent, was the one who had threatened her before. Fanny knew that he spoke English.

"What is going to happen to me?" she asked.

"You are going to die," One-Who Waits answered..

"Why must I die?" Fanny asked. "I mean you no harm."

"Do you fear death?" One-Who-Waits asked.

The shock which had allowed Fanny to take her fate so calmly before, was now wearing off. Had she been killed immediately, she would have borne up to it. But she had been kept alive, and now she was embracing life with an appetite she didn't know she possessed.

She wondered how best to preserve her life now. Should she plead for it, or should she seem to show disdain?

Another Indian stepped into the tent before Fanny could answer. He was a much older Indian, and there seemed about him an aura of dignity and authority.

"What is your name?" the older Indian asked.

"My name is Fanny," Fanny answered.

"Now, your name shall be Real Woman," the older Indian said.

Real Woman? Fanny thought. Why would they call her Real Woman? What an ugly name that was. At first, Fanny thought to protest, then, there was a twinkling spark of hope about it. If they intended to kill her, they wouldn't give her a new name, would they?

"Real Woman," Fanny repeated. "Yes, that is a good name. What is your name?"

"My name is Ottawa," the old man said. "The one who brought you here is called One-Who-Waits."

"One-Who-Waits," Fanny said. "Why do you hate me so?"

"You are my enemy," One-Who-Waits said. "It is right that I hate my enemy."

"But you seem to hate me with a special intensity."

"You have caused One-Who-Waits to lose face," Ottawa said.

"How could I have done that?" Fanny asked. "I have been the prisoner of One-Who-Waits."

"You did not show the proper fear of him," Ottawa explained. "The others respected your medicine more than the medicine of One-Who-Waits."

One-Who-Waits started to say something, but Ottawa interrupted him. "Speak in the language of the *winu*, the captive woman," he said. "Real Woman should hear the words you speak."

"The medicine of the *winu* is not stronger than my medicine." One-Who-Waits said. "I led many young men to a great victory. We killed many soldiers, and we made the soldier chief run. His name is now Soldier-Who-Is-A-Coward. That is a great honor, is it not?"

"Yes," Ottawa said. "But it is also a great honor for this *winu* to be named Real Woman."

"It is an empty honor," One-Who-Waits said. "For soon she will be dead."

"No," Ottawa said. "She will live."

"It is my right to kill her," One-Who-Waits said. "She is my prisoner."

"It is your right to claim her as your *yuza*, your slave. But as she was not killed upon the field of the battle, she cannot be killed now, except by a council ruling."

"Then I shall have a council ruling," One-Who-Waits said.

"Why do you wish that?" Ottawa said. He looked at Fanny, with eyes which showed a genuine appreciation for her beauty. "Real Woman looks soft and would be a most agreeable woman to give you pleasure."

"No!" Fanny said quickly, when she realized what Ottawa was referring to. Whereas she had managed to show a lack of fear over the possibility of dying, the possibility of having One-Who-Waits come to her was very frightening.

One-Who-Waits was quick to respond to Fanny's outcry, and he smiled broadly, as he realized he had just discovered the thing Fanny feared most. He turned toward her, and he grabbed himself obscenely, then made a thrusting motion with his hips. Fanny turned her face away.

"Yes," One-Who-Waits said. "Yes, you are right. I do not wish to kill her. I will keep her for a *yuza*."

"Please," Fanny said. "Don't I have anything to say about this?"

"You could select someone for a husband," Ottawa said. "And if the council approves, and if the one you selected approves, you can become his wife."

"Can I not say that I wish no husband at all?" Fanny asked.

"No," Ottawa said. "You are our prisoner. You must be married, or become a slave. There is no other."

One-Who-Waits continued to smile down at her, and now Fanny could see the unmistakable bulge under his loin cloth. His eyes, which had been filled with anger and hate, had undergone a subtle change, and now Fanny could see that they were filled with lust. In that, they looked much as Colonel Albertson's eyes had looked on that last night in the fort.

"What if I want a husband?" Fanny asked.

One-Who-Waits laughed. "You would choose a husband?"

"Yes."

"It must be an Oglala," One-Who-Waits said. "Who would you choose?"

"I would choose Ottawa," Fanny said.

Ottawa looked up in surprise.

One-Who-Waits laughed again. "Foolish woman, Ottawa is an old man. He cannot make you feel pleasure. If you are my slave, I will make you know pleasure."

"The look of him pleases me," Fanny said. "I wish him for my husband."

"Real Woman, I already have three wives," Ottawa said. "One-Who-Waits has no wives. Perhaps as his *yuza*, you could also be his wife. Would you not rather be the first wife of a young man, than the fourth wife of one who has seen many winter counts?"

"Are you a man of importance?" Fanny asked.

"I am a man others listen to," Ottawa admitted.

"Then it is no dishonor to be the fourth wife

of such a man," Fanny said. She was desperately
trying to avoid being forced into any kind of relationship with One-Who-Waits, and anything, even
marrying this old man, was preferable to that.

Fanny was getting through to Ottawa, she could
see that. He was flattered by her suggestion. Now,
she hoped she could interest him beyond mere
flattery. She had seen the unmistakable signs of
lust in the eyes of others as old as Ottawa. She
knew that desire did not leave men when they
grew older, it just became harder to summon.

"I could give you great pleasure," Fanny said,
and she twisted in the rawhide bindings, so that
the curve of her hip was clearly outlined by the
folds of her dress. "You do still take pleasure from
a woman, do you not?"

"I am an old man, with three wives," Ottawa
said again.

"I am a young woman," Fanny said. "An old
man needs a young woman."

"I will go before the council," Ottawa said. "If
the council agrees that you should have the right
to choose your husband, then I shall take you as
my fourth wife."

"You are a fool, old man, if you think you can
have this woman!" One-Who-Waits said angrily.
He turned and pushed through the flap of the tipi.

"I will go before the council," Ottawa said
again.

"When?"

"Tomorrow."

"But . . . must I stay here, like this?" Fanny
asked. "The bindings hurt my wrists."

"You must stay," Ottawa said, as he left the tipi.

Fanny lay tied to the stakes for the rest of the day. She had frequent guests, men and women who would come in singly, or in pairs to look at her, but no one spoke to her, even though she tried to get them to speak. Late in the afternoon several children played a game where they ran through the tipi, jumping over her, and running around her, but she could have been a rock or a tree to their game for all the attention they paid her. Once, just after dark, an old woman came in and lit a pine knot lantern. She sat in the flickering yellow light and looked at Fanny, staring in silence for several moments.

"Do you speak English?" Fanny asked.

The woman made no response. There wasn't the slightest flicker in her eyes, nor the barest hint of a change of expression on her face.

"Who are you?" Fanny asked.

The woman was silent.

"I am called Real Woman," Fanny said, hoping the name would mean something to her.

There was still no response. Finally, the woman got up and left.

Night came and the wavering orange of the campfire's glow joined with the flickering flame from the pine knot to bathe the inside of Fanny's tipi in an eerie, gold light. The Indians were celebrating their great victory, and they were dancing around the fires, chanting a strange, discordant, yet hauntingly beautiful melody. The drums pounded incessantly. She listened to the drums' crescendo, trying to reckon the passing of time. Time and space seemed to hang suspended now. She was having difficulty believing that she was actually here, in an Indian tipi, in an Indian village, tied to stakes in the ground.

Fanny closed her eyes, and in a fright-induced hallucination, she seemed to see her father.

"So, Fanny girl, your meddlesome ways have landed you in trouble, have they?"

"Father, it's you? But, what are you doing here? Have you come to help me?"

"Ah, lass, 'tis a shame but I cannot. For truly you began this journey to trouble even when you married the young Lieutenant, and against my better judgment, I should hasten to add."

"But you approved, Father. You stood up for me. You gave me away."

"I gave you away, Fanny girl, but I never approved. 'Twas your mother's wish that I give you away, lest there be some hint of a scandal. An' now I ask you, where is your fine Lieutenant now, eh? Soldier-Who-Is-A-Coward." Her father laughed. "Sure 'n that's a good name for him, I'm thinking."

One-Who-Waits came into the tipi, and the image of her father popped away. For an instant, Fanny had to tell herself where she was, to keep her sanity about her.

One-Who-Waits looked down at her, his eyes reflecting the red glow of the fires, his face looking demonic in the flickering light.

"What are you doing in here?"

"You belong to me," One-Who-Waits said.

"No," Fanny replied. "I don't belong to anyone until after the council meets tomorrow. You heard what Ottawa said."

"You belong to me," One-Who-Waits said again.

"One-Who-Waits, you'd better get out of here," Fanny said. "If you don't, I will call for Ottawa."

"Ottawa is asleep," One-Who-Waits said. "He is asleep with his three wives, and he will not hear the call of one captive woman, a *winu*."

One-Who-Waits knelt down beside her, and only then did Fanny see the blade of a knife flash silver in his hand. He put it at the bodice of her dress, and Fanny heard a tearing sound. One-Who-Waits cut her dress from the neck, all the way down to the hem. He lay the dress open, then looked somewhat surprised to see a chemise on beneath.

"Why two dresses?" he asked. He cut the under garments away too, then Fanny felt the cool air across her body, and she knew he was gazing upon her nudity.

"Woman made for pleasure," One-Who-Waits said, and Fanny felt his rough hands on her body, kneading a breast, then moving across her skin until they reached the junction of her legs. She tried to twist away from him, but her undulating body only served to enflame the Indian's desire. He leaned over toward her breast, and took one of them into his mouth.

My God, she thought. He's going to bite it off!

But One-Who-Waits didn't bite. He began sucking on it, and he pulled the nipple in between his teeth and flicked his tongue across it.

Fergus had never done such a thing to her in all the times they had made love. It was a strange, tingling sensation which was, strangely enough, quite pleasurable.

But the puzzling pleasure which coursed through Fanny at that moment failed to assuage the fear which was running through her, and the fear grew even more acute when she felt his fingers penetrating her most private part, gouging into her, painfully.

A moment later his finger was replaced by the erect appendage which thrust out from behind the loin cloth. She felt him enter and, as she was frightened, and unready for him, it was a most painful experience as he plunged his entire length into her.

Fanny closed her eyes and tried to position herself to accommodate him, thus lessening the severity of the pain. Though the pain subsided somewhat, the humiliation didn't, and Fanny bit her lips and turned her head to one side to keep from crying out. Finally she felt him grow tense, then she heard a shuddering expulsion of his breath, and she realized that he was finished.

Slowly he lifted himself from her body. She opened her eyes just in time to see him covering his maleness with the loin cloth. It looked frightening, like an angry, damp, snake.

"You will belong to me," One-Who-Waits said. "Ottawa cannot pleasure you like I can. You will see."

One-Who-Waits left her then, without bothering to put her clothes back on her, or to cover her, and she lay naked, listening to his evil laugh as he pushed his way through the tipi opening. She could hear his evil laugh for a long time, even above the drums and the singing and the dancing of the others.

7

KETTLE WOMAN walked across the common ground from her hogan to the tipi where the *winu* was being held captive. It was early in the morning, and the fires from the celebration the night before had died down. Now only the glowing of the coals, and the rich smell of roast meat remained to recall the great victory feast.

There were more than a dozen Indians sleeping on the ground, drunk from the liquor they had consumed during the ceremony. Kettle Woman picked her way through them, clucking her tongue in disgust at their behavior.

Kettle Woman was carrying a dress for Real Woman to wear before the council meeting that was to be held today. It was an exceptionally beautiful dress, perhaps the most beautiful dress in the entire village, and Kettle Woman had made it herself.

The dress was made of deerskin, which Kettle Woman had chewed until it was as soft as a feather. After she softened the skin, she dipped it into alkali water until the skin was bleached as white as winter's snow. The bodice of the dress was decorated with a design which Kettle Woman created out of red and white beads, sewing them on with thread made from the muscle of a buffalo.

It had taken Kettle Woman a long time to make the dress, and by the time she was finished with it, she had grown fat and could no longer wear it. Now, she was taking it to Real Woman, so Real Woman would impress the council, and be rewarded by the council with the right to take the husband of her choice.

The husband Real Woman would choose would be Ottawa. Kettle Woman knew this, because Ottawa told her. Kettle Woman was Ottawa's oldest wife.

Ottawa's other two wives were jealous of Real Woman. Real Woman was younger and prettier than they were, and they thought it was unfair that she should want their husband. Kettle Woman, alone, did not protest last night, and today she was giving Real Woman her prettiest dress. That would show Ottawa that Kettle Woman's love for him was real. The other wives loved Ottawa only for the position they were able to maintain in the tribe by being wives of the chief. Kettle Woman would love Ottawa, even if he weren't a chief, but simply an old warrior beyond his time of usefulness.

Kettle Woman stepped into the tipi with Real Woman, and she gasped when she saw her. Real Woman was nude, with her dress torn away from her and tossed aside. It was obvious what had happened to her. Kettle Woman was also sure of who had done it to her.

Kettle Woman reached down and began cutting the thongs which held Real Woman secure.

Sleep had been a long time in coming for Fanny last night. First, there was the pain, anger and humiliation over being raped by One-Who-Waits. Added to that was the fear of what was going to happen to her, the terrifying sounds of the dances and whoops which grew louder and more frightening as the night wore on, and finally, the aching discomfort of being tied to the ground. When sleep finally did come, it was the result of total exhaustion, and it was more fitful than restful. Now, as her bonds were being cut, she opened her eyes.

The woman who was cutting her bonds was the same woman who had come into the tipi on the day before and sat, watching. Her face was totally devoid of expression as she cut the ties.

"Oh, thank you," Fanny said. She sat up, groaning, then began rubbing the circulation back into her wrists and feet. Her back and legs were hurting.

"You wear this dress," the old woman said.

The words startled Fanny. She had tried, without success, to speak with the woman the day before, and she had decided that the woman spoke no English. Now the woman was speaking to her.

"You speak English," Fanny said.

"Yes."

"But when I tried to talk to you yesterday, you wouldn't say anything."

"Yesterday I had nothing to say," the woman said.

"What is your name?"

"Kettle Woman," the old woman said.

Fanny looked at Kettle Woman, and she decided that the name fit. She was short, and very rotund, like one of the big, black kettles used by the ladies of the wagon train.

Kettle Woman handed Fanny the dress. "I made this dress," she said.

Fanny looked at it. Fanny was quite an accomplished seamstress in her own right, and she could recognize quality workmanship when she saw it. This was quality workmanship.

"Oh, this dress is beautiful, Kettle Woman," Fanny said, and she said it sincerely.

Kettle Woman was able to recognize the sincerity in Fanny's voice, and she warmed to Fanny because of it. "When the council sees you in this dress, it will move their hearts to vote as you wish," she said.

"Oh, I hope you are right, Kettle Woman," Fanny said. She slipped the dress over her naked body, grateful to be covered again after such a long time. The dress felt soft and comfortable to her. "You see, I have to convince the council to allow me to marry Ottawa. Otherwise, I shall be forced to become the slave of One-Who-Waits."

"One-Who-Waits is a good hunter," Kettle Woman said. "Your tipi would never be without food.

He is also a young man. He would pleasure you as often as you want."

Fanny blushed. "I don't want to be pleasured by One-Who-Waits," she said. "I don't want to be pleasured by anyone."

"You don't wish to be pleasured by Ottawa?"

"No," Fanny said.

"Then why do you wish Ottawa for your husband?"

"Because I was told that I must choose a husband from among the Oglala," Fanny said. "And Ottawa seems to be a kind and good man."

"Yes," Kettle Woman said. "He is very kind and very good. He is my husband."

Fanny gasped. "Ottawa is your husband?"

"Yes."

"Oh, Kettle Woman, I'm sorry. Here I'm talking about wanting to choose him, and you tell me he is your husband. And . . . . and you've even brought me this lovely dress to help sway the council. I don't understand. Why are you doing such a thing for me?"

"I am doing it for Ottawa," Kettle Woman said. "It would please him to have you for a wife, and I wish to please him."

Fanny reached out and took Kettle Woman's hand in hers. "Ottawa is a lucky man to have such a wonderful wife as you," she said. "Whatever happens, Kettle Woman, I would like for us to be friends."

Kettle Woman smiled. "Yes," she said. "Yes, we will be friends."

Fanny heard someone shouting outside, and she

looked at Kettle Woman with an unasked question in her eyes.

"It is the call for the council," she said. "Come, we must go now."

Fanny followed Kettle Woman outside. It felt wonderful to be free of restraints, and to be walking. The walk returned the circulation to her whole body.

There were several gathered around now, crowding toward the middle of the large center circle, sitting in such a way as to leave a large circle in the middle. A smaller group of Indians came to the center of the circle and sat down upon crossed legs. In this smaller group, Fanny recognized Ottawa. Ottawa was carrying a long stemmed pipe, and he held a burning brand to the bowl of the pipe and lit it. He drew in several puffs, and soon the smoke began curling up from the bowl. He passed the pipe to the Indian on his left, holding it gently with both hands. That Indian took a puff, then passed it to the one on his left, treating it the same way Ottawa had.

"What are they doing?" Fanny asked.

"They are smoking the council pipe," Kettle Woman answered. "The smoke from the council pipe gives them *woksapa*, and it will help them to make the right decision."

After the pipe had gone all the way around the circle, and everyone on the council had taken a puff from it, One-Who-Waits was called before the council, and he was offered the sacred pipe.

"They will offer the pipe to you too," Kettle Woman told Fanny.

"Oh, no, I hope not," Fanny said. She screwed up her face in an expression of distaste. "I don't think I could smoke it."

"Oh, but you must," Kettle Woman said. "If you do not smoke the pipe, you will offend the council and the decision will surely go against you."

One-Who-Waits returned the pipe to the council.

"Real Woman," Ottawa called. "Come, take the pipe." He held it out toward Fanny, and, taking a deep breath and summoning all her courage, Fanny walked over to Ottawa and took the pipe, then took a puff the same way she had seen the others.

The Indians all grunted in a favorable response to her action.

"Kettle Woman," Ottawa said. "You will be the ears for Real Woman. You will tell her what words are spoken before the council. And you will be the tongue of Real Woman. You will tell the council what words are spoken by Real Woman."

"Yes," Kettle Woman said.

Because Kettle Woman was to have a function in the council, albeit, only as a translator, she, too, was offered a smoke from the council pipe. The pipe was handed to her and she took a puff, then handed it back and took her position beside Fanny, or "Real Woman" as she was being called, and prepared to translate for her.

"And now," Ottawa said. "As the decision of this council concerns me, I shall pass the feathered stick to Gallant Bear, who will speak for the council." Ottawa passed the stick, the symbol of his authority, to Gallant Bear.

"The council will hear Elk Heart," Gallant Bear said, with Kettle Woman translating almost simultaneously to Fanny.

Elk Heart came before the council, and Fanny recognized him as one of the Indians who had participated in the raid on the wagon train.

"Tell of the fight," Gallant Bear said to Elk Heart.

"The fight was in the sacred burial grounds of our fathers," Elk Heart said. "It was a just fight, for the white man's wagons should not have been there."

"Was it a good fight?"

"Yes. The white men had some soldiers and the soldiers and the men of the wagon train all had long guns. But there were too few of them and too many of us. Right was on our side, and our medicine was strong. We won the fight. No warriors were harmed, but all the whites were killed except three."

"I have seen with my own eyes, Real Woman," Gallant Bear said. "Who were the other whites who were not killed in the fight?"

"As I have spoken, there were three who were not killed," Elk Heart went on. "The soldier chief was not killed, and he ran from the field of battle in fear. He was named, Soldier-Who-Is-A-Coward."

At this, all the Indians in the village laughed, and whooped, and One-Who-Waits, who was credited with the victory, and with the shame of his enemy, beamed proudly.

"There was also a child who was not killed in the battle," Elk Heart said. "But when Real Woman tried to give the child to Soldier-Who-Is-A-Coward, his horse ran her down and she was killed."

"What did this woman do next?" Gallant Bear asked.

"She did nothing," Elk Heart said. "One-Who-Waits thought to frighten her, and make her plead for her life, but he could not do so. He raised his war club to her, but she laughed."

"She laughed?" Gallant Bear asked, puzzled.

"Yes," Elk Heart said. "She showed no fear of death, even when One-Who-Waits begged her to beg for her own life, she did not. It was then that we called her Real Woman."

One-Who-Waits had beamed proudly a moment earlier, when his greatest triumph was relived before the tribal council and the people of the village. Now, however, his shame was exposed, and he looked down, broodingly, as his eyes shone with hate.

"Who wishes to add to Elk Heart's story?" Gallant Bear asked, and when no one was forthcoming, he went on. "Who wishes to change Elk Heart's story?" Again there were no responses. "Then the council agrees that the battle was as Elk Heart said it was." Gallant Bear looked at One-Who-Waits. "Now, you may speak."

"The battle was as Elk Heart said," One-Who-Waits started out.

"We know this," Gallant Bear said. "We do not need your word."

One-Who-Waits glared at Gallant Bear and the council for a moment before he went on. "It is wise to remember that I was the leader of the war party," One-Who-Waits said. "I claimed coups for all who were killed."

"How many enemies did you claim coups by combat?" Gallant Bear asked.

"I claimed two coups by combat," One-Who-Waits said.

"It is the right of One-Who-Waits to claim coups on all," one of the other members of the council said.

"As the one who has claimed coups on all, I also claim coups on the white woman who is now our captive. She belongs to me, and I would ask the council to give her to me as my *yuza*."

"If she belongs to you by right of coups, why must you come to the council to ask for her?"

"Because the white woman . . . ."

"Her name is Real Woman," Ottawa reminded One-Who-Waits.

"If she is to be my woman, her name will be as I wish," One-Who-Waits said. "I do not like the name others have chosen for her."

"If the council rules for you, you may name her," Gallant Bear said. "But for now, she will use the name Real Woman."

"Real Woman," One-Who-Waits said, letting the words slide out with a sneer, "has asked for the right to claim her own husband. This is a right women of the Oglala have, but she is not an Oglala. I ask the council to deny her that right, and give her to me as the slave-woman she is meant to be."

One-Who-Waits then sat down, and Fanny was invited to speak to the council.

"First," Fanny said, "I would like to thank the council for hearing me speak. And I would like to thank the Oglala people for giving me the fine

name, Real Woman. Surely, with such a name, I
have become more than a captive woman, what
you call *winu*. I have become an Oglala, for such
a fine name is befitting an Oglala. If I have become an Oglala, then I have the right to come
before the council and make a request for a husband."

"And who would you choose for your husband?"
Gallant Bear asked.

"I would choose Ottawa."

As Fanny's words were translated, grunts and
exclamations were exchanged by the Indians. Some
of the strange, guttural sounds, were uttered with
ribald smiles and looks, and when Kettle Woman
didn't translate any of the remarks, Fanny asked
what they were saying.

"They are saying nothing of importance," Kettle
Woman mumbled.

"They ask if you can make a man my age know
cezin," Ottawa said.

"*Cezin?*"

"It means when man is stiff, here," Kettle Woman
said, and she put her hands down between her
legs to indicate a penis.

The entire camp roared in laughter, and Fanny
felt herself blushing fiercely. She knew that this
was a critical time. How she reacted at this very
moment, might very well determine how the council would rule.

"It is the duty of a wife to make herself desirable to her husband. If she does this, her husband
will know *cezin*. If I am your wife, I will be desirable to you."

"Wait," Gallant Bear said. "We will tell you our decision soon."

All the members of the council stood then, and started toward the residence of Ottawa, and because it was in the center, it was also the most important structure in the entire village. It was here that the council made decisions which would affect everyone, though, it was the Indian way that if they didn't like the decisions made by the council of one village, they were free to move to another village.

"Hear me, my brothers," One-Who-Waits called, as the council started to leave. They stopped and looked back toward him.

"You have already spoken," Gallant Bear said.

"Now, I speak again," One-Who-Waits said. "If the council does not rule in my favor, I will become a contraire."

All the Indians within hearing distance of One-Who-Waits' words gasped aloud, and even Kettle Woman gasped, as One-Who-Waits spoke.

"Kettle Woman, what is it?" Fanny asked. "What did One-Who-Waits say?"

"He has promised to become a contraire, if the council rules in your favor," Kettle Woman said.

"What is that?"

"It is a life of great sacrifice. One who is a contraire must do all things backwards. He must laugh when sad, cry when happy, sleep when rested, wake when tired, be friendly to those people he would harm, and be rude to those who are his friends."

Fanny laughed. "That doesn't make sense. How can anyone do such a thing?"

"No one can," Kettle Woman said. "Those who become contraire go crazy very soon, because it is not possible to do the things they have vowed to do."

One-Who-Waits sat down in the center of the circle and crossed his arms across his chest. He stared straight ahead, looking neither left nor right, and he waited for the decision of the council.

Jumping Bear was returning to the village from his time in the mountains and in the *initi*. A song had come to him while he was in the sweat lodge, and he was singing the song as he returned to his village.

The words of the song were very mysterious to him. He didn't know what they meant, and yet he knew they were words of great meaning. It would be his task now that he had received the knowledge, to acquire the *woksapa*, the sacred wisdom. Jumping Bear had learned a long time ago, that knowledge and wisdom were not the same thing. They were not the same thing at all.

Jumping Bear sang the song again, letting the words play against his mind, not trying to decipher them individually, but rather trying to gather the meaning of the whole.

> *"In this circle, hear what I sing.*
> *When one knows of beauty,*
> *Already there is ugliness.*
> *When one knows of good,*
> *Already there is evil.*
> *When there is,*
> *There is also, is-not.*

When there is easy,
There must be difficult.
When there is before,
There is after.
When there is the red man,
There is the white man.
In this circle, hear what I sing."

Jumping Bear sang the song many times, so he would remember clearly when he returned to the village. Perhaps Ottawa could help him know the meaning of the song.

There was a meeting going on. Jumping Bear saw the entire village gathered in the center circle, so he rode his horse into the center of the village, then dismounted and walked closer to see what was happening.

"The council returns," someone called.

"Now, we shall know," another said.

"What is it?" Jumping Bear asked someone near him. "Why has the council met?"

"Do you not know? No, that is right, you were in the mountains, weren't you?" Elk Heart said. He pointed to a beautiful white woman who was standing just inside the circle. "We took a *winu* on our war party. One-Who-Waits claimed her for his *yuza,* as he led the war party."

"Then that is his right," Jumping Bear said. "She should be his slave if he wishes."

"But wait," Elk Heart said. The *winu* showed strong medicine and great bravery. When One-Who-Waits raised his war club against her, she laughed at him."

"She *laughed* at him?" Jumping Bear said, looking at the pretty woman with even more admiration now.

"Yes. And she alone stood her ground against us, while the soldier chief ran away in disgrace. The *winu* tried to save a small girl, but the soldier chief killed the small girl. We named her Real Woman."

"That is an honorable name," Jumping Bear said.

"Real Woman has asked for the right to choose a husband," Elk Heart said. "She has asked to be the wife of Ottawa. The council has met to decide."

Jumping Bear moved closer to look at the one called Real Woman. Closer and closer he edged toward her, moving through the crowd until he was standing inside the circle, just a few short feet away from her. Then he saw her eyes, and he gasped. These were the same eyes he had seen in the white horse in his dream!

"The council has decided," Gallant Bear called to the village. He held up the stick with feathers Ottawa had given him earlier, and all who saw it grew quiet, for this was a very sacred stick. The feathers on this stick were said to come from an eagle plucked from the sky by Buffalo Cow Woman herself. It was a very old and very important stick, and whoever held the stick was the spokesman for the council. Ordinarily it would be held by Ottawa, but as Ottawa was one of the parties involved in this decision, the stick had temporarily passed to another. "Real Woman shall have the right to marry Ottawa," Gallant Bear said.

Real Woman smiled broadly and she turned to say something to Kettle Woman. At that moment,

One-Who-Waits, in a fit of rage, grabbed a spear and threw it at Real Woman. Jumping Bear saw it from the corner of his eye, and, moving instantly, shot out his hand and caught the spear as it flew by, stopping it with the broad, sharp point just inches away from piercing Real Woman's body.

Nearly all had seen Jumping Bear's great feat, and they all cheered him, and expressed their admiration for such a deed. Jumping Bear turned toward One-Who-Waits, ready to do battle with him if need be, but One-Who-Waits stomped away from the circle, walking backwards and smiling politely at everyone. He climbed onto his horse, facing to the animal's rear, and he rode away. His life as a contraire had begun.

8

FOR A MOMENT, Fanny was stunned. She stood in silence and, with the others who were present, watched as One-Who-Waits rode, backwards, out of the camp. Then she realized how close she had come to death, and she realized also, that her life had been saved by the Indian who had snatched the spear in its flight.

Fanny looked at the Indian. He was tall and handsome, and not scarred as were so many of the others. She couldn't help but notice his even, white teeth, and clear, sparkling eyes.

"Thank you," Fanny said. "You saved my life."

"No," Kettle Woman said quickly, reaching out to put her hand on Fanny's shoulder, and pulling her back. "You must not say this."

Fanny turned to Kettle Woman. "But why can't

I thank him?" she asked. "I owe my life to him."

"If you say such words before witnesses, then you give yourself to him. This, you cannot do, for the council has given you to Ottawa."

"Oh, I'm sorry," Fanny said, and she turned to apologize to the tall, handsome Indian who had saved her life, only to see him climbing onto his horse, as if totally ignorant of her presence.

"He is Jumping Bear," Kettle Woman said. "He is like a son to Ottawa. He will behave as if the words weren't spoken. But some would behave poorly, and you would be trapped."

"Your social customs are going to take some getting used to," Fanny said, and even as she uttered the words, she felt a small shudder come over her. Getting used to the customs meant that she would have to stay here for an indefinite period of time. How long would she have to stay, she wondered? And would she be able to make the adjustment, and live the life expected of her?

"In twelve days, you will be married," Kettle Woman said. "There is much to do before then."

"Am I to be tied again?" Fanny asked, rubbing her wrists gingerly.

"No," Kettle Woman said. "You are now an Oglala. The council has made you so. Oglala women are sometimes beaten, but they are never tied."

"Beaten?" Fanny asked in alarm. "Are Oglala women beaten?"

"Only when they are unwomanly, and do not behave as wives should behave," Kettle Woman said. "Then it is a husband's duty to beat his wife."

"Does Ottawa beat his wives?"

"I, myself, have never been beaten," Kettle Woman said. "But Willow Branch and Morning Flower have often been beaten. They are Hunkpapa and they are sisters. They are Ottawa's other wives. They are unhappy that you will be a new wife, for it threatens their rank with Ottawa."

"I am sorry they are unhappy," Fanny said. "Perhaps I can make friends with them."

"No," Kettle Woman said easily. "They have taken a vow to be your enemy. You cannot become their friend."

"Oh," Fanny said. "Surely if I try very hard, I can win them over."

"*Hunkpapa* are known to lie with dogs when they wish pleasure and no man is present. Willow Branch and Morning Flower are not worthy to be your friends. Do not waste your time with them. They are my enemies as well."

As Fanny and Kettle Woman walked toward Ottawa's hogan, Fanny looked around at life in the village, curious to see what was to be her home. Since the council had broken up, things had returned to normal. Women were at work again, and the men had returned to their horses, or had retired to groups, where they sat in circles telling stories and talking. Children ran free, tolerated by their elders as they darted in and out of hogans and tipis without regard as to who lived where, laughing and shouting as do children everywhere.

"Kettle Woman, why do some live in tipis, and some live in earthen shelters?" Fanny asked.

"Every summer we come to *Miniwacici* to live," Kettle Woman said. "But when the leaves turn, we leave the *Miniwacici* and follow the game. Some

have built hogans here, and some have built hogans in the place of our winter encampment, and
they move from one hogan to the other. Many pre-
fer to move their tipi, and have never built a hogan in either place."

"Ottawa has a hogan?"

"Yes, because he is the council elder, what the
whites call a chief. But often he will have his
wives put up a tipi, for he prefers to live in a tipi.
You must erect a tipi for the week-of-no-women-
but-the-new-wife."

"What?" Fanny asked. "You mean *I* have to erect
a tipi? Why, I wouldn't even know where to start."

"I will help you," Kettle Woman said.

They reached the hogan then, and Kettle Woman went through the door, and motioned for Fanny
to follow her.

There were two other women inside, consider-
ably younger looking than Kettle Woman, but both
just as plump as Kettle Woman. It became very
obvious to Fanny at that moment that being the
wife of a chief meant, at least, that you didn't go
hungry.

Kettle Woman and the two other wives began
speaking, but Fanny couldn't understand what they
were saying.

"Look, Willow Branch," Morning Flower said.
"Kettle Woman has become the slave of the *winu*
who would become Ottawa's wife."

"See how she helps the *winu*," Willow Branch
said, putting the same contemptuous sneer in her
voice as had been in Morning Flower's insult.
"Perhaps she will also hold onto Ottawa's penis, to
help him mount her."

"As you hold onto the penis of a dog to help him mount your sister?" Kettle Woman replied.

"You speak with the tongue of Ottawa's first wife now, old woman, but soon he will tire of you and he will throw your stick away. Then you will beg for scraps, and if I feel kindly toward you, I may feed you with the dogs of the camp," Willow Branch said.

"I have no fear that I will be discarded," Kettle Woman said. "You have the fear, or you would not make a vow to be the enemy of Real Woman."

"You will see," Willow Branch said. "It is not only we who shall be the enemy of the *winu*. Soon many others will be her enemy as well, for they will learn that the word of a *winu* is not to be trusted."

Fanny had no idea what the women were saying, but she could tell from the tone and texture of the conversation that it was not friendly toward her. She was glad Kettle Woman had placed herself in the position of being her defender, and she shuddered to think of how she would fare had Kettle Woman not done so.

Kettle Woman gathered several poles, then indicated to Fanny that she should pick up a large bundle. "We will go now, to put up the tipi," Kettle Woman said.

As Fanny leaned over to pick up one of the bundles, Willow Branch spit on her.

Fanny's reaction was instantaneous. She lashed out at Willow Branch. Fanny was bent over to retrieve the bundle, so she had already gathered her strength for that task. Therefore, when she brought her hand up and around in the backhanded slap, she had, by a unique set of circumstances, mustered all the strength of which she was capable. The result was a blow which not only startled Willow Branch by its suddenness, but by its strength, and the Indian woman was knocked flat on her backside. She lay on the ground with her ears ringing and her head spinning, surprised that a woman who appeared to be so small and so weak, could hit with such stunning force.

"Return her blow, my sister," Morning Flower said.

"Aiiee," Willow Branch said, sitting up and rubbing her eye, gingerly. "The *winu* has the strength of a horse."

Fanny picked up the bundle, bound not to let them see what a load it was for her to carry, and she followed a laughing Kettle Woman through the door of the hogan. As soon as they were outside, Kettle Woman began shouting, and others, nearby, began laughing.

"I have told them how you bested Willow Branch," Kettle Woman explained.

Kettle Woman walked for quite a ways through the village, and Fanny followed, tiring, but determined to bear the load without complaint. Finally, Kettle Woman looked around.

"Have you found no place you like?" she asked.

"I beg your pardon?"

"It is to be your tipi," Kettle Woman explained. "It is for you to choose the place."

"How about right here?" Fanny asked, dropping her load at her feet. If she had known that, she would have pitched the tipi right outside the hogan door.

"This is a good spot," Kettle Woman said. "You are near the water, yet far from where the horses are kept. The ground is flat where the tipi will be, but it is higher than the water so you will not get wet during the big rains. You have chosen a good spot."

Then, Fanny realized that in her way, Kettle Woman had actually chosen this spot, but had done it in such a way as to make it look as if Fanny had chosen it herself.

Kettle Woman began undoing the bundles Fanny had carried, and Fanny looked it over, trying to figure out how the thing went together. The tipi cover was made of buffalo hides, stitched together with the same type of sinew which held Fanny's dress together. In addition to the tipi cover, there were also the poles Kettle Woman had pulled behind her.

"You watch," Kettle Woman said.

Quickly and deftly, Kettle Woman tied the poles together, using the same cord which had bound the bundle. She tied them at one end, then she raised the poles with the tied end up, and she spread the bottoms out so that they formed a tripod. The remaining poles, which were as tall, but not as big around, were leaned against the tripod, until there was a cone. Next, Kettle Woman put the tipi cover in place, by tying it to a stout lifting pole and hoisting it into position. After that, the cover was unfolded around the poles, pegged to the ground along the bottom, then closed at the

seam with wooden pins. Finally, two poles were
attached to the smoke flaps at the top, and Kettle
Woman showed Fanny how to adjust the poles to
vary the size and angle of the opening. The entire
operation had taken only a few minutes, and Fanny
was amazed at how sturdy the finished product
was.

"Take it down," Kettle Woman instructed.

"What? Why, I think it is good," Fanny replied.

"It is good," Kettle Woman said. "But you must
do it. Take it down, then put it up."

Fanny sighed, but she appreciated what Kettle
Woman was doing for her, so she disassembled the
tipi, then started to put it back up.

"No," Kettle Woman said. "First you must prepare to move. Then you put it back up."

Fanny tried to remember how the bundle had
been wrapped and how the pegs and poles were
arranged, and finally she was able to get it into
condition so that it could be moved. Kettle Woman
inspected everything with as critical an eye as
any Sergeant Fanny had ever seen inspecting the
troops at Fort Laramie. Finally, with a grunt, she
approved the packing.

"Now, put the tipi up," Kettle Woman said.

Fanny unpacked the bundle, and, remembering
what she had seen, began erecting the tipi. She put
up the tripod, then the poles, and finally, remembering to use the lifting pole, put the tipi cover
in place. When it was all done and pegged down
around the sides and held closed with the lodge
pins, she looked at Kettle Woman and smiled
proudly. "I did it," she said.

"It is wrong," Kettle Woman said, matter of factly.

"Wrong? What's wrong with it?" Fanny asked.

"Where does sun come up?"

"Where does the sun come up? In the east, of course. What does that have to do with it?"

"The sun comes up there, over that mountain," Kettle Woman said, pointing to the east. "The tipi and the hogan must always open to the direction of the morning sun."

Fanny glanced over toward the other tipis and hogans in the village, and only then did she notice that Kettle Woman was correct. Every door in the village was pointing east.

"Very well," Fanny said. "I shall change it."

Patiently, Fanny pulled up all the ground pegs, then she took the lifting pole and hoisted the cover around until the door opening was facing east. Then she repositioned the ground pegs, reclosed the seam, and repositioned the smoke flaps. Finally she looked toward Kettle Woman again, this time not with a proud smile, but with a hopeful glance.

"It is good," Kettle Woman said. "You will live here until you are married." Kettle Woman turned and started to go back to the hogan.

"Thank you for helping me," Fanny said. She turned back toward the tipi which was now 'hers', then she caught the smell of roasting meat, and suddenly she realized that she was hungry. She had eaten nothing since the raid on the wagon train the day before.

"Kettle Woman," she called.

Kettle Woman stopped and looked back toward her.

"Kettle Woman. . . . I have nothing to eat."

"It is for One-Who-Waits to feed you," Kettle Woman said.

"One-Who-Waits?"

"It was he who captured you," Kettle Woman said. "He must feed you until you are married. That is the law."

"Oh, splendid," Fanny said sarcastically. "If I have to depend on him, I'll probably starve to death."

Kettle Woman turned without another word and started back toward her hogan. Fanny watched her for a few moments, then she looked down toward the stream. She squared her shoulders. Surely, there were fish in that stream. If so, she would not starve.

Fanny walked down toward the stream and stood on the bank looking into the water. After a few moments she saw the quickly moving flashes of silver, as trout darted around the rocks, swimming in the icy water. Yes, she thought. The trout would make a fine meal. All she had to do now was catch one.

As Fanny stood on the bank of the stream looking down at the trout trying to figure out how to catch a fish, One-Who-Waits approached the stream from the other side. He was mounted on his horse, and he was riding backwards. He swung down from his horse, and, walking backward, splashed across the stream. He was carrying two rabbits.

"Oh, One-Who-Waits," Fanny said. I wasn't sure you would come back. I mean you were so angry. I never thought I would say it, but you are a welcome sight. Especially, with the rabbits."

"These are not for you," One-Who-Waits said, handing the rabbits to her.

"What?"

"These are not for you!" he said again, more impatiently. Again he handed the rabbits to her.

"Then why are you handing them to me?"

"Do not take them."

"Alright, I won't," Fanny said, putting her hands behind her back.

"Do not take them!" One-Who-Waits said again, much louder than before.

"Take them, Real Woman," a voice said, and Fanny saw a young boy of about twelve.

"I don't understand," Fanny said. "He says don't take them, but he keeps handing them to me."

"He is a contraire," the young boy explained. "He does everything backwards."

"Oh," Fanny said, reaching for the rabibts. "Oh, yes, I remember now." As soon as Fanny took the rabbits, One-Who-Waits smiled, and backed across the stream to his horse. "Will you eat some of the rabbit?" Fanny called to him.

"Yes," One-Who-Waits said.

"Yes, that means no, doesn't it?"

"No," One-Who-Waits said. He climbed onto his horse, slapped his legs against the animal's side and the horse started away, with One-Who-Waits hanging on, still riding backwards.

"Heavens, will he be like that for the rest of his life?"

"No," the young boy said. "He will either do a brave thing, or he will go crazy in the head. I would eat some of the rabbit if you will have me."

Fanny smiled at the young Indian. "Of course

I will have you," she said. "What is your name?"

"Running Rabbit," the young Indian said.

"Well, Running Rabbit. Let us hope that neither of these animals is your relative," she teased.

"All animals are the relatives of all Oglala," Running Rabbit said seriously. He looked around. "You do not have *peta*?"

"*Peta*," Fanny asked, confused by the term.

"A fire," Running Rabbit explained.

"No," Fanny said. "I don't even know how to start one without a match."

"You gather wood," Running Rabbit said. "I will bring fire."

Fanny decided to take help when and where she could find it, so she gathered the wood and made a pile in front of the tipi. Running Rabbit returned a few moments later with a burning brand, and he used it to start a fire going.

Fanny looked at the two dead rabbits, then Running Rabbit, realizing that she had no knife, gave her his own so she could skin and clean them. A short time later, the rabbits were spitted, and turning slowly over the fire, and the aroma of her own cooking joined with that of the other fires of the camp.

Over the next several days, Running Rabbit proved to be as invaluable to Fanny as Kettle Woman. Running Rabbit brought several things to Fanny. He brought her two more knives and a cooking kettle, as well as several water jugs, eating bowls and spoons. Kettle Woman brought Fanny buffalo robes and more clothes, and she helped Fanny make a soft bed of stretched skin and fragrant grasses. One-Who-Waits made his appearances at odd times during the next several days, bringing rabbits, or squirrels, or fish, or game birds. His strange behavior didn't frighten Fanny quite as much as it did earlier, though she couldn't help but feel that he was a bomb with a slowly burning fuse. At any moment, he might go off, and she hoped that she wasn't alone with him when it happened.

Several times, Fanny saw the handsome Indian Kettle Woman called Jumping Bear, and she was certain that he was looking at her, but when she looked at him, he always looked away.

On the morning of the twelfth day, the day Fanny was to become Ottawa's wife, she was awakened from her sleep by a call outside of her tipi.

"Ho, Real Woman. Ho, Real Woman. Come outside."

Fanny stepped outside. The village was silent with sleep. It was still very early in the morning, so early that the sun was red, and the mist upon the valley had not yet burned away. There was dew on the grass, and the dew sparkled in all the colors of the rainbow. There, standing before her tipi, holding the reins of a horse, stood Jumping Bear.

"I bring you this gift from Ottawa," Jumping Bear said. He handed the reins to Fanny.

"A horse?" Fanny said. "You mean I am to have my own horse?"

"It is your wedding gift."

Fanny walked up to the animal and patted it

affectionately on the neck. "Oh, it is such a beautiful horse," she said.

"It is the swiftest of all Ottawa's ponies," Jumping Bear said. "It is a great honor to be given such an animal."

"Tell Ottawa I am greatly pleased by his wonderful gift," Fanny said.

Jumping Bear said nothing. He just mounted his own horse and started riding back through the early morning quiet of the village.

Fanny stood, petting the horse for several moments, talking to him softly, then she looked down toward the stream and beyond the stream to the rolling prairie which stretched out, endlessly, before her. Somewhere out there was Fort Laramie, and the world she had known before entering this world.

Somewhere out there was freedom.

Then, with absolutely no thought or prior planning, Fanny decided to leave. She climbed onto the back of the horse, and, moving quietly, rode him across the stream away from the village. She was free!

9

ONCE FANNY was far enough away from the village so that she couldn't be heard, she slapped her legs against the side of her horse, to start him running.

"Go horse, go!" she urged.

The horse burst forward like a cannon ball, reaching top speed almost immediately. Fanny bent low over the pony's neck, holding on tightly, laughing into the rush of wind with the pure thrill of the run and the exaltation of the escape. For the moment, she felt as if she and the horse between her legs were one, sharing the same muscle structure and bloodstream. The horse's hooves kicked up little spurts of dust behind him as he galloped across the plains. Jumping Bear had said this was the swiftest of all Ottawa's war ponies, and as she slapped her legs against him again, she believed him. She pushed the horse on, faster and faster, until she had the dizzying sensation that she was going to fly!

Suddenly, and seemingly from out of nowhere, Jumping Bear appeared in front of her. He rode out from behind a rise of ground, and Fanny's horse, startled by him, stopped and reared up. Fanny slid off the horse's back, falling painfully to the ground.

"What the devil!" she called. "What are you doing here?" She got up and began dusting herself off, thankful that she wasn't hurt. The horse she had been riding turned, and ran back to the village without her.

"Where do you go?" Jumping Bear asked.

"Where do I go? I go home, that's where I go," Fanny said angrily.

"That is home," Jumping Bear said, pointing to the village.

"That is *not* home," Fanny said. She looked at Jumping Bear. "Oh, please, you once saved my life. Let me go, won't you? I won't cause anyone any harm. I'll just go back where I belong, and you'll never see me, or hear of me again."

"I cannot do that," Jumping Bear said. "Today you must become the wife of Ottawa."

"I do not *want* to become the wife of Ottawa. Can't you understand that?"

"No," Jumping Bear said. "I cannot understand. You went before the council to ask to become the wife of Ottawa."

"I only did that to get away from One-Who-

Waits," Fanny said. "I assure you, I have no desire
for Ottawa, or for the social standing marrying
him would bring. Now please, can't you see it
would be better for everyone if you just let me
go?"

Jumping Bear reached down and took Fanny by
the upper arm, then lifted her onto his horse in
front of him. He had incredible strength, and he
picked her up as easily as if she had been a child.

"Come," he said, as if tired of the discussion.
"We will go back to the village and find your
horse. Do not try to leave again. I will not speak
of this, this time."

"I hate you," Fanny said. "I hate all of you, and
I want to go home." She began to cry then, and
because it was the first time she had cried since
her capture, all the pent up emotion; fear, heart-
break, sadness over the deaths of so many, anger,
humiliation, and frustration, all came forth to cause
her to cry bitter tears of anguish.

"We will stay here until all your tears are gone,"
Jumping Bear said, halting his horse, and Fanny
noticed, even through her racking sobs, how amazingly gentle and solicitous of her, Jumping Bear's
voice was.

Would she ever leave this place again, she wondered?

Fergus Kelly stepped into the orderly room of
the Commandant's Building, and saw the Sergeant
Major sitting at his desk.

"Colonel Albertson sent word he wished to see
me?"

"Yes, sir," the Sergeant answered. "Go right in, sir."

Fergus had no idea what the Colonel wanted. The Colonel had been most concerned for his welfare ever since he and Parker, and the Davises had returned to Fort Laramie with news of the massacre. Fergus had spent several anxious days since then, wondering if Colonel Albertson would find fault with him because of the incident, and if so, would that cost him his promotion? Fergus was particularly worried about his promotion, for it had not been mentioned once, since his return from the field.

Colonel Albertson was standing near a window, looking out over the parade ground at a drill which was being conducted beneath the flagpole. He had his hands behind his back, and when Fergus came in, he called out to him, without turning around.

"Have you seen 'C' Company's drills, since Lieutenant Masters has been working with them?" the Colonel asked. "He has done an excellent job."

Lieutenant Masters was in direct competition with Fergus for the promotion. If the Colonel was impressed with his handling of the parade drills, perhaps that would be all the excuse he would need to promote Masters over him.

"Yes, sir, I have seen their drills," Fergus said. "They are most impressive, and Lieutenant Masters should be commended for doing an excellent job with their training."

Colonel Albertson chuckled, then turned around and held his arm out, indicating that Fergus should be seated.

"Yes," the Colonel said. "Our dear, young Lieutenant is quite good at training. But the question is, how would he hold up under the rigors of battle, eh?"

"That's the question, sir," Fergus said, not sure of where this conversation was going.

"Yes, well, it's no longer a question with you, is it, Fergus?"

"I beg your pardon, sir?" Fergus asked.

"I mean you have met the enemy in the field, and you behaved in the highest traditions of the service, and, as a fellow graduate, I might say, in the highest traditions of the corps."

"I did my duty as I saw my duty, sir."

"Yes, and what a magnificent duty that was, too," Colonel Albertson said. "Listen to the dispatch I have sent to Washington." Colonel Albertson picked up a sheet of paper, cleared his throat, and began to read.

"Lt. Fergus D. Kelly, on the 28th day of July, 1864, did, while leading a detachment of ten men in the escort of a wagon train, defend same from a devastating attack launched by over 250 Sioux Indians. Though outnumbered 25 to one, Lieutenant Fergus Kelly fought gallantly, rallying his men and the members of the wagon train party to super-human efforts in their attempt to defend themselves. He watched a little girl in his wife's charge be slain by an Indian's war club, and then he saw his own wife brutally murdered."

Colonel Albertson paused for a moment, and swallowed. "It is still hard to believe that such a lovely . . . . lovely woman," he started, then he cleared his throat and went on reading from the paper, without finishing his thought.

"When the last man of his command, and the last member of the wagon party were killed, and only then, Lieutenant Fergus Kelly braved the gauntlet of warriors, and escaped. His primary concern was the lives of the three wagon party members who had become separated from the main train, and he found them still alive, then, through the exercise of good leadership, led them through hostile territory, back to the safety of Fort Laramie."

Colonel Albertson looked up. "Does that about sum up your report?" he asked.

"I would say, yes, sir," Fergus said. "It is a most accurate description of what happened out there."

"I want to tell you again how sorry both Mrs. Albertson and I are, over the unfortunate demise of your lovely wife, Fanny."

"Yes," Fergus said. "Watching her struck down was quite a blow."

"I know nothing can replace the love of a good wife," Colonel Albertson said. "But I do have two things which I hope help to ease the pain you're going through."

"What two things, Colonel?"

"First, I have this," Colonel Albertson said. He picked up the paper. "I didn't read all of it to you. Now I shall finish it." Colonel Albertson cleared his throat, then studied the paper for a moment before he went on. "There is one more paragraph." He read again. "Therefore, I hereby

request that Lieutenant Fergus D. Kelly be award-
ed the Medal of Honor."

"The Medal of Honor?" Fergus said. He gasped,
unable to believe what he heard.

"Yes, Fergus, the Medal of Honor," Colonel Albertson said. Colonel Albertson's eyes beamed
proudly, and he stepped forward to shake Fergus'
hand. "We will show those back east, that it is
not only the officers and men who are engaged in
the War of Rebellion who are capable of acts of
glory and honor. We, here on the plains in the
Indian wars, are equally capable of valor. I am
proud to be your commander, *Captain* Kelly."

"*Captain* Kelly? Did you say *Captain* Kelly, sir?"

Colonel Albertson chuckled. "That I did, Fergus."
He reached for another piece of paper on his
desk. "Here are your orders of promotion. Congratulations, Captain."

"Thank you, sir," Fergus said.

"It's a shame Mrs. Kelly couldn't have lived to
see this proud moment," Colonel Albertson said.

"Yes, isn't it?"

"It's strange that the burial detail was unable to
find her body," Colonel Albertson said. He rubbed
his chin. "You are certain she was killed?"

"Colonel, do you think for one moment I would
have abandoned her, had she lived?"

"No, of course not," Colonel Albertson said. "It's
just that, without a body, one can always have
hope."

"I have no hope, Colonel, because I have no il-
lusions," Fergus said.

"Well, here is some more good news for you,"
Colonel Albertson said. "I have requested permis-

sion from Washington to mount a punitive campaign against the Indians."

"A . . . . a punitive campaign, sir?"

"Yes. We will launch it this winter, when the Indians are in their winter encampment. You will lead it." Colonel Albertson smiled broadly again. "You will have your revenge, Captain."

"Yes," Fergus said. "Yes, I shall look forward to that with most eager anticipation." Fergus saluted Colonel Albertson, then did a sharp about-face, and left the Colonel's office. The Sergeant Major approached him and offered his congratulations.

"I knew of the promotion, Cap'n, but I couldn't say anything," he said. "The Colonel wanted to be the one to break the news. Congratulations."

"Thanks," Fergus said, barely hearing the Sergeant Major's words.

Fergus stepped out of the Commandant's Building, onto the wooden porch. The two soldiers who were standing sentry duty just outside the door came to attention and brought their rifles up in the prescribed presentation of arms. Fergus returned their salutes, then stepped off the porch and out into the sun and the dust of the quadrangle.

A punitive expedition, he thought. That meant he would have to face those heathen devils again! Fergus felt his hands beginning to shake in fear, and he felt a nervousness in the pit of his stomach.

He couldn't face them again! He was nearly killed the last time . . . . surely he would be killed this time! Why would Colonel Albertson send him against them again? Doesn't he understand?

For one, long, nervous moment, Fergus Kelly, newly appointed Captain of the Mounted Infantry, considered running away. He would desert. That's what he would do.

No, he couldn't do that. If he deserted and if he were caught, he would be disgraced . . . . maybe worse. In time of war, deserters were hanged. Colonel Albertson would have that authority, and Fergis didn't doubt but that he would exercise it.

Fergus was trapped. He would have to stay, and he would have to lead the expedition.

But wait, he told himself, growing somewhat calmer. The expedition isn't until winter . . . that's a long way off. Much could happen between now and winter. Let us not do anything yet, he told himself. Let us wait until winter.

Fergus took several deep breaths, then, thankfully, felt his stomach settling again. He saw the Sutler Store, then he thought of the Captain's shoulder boards which the Sutler had ordered for the officer who would be promoted. He smiled, and went in to get them. He would put them on, then, casually, walk out to observe Lieutenant Masters drill with his company.

Matt Parker stepped up to the bar of the saloon and wiped the back of his hand across his mouth. When the bartender stepped over to him, Matt asked for a glass of beer.

"I've got some good whiskey," the bartender said, drawing the beer from a barrel behind the bar. The golden liquid filled the mug and a white head of foam built up on top of the gold. "You want a whiskey, too?"

"No, thank you," Matt said. "I've been riding pretty hard for the last couple of days, and I need something to cut the dust out of my throat. Beer will do."

The bartender set the beer on the counter and Matt gave him a nickel, thanked him, then lifted the mug for a long, satisfying swallow.

"Where've you been ridin'?" the bartender asked.

"North."

"North? That's Indian territory, mister. You're lucky you wasn't scalped."

"I know it's Indian territory," Matt said. "I've been looking for someone."

"An Indian?"

"No."

"Well the chances are if they ain't Indian and they're up there, they're dead now."

"She's not dead," Matt said. "I know she isn't dead."

"She? You're lookin' for a woman up in Indian territory? A *white* woman?"

"Yes," Matt said.

The bartender wiped the counter in front of Matt, using a damp cloth. "I don't know why you're a'wastin' your time, mister. Even if she's alive, she wouldn't be no good to you now, not if she's been with the Indians all this time."

Matt's eyes narrowed menacingly, and he glared at the bartender. "You mean I should shoot her if I find her, is that it?"

The bartender measured the danger in Matt's eyes, and backed away from any further confrontation.

"No, sir, I didn't mean nothin' like that," he said. "I didn't mean nothin' 'tall. I hope you find her, mister, really I do. 'N if I hear anythin', I'll let you know right away."

Matt looked at the fear in the bartender's eyes, then he sighed, a sigh of disgust. How could he blame the bartender for feeling that way when Fanny's own husband felt that way? Fergus Kelly swore that Fanny was dead, that he had seen her killed with his own eyes, but Matt didn't believe him. Not for a moment did he believe him.

Fanny was alive, and he was going to find her. &

10

TRUE TO HIS word, Jumping Bear said nothing about Fanny's attempt to escape, and by noon the rest of the village had already begun the celebration of the marriage which would take place at sundown. Gifts of flowers were piled high around Fanny's tipi. In addition to the flowers, there were other gifts, such as eating utensils, robes, blankets, and baskets of corn and turnips.

Kettle Woman was in Fanny's tipi, having come by to help her prepare for the wedding. As they worked on Fanny's dress, Kettle Woman continued with her language instruction, and with the lessons on the customs of the Oglala.

"It is important for you to learn the language as quickly as possible," Kettle Woman said. "For once you know the language, the *Wanagi* of the Oglala will come to live in your body."

"The *Wanagi*," Fanny said. "That means soul, doesn't it?"

"Yes," Kettle Woman said. "Do believers in the *Jesus-Wakan* have a soul?"

"Catholics believe in a soul, of course. But what is *Wakan?*"

"The Great Spirit which is over everything," Kettle Woman explained.

"God," Fanny said. "We call the Great Spirit over everything, God."

"Yes, I have heard that," Kettle Woman said. "Do you believe in the Jesus-God?"

"Yes," Fanny said. "And Kettle Woman, even though I want to become a good Oglala, I will not stop being a Catholic, a believer in the *Jesus-Waken.*"

"It would not be good if you stopped believing in your *Jesus-Wakan*," Kettle Woman explained. "For then your medicine would be weak. It is important that everyone have a *Wakan* to pray to. Without *Wakan*, we would be nothing. But the Oglala believe every person must find their own *Wakan*. In the life of the Oglala, there is one thing more important than all other things. The *Wanagi*, what you call the soul, is the most important. When the Oglala awakens in the early morning and sees the rising sun, it is a good time to pray. When the Oglala sees food which the *Wakan* has put on earth, it is a good time to pray. When the Oglala sees lightning, or hears thunder, it is a good time to pray. When the *Wakan* takes the sun from the sky and makes night so that one can sleep without the pain of bright light in the eyes, it is a good time to pray."

"Catholics pray for all these things as well," Fanny defended.

"Ah, then this is good," Kettle Woman said. "For if the *Jesus-Waken* who came to the whites is the true Great Spirit, then he hears all prayers . . . . the prayers of the whites and the prayers of the Oglala. If the *Jesus-Wakan* is not the true Great Spirit, then the true *Wakan* hears the prayers."

"There is one thing which bothers me," Fanny said. "I already have a husband. He is the one the Oglala call Soldier-Who-Is-A-Coward. His real name is Fergus Kelly."

"Soldier-Who-Is-A-Coward is your husband?" Kettle Woman asked.

"Yes," Fanny said. "As a Catholic, I can only have one husband."

"But he has brought disgrace to you."

"That doesn't matter," Fanny said. "He is still my husband."

"It is easy to divorce him," Kettle Woman said. "Divorce him and when you marry Ottawa, you will only have one husband. That will satisfy your Christian law."

Fanny laughed. "Kettle Woman, a bill of divorcement is very, very difficult to get, even for one who is not a Catholic. I cannot divorce him."

"For the whites it is difficult. For the Oglala it is easy. You are going to be married by Oglala law, you will divorce Soldier-Who-Is-A-Coward by Oglala law."

"How would I do that?"

"Do you have something which belongs to Sol-dier-Who-Is-A-Coward?"

"No," Fanny said. "I have nothing now. Every-thing was lost when the wagon was . . . ." Sud-denly Fanny thought of her wedding band, and she touched it. "Wait," she said. "Fergus gave this to me."

Kettle Woman looked at the ring. "Yes, I have seen such things. It is the marriage symbol of the whites. Tonight, before Ottawa takes you for his wife, you must remove the yellow metal from your finger and throw it away. As you throw it away, say the word, *tawamiciya*. This means, 'I am free of other men'."

"But even if I do this," Fanny said, "I will not be free of him by the law of the Catholic Church."

"If you marry Ottawa by the law of Oglala, will you be married to him by the law of your church?" Kettle Woman asked.

"No."

"Then, by the law of the church, you will still have only one husband. And by the law of the Oglala, you will have only one husband. So where is the wrong?"

Fanny laughed. "Kettle Woman, you are a wise woman. I must give you credit for irrefutable logic." She sighed. "Besides, I really have no choice, so I will do as you say. But, does it not bother you to know that I will be marrying Ottawa, who is already your husband?"

"If it pleases Ottawa to take you as his wife, it pleases me," Kettle Woman said. "And it also pleases me that you will soon be my *teya*. That is the word for the kinship between two women who have the same husband. I will be very happy to be your kin."

Fanny reached out and squeezed Kettle Woman's hand. "And I will be happy to become your kin as well," she said.

"Real Woman," Running Rabbit called. "May I enter your tipi?"

"Of course," Fanny said.

Running Rabbit came into the tipi, and, seeing that he was the only male present, moved immediately to the right side of the tipi to assume the position of respect due his sex, even though he was still very young. He sat down, and began eating the piece of meat he had brought into the tipi with him.

"Uhmm," he said. "This is very good. There is much food like this being prepared for the marriage. I wish many more would marry, so that there would be such a feast every day."

"It is good that this is not so," Kettle Woman said. "For if there were many more feasts, you would soon be as fat as I am, and you would not be a swift runner. When you grew older, you could not become a skilled warrior."

"I am a skilled warrior now," Running Rabbit said, stung by the inference in Kettle Woman's remark, that he may still just be a child.

"I know you are a skilled warrior now," Kettle Woman said, easily pacifying his youthful vanity. "Please forgive me. I did not mean otherwise."

"One-Who-Waits does not realize this," Running Rabbit said. "That is why I do not like him. I am glad he has become a contraire. That means he will not be in the village for the feast. He has ridden into the hills."

"I, too, am glad he won't be here," Fanny said.

"Jumping Bear will not be here either," Running Rabbit went on, sucking noisily on the bone, now that the meat had been eaten.

"Where is Jumping Bear?" Kettle Woman asked.

"He says he is going to find the buffalo herd to see how fast the fur is growing, so that he may know how long before the snows come. But I do not believe this. I believe Jumping Bear would like to have Real Woman for himself, and does not wish to see her become Ottawa's wife."

"Oh, Running Rabbit, surely you are wrong," Fanny said, with an expression of shock in her voice.

"No," Running Rabbit said easily. "I am right."

"Yes," Kettle Woman agreed. "It is easy to see that Jumping Bear would have you for his own if he could. In his eyes I can see that he desires to have pleasure with you."

Fanny thought it was strange that Kettle Woman and Running Rabbit could talk about such a thing so easily, without the slightest hint of shock or condemnation of Jumping Bear. And yet, surely, it was no more strange than her own behavior, for she was actually about to take an Indian husband. She, Fanny Marie Kelly, nee O'Lee, a girl who had once considered becoming a nun, was about to become an Indian's squaw.

* * *

When Fanny and Kettle Woman went to the ceremony that night there was a ring of campfires burning brightly around the outer edge of the center circle of the camp. A circle, Fanny knew by now, was very important to the Oglala. The power of the world worked in a circle, or so the Oglala believed. They reasoned that the sky is round, the moon is round, and the earth is round, and that was not without purpose. The seasons also form a circle, always coming back again. The nests of birds are round, tipis are round, and hogans are round. The tipis and the hogans are always set in a circle, and all meetings and ceremonies take place in the center of that circle.

Fanny looked toward the other side of the circle, and she saw Ottawa standing there, dressed in his ceremonial finest. He wore a feathered headdress which was so long that the end of it trailed all the way to the ground. He carried the sacred feather stick, and his jacket and trousers were decorated with brightly colored beads. His eyes glowed in the reflected light of the many campfires as he looked over the assemblage. At that very moment, the drums and the chanting grew quiet.

Ottawa started toward the middle of the circle, and when he reached the middle of the circle, he held his hand out toward Fanny. Fanny just stood where she was for a moment, awed by the absolute silence which had come over the camp. Over the last two weeks she had grown used to the constant noise of the village; the drums, the chants of the men, the babble of the women, and the laughter of the children. Now there was no sound except the snapping and popping of the wood in the dozen or so campfires.

Several hundred faces were looking toward Fanny now, all of them bathed orange by the flickering light of the fires. For Fanny, there was a surrealism to the moment which made it all seem like a dream. It couldn't be real . . . . and yet, despite all logic, it was.

"If you would divorce Soldier-Who-Is-A-Coward, you must do so now," Kettle Woman whispered. "Take off the yellow metal."

Fanny felt of her ring. She knew that the Indian divorce of Fergus would have absolutely no validity in her own world, but, she also knew that it would have a great symbolism for the Indians. And, she thought, for herself as well. She smiled, and she wished Fergus could be here at this very moment to see her act of defiance toward him. She pulled the ring off and held it up. It glistened in the light of the fires.

"This is the ring of my white *Wicaha,* my husband," Fanny said. "He is the one called Soldier-Who-Was-A-Coward."

There was a murmuring reaction to her statement. Most of the Indians had never even considered whether or not Fanny was married. When they learned that she was not only married, but was married to the soldier chief who had disgraced himself, they were surprised by the revelation.

Fanny threw the ring as far as she could, and it disappeared into the blackness, beyond the nearest campfire. "*Tawamiciya!*" she yelled. And then, in English, so that it would have more meaning to her; "I am free of this man!"

"Hi, hi, hi, hi!" the Indians shouted gleefully, and at that very moment, Fanny felt a peculiar sense of pride over the fact that her dramatic act had greatly pleased them. She walked to the center of the circle and stood before him.

"*Mitawicu*," Ottawa said. "I take this woman for my wife."

"*Miwicaha*," Fanny replied. "I take this man for my husband."

Ottawa sat down then, sitting on crossed legs. Fanny sat down, remembering to sit with her legs to one side, as was prescribed for a woman, and food was brought to them. When they took their first bite, the others in the village started eating, and the feast began.

Midway through the feast, Ottawa stood, and beckoned for Fanny to follow him. He led her through the circle, and into the darkness beyond the campfires, until they reached her tipi. Just outside the tipi, he motioned for her to go inside.

"It is not for me to enter the tipi before my husband," she said.

"I do not go into the tipi with you," Ottawa said.

"What?" Fanny asked, surprised by the strange statement. "What do you mean? Why not?"

"Hear me," Ottawa said. "I am a man of many winter counts. I am old, and set in my ways, and I find peace in the quiet times. You are a young woman, and I fear your blood will be too hot and your desire too strong. I cannot share the hot blood and the strong desire. I cannot make *cezin*, even with one as desirable as you. And I do not wish to try."

"I don't understand," Fanny said. "Why did you marry me?"

"Did you wish to marry One-Who-Waits?"

"No," Fanny said. "Absolutely not!"

"Then it was good for you to marry me, for now One-Who-Waits has no claim on you. You are safe."

Fanny realized then what Ottawa had done for her, and never had she felt a greater sense of gratitude for anyone.

"Ottawa, I thank you," she said. "From the bottom of my heart, I thank you, for what you have done for me. And I will try to be a good wife for you in whatever other way you wish."

"It is good that you are pleased by what I have done," Ottawa said. "And now I have done something more to please you."

"Something more? What more could you possibly do?" Fanny asked. It was too much to believe that he was going to let her go home.

"I know that you have hot blood and strong desire. You will not be a woman without a man on her marriage night."

"What?" Fanny asked, not certain that she understood what Ottawa was suggesting to her.

"Go inside your tipi," Ottawa said.

Fanny, curious as to what he was talking about, slipped into the tipi.

There was a fire in the center of the tipi, and though most of the smoke was being evacuated by the smoke flap at the top, some was trapped inside, providing a diaphanous haze to partially obscure the interior. Despite the haze, and the dim, shadowy light, Fanny was able to see quite well, and she saw, instantly, what Ottawa was talking about. For there, lying on the soft furs, wearing only a loin cloth, and propped up on his elbow and staring toward her, was Jumping Bear.

Fanny felt a quick fear. Despite that fear however, deep down inside, equal in intensity with the fear, was a racing thrill. Ottawa expected her to go to bed with Jumping Bear.

"No," she said. "No, I can't do this." She took a step back toward the tipi opening.

Jumping Bear made a motion with his hand, inviting her to come to bed with him.

"I . . . . I can't," Fanny said. "This isn't right, I'm married to Ottawa."

"It is for Ottawa that we do this," Jumping Bear said.

"But you can't just, I mean we shouldn't just . . . ." Fanny stopped in mid-sentence. Why was she fighting this? After all, hadn't she made up her mind to go to bed with Ottawa? Was it any more right to go to bed with Ottawa, than it would be to go to bed with Jumping Bear? No, of course not. Despite the Indian divorce, and marriage, she was still married to Fergus and she knew it. So it wouldn't have been right to go to bed with Ottawa either. Why then, did this situation seem more dangerous to her?

And then Fanny realized the answer to her own question. She would have gone to bed with Ottawa in the belief that she really had no alternative, she was being forced into it. But, if she went to bed with Jumping Bear, it was because . . . God help her . . . she *wanted* to. At that very moment Fanny knew that she was going to give herself to him. Without another word, she reached up and unfastened the bone clasp which held the dress together at the shoulders. With one, deft action, she let the dress fall to her ankles, then she stepped out of it, and stood by the fire with her loveliness bathed by its light so that her body shined in a soft, shimmering glow.

Jumping Bear put his arms up to invite her to his bed, and she lay down with him, body against body, feeling at once that Jumping Bear had no problem with the *cezin* which had so worried Ottawa. Jumping Bear's hands moved slowly over Fanny's body, pausing lightly on her breasts, then moving down to that part which was the wellspring of her sensitivity. His hands lingered there to bring on the most exquisite pleasure, and to send bubbles of fire throughout her body.

They lay against each other, naked and unashamed, with their body heat transferring from one to the other until they were on fire with desire for each other. Fanny felt the muscles of Jumping Bear's chest, and the iron-hard strength of his thighs. She was very aware of the eager thrust of his maleness, and then, because she could wait no more, she lay on her back and pulled him onto her.

Fanny felt his weight move over her, and riding the crest of the tide of passion, she guided him into her with a small groan of pleasure.

Jumping Bear took her with more tenderness than Fanny had ever known that a man could possess, and their bodies moved as one in the urgent rhythm which would bring them to the desired climax. Now, Fanny was no longer the *winu*, the captive woman, nor the *yuza*, the slave, nor even Fanny Kelly, the wife of an insensitive husband. She was a creature of flesh and spirit, ignited by a passionate fire in a quest for pleasure. She was a woman with an unquenchable erotic thirst. When the first peak of sensation hit her, it was an orgasmic fireburst, which licked at her with tongues of flame, igniting and reigniting rapture as wave after wave of pleasure swept over her.

They lay together for several minutes afterward, while Fanny floated with the pleasant sensations which lingered on in her body, long after they had finished making love. Jumping Bear put his hand gently on her hip, and she could feel the strength of it as it lay across the sharpness of her hip bone and the soft yielding of her flesh. And, for the moment at least, there was nothing in the world which seemed more right to Fanny than this.

11

Matt pulled his parka about him more tightly and, standing in the stirrups of his saddle, looked down on the other side of the mountain he had just climbed. The world before him was harsh white and stark black, covered with the blanket of new-fallen snow. About a mile and a half below him he saw a small encampment, consisting of two tipis and a campfire.

Matt did not happen upon the encampment by accident. He had smelled the woodsmoke when he awoke earlier this morning, and he merely followed his nose to this point.

"Well, horse, they appear to be Indian," Matt said quietly. Matt often spoke to his horse, just to hear the sound of a human voice, even though it be his own. Matt leaned over and patted his horse on the neck. "I hope they are friendly, and in the mood for a little trading."

Matt had some flour, beans, coffee, and salt. He had no meat because he was in Indian territory and he wasn't sure how they would react to a white man poaching their game.

Matt started down the mountain toward the camp below. He could see a woman working around the fire, and, a short time later, he saw two more figures in the encampment . . . . another woman and a man. He knew also that they had seen him, for his approach was as visible as black ink on white paper. His horse left a trail in the snow behind him, a long, dark scar on the face of the white mountain.

"Hello the camp," he called when he was within hailing distance.

"I know'd you was a white man from the way you was ridin'," the man at the encampment answered, and his voice confirmed the suspicion Matt had harbored for the last several minutes; that the camp consisted of one white man and two Indian women. "D'ya have 'ny coffee?"

"Yeah," Matt said, swinging down from his horse. He opened the saddle bag and took out a small pouch. He had measured his coffee into pouches, the better for trading, and he flipped the pouch to one of the Indian women.

"The name is Charles M. Gwaltney," the white man said. "But most folks jes' call me Mountain Charley."

Mountain Charley was a big bear of a man,

with a full, bushy, red beard, and long, scraggly red hair. He was dressed in buckskins and buffalo robes.

"I've heard of you," Matt said. "My name's Matt Parker."

"Be ye' wantin' some terbaccy for the coffee?" Mountain Charley asked.

"No," Matt said. "I'd rather have some meat, if you've some to spare."

"I can spare you some," Mountain Charley said. "Fac' is, the women are cookin' up a meal right now. Why don't you stay with us a spell and eat a bit?"

"I thank you kindly for your generous offer," Matt said. He looked at the two women with Mountain Charley. One was moon-faced and chubby, the typical Indian squaw, but the other was thinner and younger, with large, doe-like eyes and clear, olive skin. She looked at Matt with undisguised curiosity, and he could appreciate her loveliness, even beneath all the winter clothing she was wearing.

"I see ye' be lookin' at my women," Mountain Charley said with a chuckle. "This here one is my wife, Sasha, 'n the little one is her sister, Tanteo. Tanteo's winterin' with us."

"Has it been a good season for trapping?" Matt asked.

Mountain Charley stuck a handful of tobacco in his mouth and chewed for a while. He squirted a stream of tobacco juice onto the snow, browning its crust, before he answered. He squinted at Matt.

"Now I can't say as it's been too good, 'n I

can't say as it's been too bad," he said. "I've taken some. How goes it with you, Matt Parker? Be ye' trappin' fur?"

"No," Matt said. "I know better'n to trap fur without getting the approval of the Indian council."

"Then what brings you out here in the winter?"

"I'm looking for someone," Matt said. "A woman . . . . a white woman. I believe she is a captive of the Sioux."

Mountain Charley squirted another stream of tobacco juice onto the snow, then spoke to the two women in their own language. Sasha, the older woman, answered him.

"My wife says she had heard talk of a *winu*," Mountain Charley said.

"A *winu*?"

"A captive white woman," Mountain Charley said.

Tanteo spoke then, and her voice had a clear, musical sound to it, like the whisper of wind in the pines.

"Tanteo wants to know if the *winu* is your wife," Mountain Charley said. He laughed. "I think she's taken a fancy to you."

"No, the *winu* is not my wife," Matt said. "She is my friend."

Tanteo spoke again, and again Mountain Charley translated. "She said the *winu* she's heered tell 'bout was the wife of a white man before she divorced him Indian style."

"Divorce?" Matt said. He shook his head. "I don't think Fanny would divorce her husband, scoundrel that he is. What is the *winu's* name?"

"She is called Real Woman," Mountain Charley

said, translating for the women. "She is the wife of Ottawa."

"No, I'm sure this isn't the same woman," Matt said. "Though, if she is a white woman, who else could it be? After all, how many white women are captives of the Indians?"

"I'd say nigh onter a dozen," Mountain Charley said easily.

"What? Are you serious? But, why isn't that known?"

"Most of 'em don't want it known," Mountain Charley said. He chuckled. "The truth is, them that's smart, soon enough work themselves into a pretty good thing with the in'juns. What would happen to 'em if they went back? You think they'd be accepted? I can tell you now that if you really think so, you're jes' dreamin'. No, sir, oncet they've been captured, they've no stomach for goin' back. 'n them that lost 'em in the first place don't want 'em back. So they all p'ertends, you see. The white men folks p'ertends that the women was all kilt, 'n the women p'ertends they can't escape. It all works out that'a'way."

There was a low rumble, rather like thunder, though the sky was cloudless, and the rumble lasted longer than thunder, and it shook the ground.

"That'd be snow slides up in the high passes," Mountain Charley said. "Was you plannin' on tryin' to get through that'a'way?"

"Yes," Matt said.

"Best you don't," Mountain Charley said. He walked over to the pot which was steaming over the campfire, and stirred it, then dipped the spoon in for a bite. He smacked his lips appreciatively. "That's a fine stew there," he went on easily. "The truth is, we've got plenty of meat 'n the women folk cook right good. You're welcome to stay with us a spell, until the snow has stopped slidin' aroun'."

"I don't know," Matt said. "I wouldn't really want to put you out any."

"You wouldn't be puttin' us out none a'tall," Mountain Charley said. "I'd be welcomin' some white-man talk, 'n the young woman there'd more'n likely welcome havin' a man to curl up to at night. It gets powerful cold sleepin' alone in this kind of weather, though I figure you've done found that out."

Mountain Charley's suggestion, so easily made, at first shocked, then titillated Matt. He looked over at the young Indian girl and saw with astonishment that she was smiling in embarrassed pleasure.

"She knows what you just said," Matt said, surprised at the discovery.

"Yeah, she can speak the white-man's lingo," Mountain Charley said. "Both of 'em can, but they don't like to give it away to 'jes anyone who comes along. What about it, Tanteo? Do you think you could keep this here feller warm?"

"It is for him to say," Tanteo said. "I will share my blankets if he wishes."

Matt felt a sudden heat in his blood, warm enough to cause him to forget the numbing cold. "I, uh, might stay on for a short time," he said.

"Good, good," Mountain Charley said. "Now maybe Sasha will quit bellyachin' over her sister havin' to sleep alone on these cold nights. She's been after me to take her on as a second wife, but I ain't 'a'gonna do it. It's hard enough keepin' all the laws of one Sioux wife, let alone two. 'N what with me trappin' in Sioux territory all the time, I gotta follow their rules. Iffen I don't, this ugly hair of mine will be hangin' from the lodgepole of one of Sasha's relatives."

"Look here," Matt said. "If I do share her blankets . . . . that doesn't make us married does it?"

Mountain Charley laughed. "No, not unless you go through the ceremony. It's different with me, though. I'm already married to her sister. All I got to do to make Tanteo my wife, is to let her come into our tipi one night. One night, that's all." He pointed at the two tipis which were pitched in the camp. "That's why we've always had two tipis, where ever we've camped." He tapped his finger to the side of his head. "I'm pretty smart when it comes to lookin' after my own skin."

"Eat now," Sasha said, and she began dishing the stew into bowls. Matt took his skillet from his saddlebag and held it out as Sasha ladled food into it. He carried the steaming serving over to a log which Tanteo had cleaned of snow, and sat down beside her at her invitation.

"I have been to school," Tanteo said, proudly. "I know George Washington. He is pres-i-dent," she said, saying the word awkwardly.

"He was the president," Matt said. "Abraham Lincoln is the president now."

"Why is George Washington not pres-i-dent?"

"He's dead."

"Oh," Tanteo said. She looked down sadly. "I am sorry to hear this."

Matt thought he should explain it to her, but decided not to. It would only complicate things. "How old are you?" he asked. He looked at her. "You look like a child."

"I began *isnati* five winter counts before this," Tanteo said resolutely. "Already, I have seen seventeen winters."

"*Isnati?*" Matt looked toward Mountain Charley with a puzzled expression on his face, and Mountain Charley, holding a bone and pulling the meat away with his teeth, laughed. "Her time of the month," he said. "She's been of breedin' age for five years."

"I meant no disrespect, Tanteo," Matt apologized. He smiled. "I meant it as a compliment . . . . a way of telling you that your looks pleased me."

Tanteo's face broke into a wide smile. "I am glad I please you, Matt Parker," she said.

After the meal, Matt unsaddled his horse and hobbled him so that he could forage for grass, but wouldn't be spooked and run away. He moved his saddle and gear into the tipi of Tanteo, then asked Mountain Charley how he might repay the hospitality.

"I've got a line of traps run along the creek bed down yonder a way," Mountain Charley said. "You might go down 'n check 'em out for me. I'll hike back a mile or so to my other trap line 'n fetch the pelts there. You got a long gun?"

"Yes, why?"

"Sometimes the wolves like to hit the animals I got trapped. If you got a long gun, you can discourage 'em," Mountain Charley said.

"I'll get to them now," Matt said, and he ducked

into the tipi to get his rifle, then he started down
along the creekbed to check the traps.

Between the two of them they brought back
more than a dozen beaver pelt, and they stayed
busy cleaning them for the rest of the day. That
night, around the campfire, Mountain Charley en-
tertained Matt with stories of his years as a trapper. It was obvious to Matt that Mountain Charley wanted to talk as much or more than he wanted to listen, and Matt was willing to provide him
with a willing ear.

"I come out here," Mountain Charley was saying, "that much of a fool that I said I'd never let
mountain fever drive me into marryin' a squaw.
I'd seen many a good man go that way. One winter he'd be huntin' pelt, free to go here or there
where ever he pleased, 'n then the next winter he'd
have a squaw taggin' along behind him. Next thing
after the squaw'd come a passel o' kids, 'n he'd
either wind up abandonin' the squaw 'n kids, or
else he'd leave the trappin' life. But then I met
Sasha."

"How did you meet her?" Matt wanted to know.

"Its the damndest thing," Mountain Charley said.
"Here I'd been pokin' aroun' in these mountains
for better'n ten years without nary a scratch. Then
one day I fell on some wet rocks 'n damnme if
I didn't bust up my leg. It hurt somethin' awful,
and started swellin' up 'n turnin' blue. I couldn't
do anythin', so I jes' lay on the bank of the river,
a'waitin' ter die. Well, Sasha, she come along, took
one look, 'n knowed jes' what I needed." He chuckled. "The first thing she done was to take a rock
'n break it again. You think *that* didn't hurt like
the bejesus. I tell you, I thought she was some

squaw woman bent on torturin' me 'cause I was white, 'n I pure passed out from the pain, never suspectin' to see the light of day again. But I woke up sometime later 'n my leg was all bandaged 'n splinted. She broke it, you see, 'cause it was healin' crooked. She kep' me from bein' a cripple. Not only that, she nursed me through it all, 'n I tell you, the more I looked at her ugly round little ole' face, the prettier she got. Soon I figured she was beautiful, 'n 'afore you knew it, I was marryin' up with her."

At the conclusion of his story, Mountain Charley looked over at Sasha and smiled, and she smiled back at him. Though he did not put it in actual words, Mountain Charley had just told Sasha how much he loved her.

Mountain Charley asked Matt about the war between the states, and Matt gave him the information he had seen in the latest issue of *Harper's Weekly*.

"Damn fools back there killin' each other off for no good reason," Mountain Charley said. "I'm glad I was out here when it all started. The truth is, I don't know which side I'd be for. I think they are both damn fools."

"I'm inclined to agree with you," Matt said with a disparaging laugh. "In fact, that is precisely why I am out here."

Mountain Charley filled a pipe with tobacco, then took a burning brand from the fire and lit it. As he drew on it, the bowl turned bright orange, and several glowing ashes escaped from the bowl and rose in the night. The flames of the fire had died down now, and only the banked embers provided warmth and light. The four figures around the campfire were orange-lit from the front, and shadowed in the rear. A spiralling column of smoke climbed the heat column lazily up into the night sky, reaching for the star-dust which lighted up the heavens. On the nearby mountain tops large pine trees thrust up as if they were supporting columns for the heavenly display of lights. In the distance, a lonely wolf called for its mate.

"Tell me about this gal you're a'lookin' for," Mountain Charley said. "What's her name?"

"Fanny Kelly," Matt said. "She is the wife of Army Captain Fergus Kelly."

"If she's this fella Kelly's wife, why ain't he out lookin' for her instead of you?"

"He says she is dead," Matt said.

Mountain Charley chuckled. "He prob'ly wishes she was. It seems the husban's is the ones who most don' want their women back."

"He says he saw her killed," Matt said. "But we found everyone's body but hers, so I don't believe she was killed. Not for a moment do I believe she was killed."

"You set quite a store by her, don't you?"

"I feel responsible for her," Matt said. "I was in charge of the wagon train."

"Say, was this here wagon train goin' through the Oglala holy grounds?" Mountain Charley asked.

"Yes," Matt said.

"That was a damn-fool thing to do, mister," Mountain Charley said. "Hell, if you hadn' gone through their holy grounds, the Oglala would'a let you through with no trouble 'a'tall."

"I know," Matt said. "I tried to explain that to Kelly. He was the military commander. He insisted that the wagon train take the most direct route . . . . and that was through the holy ground."

"I thought you was in charge."

"I wasn't in charge of the military escort," Matt said.

"I heered about that wagon train," Mountain Charley said. "And 'pears to me that I heered they was a woman captured then."

"Yes!" Matt said excitedly. "Yes, that would be her! Is she still alive? Where is she?"

"Now hold on, hold on," Mountain Charley said. "Them was Oglala did all that, 'n these here girls are Minneconjou. I don' know too much about the Oglala . . . . but I'll tell you what. In about a week I'll be takin' all my pelt into the winter camp of the Minneconjou under Wounded Foot, and we can ask him. If anyone'd know about your lady friend, Wounded Foot would. He keeps up with all the gossip of all the tribes better'n any woman gossip I ever knowd." Mountain Charley laughed at his own statement, then he stood up and stretched. "Well, Sasha, let's me'n you go to bed, what do you say? I'll see you in the mornin', Matt Parker."

Matt watched Mountain Charley and Sasha disappear into their tipi, then he turned toward Tanteo. She stared at him with large, brown eyes, then she looked down at the ground in embarrassed silence.

"Well, Tanteo, the moment of truth has arrived," Matt said. "Here is where we both find out if we are going to go through with this."

"I go first," Tanteo said. "You wait until I call for you."

"Very well," Matt said, smiling at her. "If you

want to play the shy maiden, it's all right with me."

Matt watched as Tanteo disappeared into the darkness of the tipi, and he waited outside for her to call him. He was the only one left now, and he looked around the silent camp. His horse had long since joined with the other horses, and they stood near a break of trees, dark, unmoving shadows in the night. A wolf called again, and then, much closer, an owl. A coal popped in the fire, and a shower of sparks fountained up, then dropped back down. The popping ignited a small flame which danced for a moment then died into an orange glow once more.

"Matt Parker," a soft voice called from inside the tipi.

Matt stepped into the tipi, then pulled the flap closed behind him. It was pitch dark inside, and he stood still, lest he stumble over her.

"I can't see you," he said quietly.

"I am here," she said, and her voice was very close, and warm, and intimate, and he felt his blood run hot.

"Just a minute," he said, and quickly, he undressed in the dark. He could feel the cold night air on his nude body as he stood there, and he felt around with his bare feet until he could feel the buffalo robe which covered the blankets. He dropped down to his knees, then crawled forward, feeling with his hands, until he felt the resiliency of soft, smooth, warm flesh, and a hard, tight, nipple. With a quick intake of breath he realized he had just felt her breast.

Tanteo lifted the blanket and Matt moved under it, pressing his nude body against that of the young

Indian girl. The heat of their bodies quickly warmed the robes, so that they were oblivious to the cold around them, and cognizant only of the cocoon they shared.

Matt ran his hands across her body, feeling the delightfully smooth flesh, seeing with his fingers what darkness denied his eyes. His hands moved from her breasts across her flat stomach, and out along the flare of her hips, then across her thighs until they were at the warm, moist . . . . Matt jerked his hand back in shock! There was no hair! Was he in bed with a mere child? Then, he remembered how sparse an Indian's body hair is, and he put his hand back before Tanteo, now flush with passion, realized he had taken it away. She may be sparse of body hair, he thought, but she was certainly a woman in every other respect.

Tanteo's own hands were exploring Matt, and he felt the delicate touch of her fingers, as she touched, explored, and stroked until, with his heart pounding, and the blood rushing with white heat through his body, he moved over her, and into her.

Tanteo changed from the young, almost virginal girl she was at the moment, to a creature who was alive with passion. She writhed beneath him, and she nibbled at his neck and shoulders, and made little sounds of joy in his ears, as she received him. Matt felt her grow tense for just a moment, then she slid across the moment into ecstasy, and as she did so, he dissolved into his own rapture, spending himself into the womb of the young girl beneath him. For that brief instant, he and Tanteo were in touch with the primeval forces of the universe.

12

I⠀T WAS TEN days before Matt and the others rode
into the village of Wounded Foot. The village was
a large, winter encampment of Minneconjou Sioux,
and the tipis were pitched in a circle along the
banks of a river which was choked with ice along
the edges, but flowing free in the middle.

The Minneconjou of Wounded Foot were fur
traders, and the village held most of the winter's
pelts. Mountain Charley was going to store his
skins with the skins of the other trappers, and as
he had been doing this for several years, he had
no qualms about the safety of his furs.

Matt had never ridden into an Indian village
for any reason other than trading, or some other
specific business. At first, he was a little appre-
hensive, but Mountain Charley and the women assured him that his apprehension was misplaced.

n my fire, Parker," Wounded Foot

rley smiled broadly. "Hey, what
ut that?" he said. "He's accepted

Matt said. "Can we ask him about

to it," Mountain Charley warned.
lay around a bit, 'n prolong the
', a'fore the business gets started

rley began talking to Wounded
  language, and Matt sat quietly
ents. He looked around the tipi,
s, the women and children, who
  At one point he heard his name
me mentioned, then everyone in
g the women and children, looked
hed out loud.
self blushing profusely, and he
Mountain Charley what was being
ught it best not to interrupt. Fi-
Mountain Charley ask a question
he knew that was his invitation
the council.
ot, my friend seeks information
man's wagon train which was de-
lala."

wish to know?" Wounded Foot

people killed?" Matt asked anx-

hildren?"

"See, there's this about the injuns that the white
men could learn," Mountain Charley said. "Iffen
one injun accepts you, then all the other injuns in
that injun's family and village accepts you too.
You'll be goin' in with Tanteo, I'm goin' in with
Sasha, that's all there is to it. No one will give
us a second look."

Matt Parker thought that was a little hard to
believe, but as they rode into the village, he was
relieved to see that Mountain Charley was right.
They received a few curious glances, but the curiosity was that for any traveller arriving in a winter encampment, and there was no hostility evi-
denced in the curiosity.

Smoke curled from a hundred tipis as most of
the villagers stayed inside where it was warm.
Those outside who had noted Matt's arrival, were
generally outside as a matter of necessity, to gather
wood, or water, and, once their task was done,
they too, hurried back into the warmth of the
tipis. The village might have been deserted for
all one could tell.

"You ladies find a good place to pitch the tipi,"
Mountain Charley said. He swung down from the
horse with the groan of one who has ridden far,
and is thankful that the journey is ended.

"There aren't many people outside," Matt com-
mented.

"Hell, no, they're inside where it's warm," Mountain Charley said. "Where *we're* gonna be soon's
the women get the tipis up."

Matt looked around the quiet, snow covered village, with the practiced eye of an ex-wagon master, and ex-military commander. "It doesn't look
as if they have any guards posted," he observed.

"Who would they guard against? The injuns don't make war in the winter, and the Minneconjou are traders, so there ain't no trouble with the whites. Besides, would *you* stand guard when it's this cold?"

"It wouldn't be very pleasant duty," Matt agreed.

"That's the way the injuns look at it."

"But someone should do it, shouldn't they?"

"Who?" Mountain Charley asked.

"I don't know, I'm not in command here," Matt answered, exasperated by Mountain Charley's strange comment.

"That's jes' it," Mountain Charley said. "The truth is, they ain't *no one* in command here. No injun can tell another injun what to do. If a guard is posted, it's because someone took it on hisself to stand guard, not 'cause someone told him to do it. If an injun gets too cold, or wet, or hungry, or sleepy, he's likely to jes' walk away from his guardin' duty, 'n there ain' no one can say anythin' to him about it."

"That seems dangerous," Matt said.

"It's always been so, 'n it always will be. Now come on, le's you'n me go talk to Wounded Foot. If anyone's heard about your Fanny, it'll be him."

Matt followed Mountain Charley to a nearby tipi, crunching through the snow as they walked. Their breath hung in front of them in clouds of vapor, and Matt's nose was so cold that it was numb.

"They's a few things you should know about enterin' another fella's tipi," Mountain Charley said. "The injuns, they set a great store by doin' things right, so pay attention to what I say."

"All right," Matt said.

"Normally [...] on in. Whe[...] out from ou[...] bein' winter, [...] get invited i[...] don't cross [...] real bad ma[...] Wounded Fo[...] time to leave[...]

"Yes," Matt[...]

"Iffen ye' g[...] Charley said. [...]

They stopp[...] rated with a [...] colored design[...]

"Ho, Wound[...] "Can you see[...]

The tent fla[...] looking, round[...] enter. Inside t[...] smoke, heavy [...] the nose, ever[...] taking most o[...] Charley aroun[...] like Mountain [...] ground. As so[...] from the smok[...] study Wounded[...]

Wounded Fo[...] hundred years [...] full of wrinkles,[...] though, his eye[...]

"This is Matt[...] "He is a friend[...] I ask that he b[...]

"Take heat fr[...] said.

Mountain C[...] do you think a[...] you right away[...]

"I am glad," [...] Fanny?"

"Don't rush [...] "Injuns like to [...] time 'o sociali[...] in earnest."

Mountain C[...] Foot in his o[...] for several m[...] and at the ot[...] were also insi[...] and Tanteo's [...] the tipi, inclu[...] at him and l[...]

Matt felt [...] wanted to as[...] said, but he [...] nally, he hea[...] in English, [...] to participate[...]

"Wounded [...] about the wh[...] feated by th[...]

"What do [...] asked.

"Were all [...] iously.

"Yes."

"Women[...]

"Yes."

"But, isn't there a chance that someone may have survived the massacre, and be living somewhere now, with the Indians?" Matt asked.

"Yes," Wounded Foot said again.

"Where? Where would such a person be?"

Wounded Foot just looked at Matt, without answering his question.

"Could a woman have survived?"

"Yes."

"Could she be with Oglala now?"

"Yes."

"*Did* a woman survive?" Matt asked, now growing more excited by the possibility.

"Yes."

"*Is* she with the Oglala right now?"

"Yes."

"Mountain Charley, where is the winter encampment of the Oglala?" Matt asked excitedly. "She's there. Fanny is there."

"Hold on," Mountain Charley said with a chuckle. "Ole' Wounded Foot here was jes' tryin' to be nice to you."

"Nice to me? What do you mean?"

"He didn't want to upset ye' none with his answers, so he jes' answered yes to ever'thin', figurin' you was answerin' your own questions the way you was askin' 'em. Let me ask the questions, I think we'll get a bit further."

"All right," Matt agreed.

"Wounded Foot, I have heard talk of a woman, a white woman, who survived the attack on the wagon train. Tell me what you have heard."

"The wagon train passed through the holy buri-

al ground of the Oglala," Wounded Foot said.
"The spirits did not like this, and they asked that
the whites be punished. One-Who-Waits heard
the spirits and it was he who led the attack."

"What happened then?" Mountain Charley asked.

"Soldier-Who-Is-A-Coward ran from the battle
when all were dead except Real Woman."

"Real Woman?" Matt asked.

"She show much bravery," Wounded Foot said.
"She laughed at death, and was named Real Woman."

"I have heard she is the wife of Ottawa the
chief," Mountain Charley said. "Could this be
true?"

"Yes, this is true."

"But would she not be the *Yuza* of One-Who-
Waits?"

"I do not know why she is not the *Yuza* of One-
Who-Waits," Wounded Foot said.

"Tell me more about the soldier coward," Matt
asked.

"I know nothing more," Wounded Foot said.

"You think this here soldier-coward fella is
Kelly?" Mountain Charley asked Matt.

"I know damn well it is," Matt said. "It would
be like him to run away in fear and leave his wife
behind to die. I wish I had a description of him.
Ask him what the soldier coward looked like."

"It won't do any good to ask," Mountain Charley
said. "When someone's disgraced like that, the injuns don't flatter 'em none by passin' in their description."

"What about the Oglala encampment? Does he
know where it is?"

Mountain Charley asked Wounded Foot in his own language, the location of the Oglala encampment, and Wounded Foot answered him.

"It's about ten days ride in the direction of the summer home of the goose," Mountain Charley said. He chuckled. "That's north, 'case ye' didn't figure it out."

"Mountain Charley, I'm going up there," Matt said.

"When?"

"Today," Matt said. "Right now."

"It wouldn't be any too perlite ye' takin' out right now," Mountain Charley said. "It would make Tanteo lose face in front of all her people. Ye' need to wait a bit before ye' go."

"How long do I have to wait?" Matt asked.

"Ye' could leave in the mornin' 'n it would be all right," Mountain Charley said. "Besides, it's gonna come up a snow tonight anyway. Ye'd be better off waitin' until tomorra."

"All right," Matt said. "But tomorrow morning, the very first thing, I'm leaving. If she's up there, Mountain Charley, I've got to find her. I hope you can understand that."

"I can understand it, all right," Mountain Charley said. "The question is, can Fanny?"

"What do you mean?"

"Well, she's already been up there for six months now. What makes ye' think she'd want ter come back, even if ye' find her?"

"Ah, Running Rabbit, you have done well," Fanny said, tasting the stew which simmered over the cooking fire in the middle of the great tipi. "Surely no other stew pot in this camp has as much meat as this. You are a good hunter."

"It is good that I am a fine hunter," Running Rabbit said. "I must keep the pot full for Ottawa and four wives. Ottawa is much too busy to do so."

"Ottawa grows old and lazy," Morning Flower muttered. "If the others knew how the wives of a chief must depend upon a boy for their food."

"Morning Flower, you know only bad things to say. Never have I known anyone in my white-before life, or my Indian-now life, who could complain as long and as loud as you," Fanny said. Fanny had learned the language of the Sioux, and now all conversation was in their own language.

"You have it easy," Willow Branch said bitterly. "You have the honor of a husband, and the pleasure of a lover. Do you think Ottawa would allow Jumping Bear to visit Morning Flower or me?"

"Do you think Jumping Bear would *want* to visit you?" Kettle Woman asked, laughing.

Ottawa had been sleeping near the edge of the tipi, and he turned over and grumbled in bad humor.

"Aiyee, why was I ever cursed with *four* wives? Your tongues rattle like dry reeds in the wind. It is winter . . . . it is the time of quiet and meditation. Can you not do this?"

All four of the women, including Fanny, were duly chastised by Ottawa's sharp words. Fanny felt a sense of satisfaction in the rebuff though, because she realized that it was aimed primarily at Willow Branch and Morning Flower, who had grown more and more sullen since her coming.

Fanny walked over to her sleeping place and sat down, looking over the tipi, at the others who shared this home with her. She had been here for over six months now, and sometimes it seemed as if there had never been any other place for her.

At first Fanny thought someone might come looking for her, but after several weeks it became apparent that no one was coming. It wasn't too long after that that she accepted her fate for what it was. She was destined to spend the rest of her life here, with these Indians.

Once Fanny had accepted her fate, it became increasingly easier for her to live the life she was now living. She took every day, one day at a time, and she cut all ties with her past and didn't think of her future.

"Real Woman," Running Rabbit said, bringing a bowl of the stew to her when it was ready to eat. "Today, when I went for wood, I heard that Jumping Bear will return tonight."

"Where did you hear this?" Fanny asked.

"There were two Sans Arcs who have come to visit our camp. They saw Jumping Bear this very morning. He has found a buffalo herd and he comes to move the village to the winter encampment tomorrow."

Fanny looked toward Ottawa with an expression of hope on her face. Ottawa smiled at her.

"Yes, this is true," Ottawa said. "I too have heard that he will return tonight. My heart soars in happiness for you, that you will see him tonight."

"Oh," Fanny said. "There is no fire in my tipi. He will think me unworthy to welcome him back with a cold tipi." Fanny put the bowl down beside her. "I must go quickly and gather wood."

"Stay," Running Rabbit said, putting his hand on her arm. He smiled. "I have gathered the wood for you. All you have to do is light the fire."

"She has not been with Jumping Bear for many days," Kettle Woman said with a ribald laugh. "I think they will start many fires together, tonight."

Everyone laughed at Kettle Woman's joke, even Morning Flower and Willow Branch. Fanny joined in the laughter, no longer embarrassed by a sense of false modesty.

"I must go to the tipi to wait for him," Fanny said, and she walked over to the fire, took two cold pieces of wood and picked up a burning brand so that she could carry the fire with her.

"Come back with a kettle for some stew," Kettle Woman invited. "There is much left."

"Thank you," Fanny said.

The distance between the two tipis was no more than thirty yards, but by the time she had crossed the cold, snowy ground, she was freezing. She put the burning brand into the pile of wood Running Rabbit had prepared for her, and, within a few moments, had a good, roaring fire going. Once the fire was going, she hurried back across the distance between the two tipis, carrying a kettle, then she took the stew she would share with Jumping Bear back, and hung it near the fire, arranging it expertly so that it would continue to simmer and stay warm, but would not cook away and burn.

Fanny's relationship with Jumping Bear was no longer hidden from the others. When they saw that no one was injured by the arrangement, they accepted it as calmly as if Fanny and Jumping

Bear were actually married. Promiscuous relationships raised eyebrows only when there was bitterness and jealousy. When all was harmonious, the other members of the tribe were willing to accept it as the natural order of things.

Fanny had just finished arranging the robes and blankets for their bed, when the flap of the tipi opened, and Jumping Bear came in.

"Real Woman," he said. "For many days now I have seen your face in the clouds, and I have heard your voice in the trees."

"My tipi has been silent without your laughter, my bed empty without your breathing," Fanny replied, and they embraced in their mutual pleasure.

As Fanny felt his strong arms around her, pulling her to him, she wondered if this was love. Certainly she had never felt the same sense of joy at seeing Fergus after an extended absence. And yet, how could this be love? She shared nothing with Jumping Bear except the pleasures she took from his body, and the island of tenderness in a sea of harsh reality.

The snow fell heavily, in large, white flakes which drifted down from the black sky and added inches to that which was already on the ground. It fell silently, and its presence deadened all sound, so that the movement of horses, and the stirrings of the villagers in their blankets, were unheard.

The doors of all tipis were laced tightly shut, and wisps of blue smoke curled up from the smoke flaps, providing a scene of peaceful tranquility to the village. The smell of a hundred simmering stews told the silent story of a night when no one went hungry, and when everyone was warm and snug against the elements.

Two hundred yards away from the village lay the lower reaches of a great pine forest, and from the darkness of those trees, came shadows emerging from shadows, a long line of riders. The horses moved silently, as if treading on air, and only their movement, and the blue vapor of their breath, gave an indication of life.

A small, chinking sound of metal on metal came from the party, a sound which was unnatural to the drift of snow and the soft whisper of trees. In the village one warrior heard it while in the deepest recesses of his sleep, and his eyes came open and he lay beside his woman and wondered what could have caused the sound. But the bed robes were too warm, and the flesh of his woman too sweet, and as he looked at his children sleeping undisturbed, he realized that he must have dreamed the unusual sound, so he rolled back into the inviting curve of the sleeping form of the body of his woman, and he went back to sleep.

Outside, the silent horses and the quiet men approached.

13

Tanteo opened her eyes. Besides her she could feel the warm, muscled body of Matt Parker, and she could hear his soft, easy breathing. In the middle of the tipi she saw the dim glow of embers from last night's fire. The embers were still giving off some heat, but very little light. The inside of the tipi smelled comfortably of cooked meat and burning wood, and the lingering musk of love-making from the night before.

Tanteo recalled the long, languorous moments spent making love, and she felt a still-lingering sense of pleasure. She pressed her nude body against his muscled leg and felt the heat stirring anew within her. She wondered if she dared awaken him, to tease him into making love to her again.

Perhaps if she built a warming fire, and cooked

his breakfast, he would be moved to make love again before the sun rose. That would mean leaving the tipi for more wood, but it would be worth it. Besides, if she made herself important enough to him, he may suspend his search for the *winu*.

Tanteo felt a moment of jealousy for the *winu* and she hoped that the *winu* would do something to cause the Oglala to kill her.

No, that is a bad thought which will cause evil to befall her, and, quickly, she mouthed a small prayer to the *Wakan*, and watched as the smoke carried her prayer through the smoke flap at the top of the tipi. Maybe the *Wakan* would look kindly on her prayer now . . . . after all most were still sleeping so he wouldn't be disturbed by the prayers of others, and the smoke was rising strongly so that the prayer would get there quickly. Also she was in the proper state of contrition, being most sorry for her evil wish of a moment before. She prayed that she would be Matt Parker's woman for the rest of her life.

Tanteo slipped out of bed, put on shoes, then wrapped a buffalo robe around her nude body, opened the tipi flap and stepped out into the cold, dark morning, to find wood for the fire.

Captain Fergus Kelly sat in the saddle and looked toward the sleeping Indian village which lay before him. It was still two hours before dawn, and his advance scouts had not only located the village, they had also confirmed that there were no sentries on duty. This would be a glorious victory, and a magnificent conclusion to the orders he had been given before he left Fort Laramie.

"This is what we've been waiting for," Colonel Albertson had told him on the day the orders were given. Albertson read aloud the orders he held in his hand. They had come from the War Department, and were authorized by Secretary of War himself. To have issued such orders concerning Indians, in the midst of a great Civil War, was quite a recognition of them, Colonel Albertson confided. He cleared his throat. "You will locate the winter encampment of the Indian tribe responsible for the massacre of the Parker Wagon Party, and strike against them, causing as much havoc and destruction as possible. The purpose of this mission is punitive, to show the savage that any future action he might consider against the whites will be met with a terrible response. In this way, the Indian will soon see the futility of hostile acts."

"Am I to have full authority in the field, Colonel Albertson?" Fergus asked. He had long since decided how the campaign would be conducted, if he did have the authority.

"Yes," Colonel Albertson had answered. Albertson had put his hand on Kelly's shoulder then, in a show of fatherly affection. "My boy, you don't know how much I wish I could be going with you on this mission. But I know what a personal investment you have and I would not want to do anything which would interfere with your right to get revenge from those heathen devils. You will have five reinforced companies of mounted infantry."

As Kelly recalled the assignment of his orders, he looked around at the men who were with him.

He held two companies on the east side of the village, and he sent two more companies around to the west side. One company guarded the north side while the south side of the village was bounded by the river. Once the attack started, escape would be virtually impossible.

"Captain Kelly," Lieutenant Masters said. "I still think we should wait until first light before we attack."

"It's too late now," Fergus answered. "The other two elements are waiting for a co-ordinated attack, set to begin at five o'clock."

"But it will still be pitch dark, sir," Masters said.

"Of course it will, Lieutenant," Fergus replied. "That will provide us with the element of surprise. Surprise is the most effective ally of any attack. Surely you remember *that* much from your lessons on tactics."

"Yes, sir, I remember that, sir," Masters said. "But I am concerned about the women and children of the village. In the dark, it will be difficult to tell one Indian from another. There may be some casualties among the women and children."

"Lieutenant Masters, this is a *punitive* campaign against the Indians," Fergus said, as if explaining something to a child. "There is nothing in my orders which requires me to differentiate between warriors and any other Indian. On the contrary, I have been ordered to extract a terrible toll. What more terrible toll could we extract than to attack them ruthlessly?"

"Women and children, sir?" Masters asked weakly.

"Were the women and children spared when the wagon train was attacked?" Fergus replied. "Didn't I see little Mary cut down before my very eyes?"

"Yes, sir, that you did, sir," Masters replied. "But I was also thinking about Mrs. Kelly."

"What about her?"

"Captain Kelly, you know yourself, sir, that we keep getting these rumors of a white woman who was captured alive when the rest of the wagon train party was massacred. I can't help but wonder if it could be Mrs. Kelly. I know how wonderful it would be for you to find her safe and sound, so I ask myself if we aren't taking an unnecessary risk by attacking in the dark? I mean, just on the off chance she's still alive. We could completely miss her in the dark."

"Lieutenant, no one would be more greatly pleased than I, to discover that I was mistaken. But I assure you, my wife is not alive. I saw her killed. Wouldn't I know?"

"I'm sure you believe she is dead, Captain, or of course you would never have left her. But what if she was just knocked unconscious and managed to recover? After all, Matt Parker believes she is still alive. He has spent the last six months looking for her."

"Matt Parker is a man ridden with guilt over his failure," Kelly said. "Parker was the wagon master, and as such, responsible for the safety of everyone in his charge. He failed that responsibility, and was safely to the rear with a straggler, when he should have placed himself with the main body of wagons."

Lieutenant Masters was about to reply, when two men approached the two officers, bringing with them an Indian captive.

"Look what we got, cap'n," one of them said.

"Who is that?"

"Some squaw woman we found gatherin' wood."

"Did she have time to sound the alarm?"

"No, sir," one of the two men said. "We seen her comin', 'n we grabbed her 'afore she knowed what hit her."

"Do you speak English?" Kelly asked.

The woman didn't answer.

"Get Cut Ear up here," Kelly said, sending for one of his two Indian scouts. "Maybe he can talk to her."

"And look at this, Cap'n," one of her guards said. He put his hand on the buffalo robe the woman was wearing and jerked it open. The Indian woman proved to be young, beautiful, and, beneath the robe, naked.

Kelly heard a quick intake of breath from the men who were close enough to see what was going on. He was, himself, affected by the sight, and for a moment he thought of declaring her 'spoils of war,' so he could enjoy her later.

"Cover her," he said quickly. "She could be quite a distraction to the men."

"Yes sir," the guard said, putting the robe back in place. "I just thought you might appreciate a little peek, that's all."

Cut Ear arrived then, and Kelly pointed to the girl. "Ask her how many Oglala are in the village," he said.

Cut Ear looked at the girl, then looked at Kelly.

"This girl not Oglala," he said. "This girl Minne-conjou."

"Minneconjou, eh?" Kelly said, rubbing his chin as he studied her. "Then she must be a prisoner of the Oglala."

"Oglala do not make prisoner of Minneconjou," Cut Ear said. "Minneconjou are brothers to Og-lala."

"Oh?" Kelly said. He smiled. "Well, in that case, it doesn't make any difference. If they are brothers to the Oglala, then they are sympathetic to the Oglala, and they are just as guilty."

"Captain, you mean you intend to carry on this attack, even though this isn't the right village?" Lieutenant Masters asked.

"Minneconjou are Sioux," Kelly said resolutely. "That's all I need to know. The attack goes as planned."

Suddenly the girl escaped from the grasp of the two guards. She did it by the simple expedient of slipping out of the robe, leaving them holding her coat, while she started dashing, naked, across the snow, headed back for the village.

"Don't let her get away!" Kelly called. "She'll give the alarm!"

One of the soldiers who was standing close by drew his rifle from the saddle scabbard, aimed, and fired. The bullet hit the fleeing girl in the back of the head and she pitched forward, spray-ing the white snow with red blood. Her nude body lay face down on the snow.

There was a shout from the village.

"Damn!" Kelly said. "Charge! Charge now, be-fore they can react!"

The bugler sounded the charge, and the mounted soldiers started toward the sleeping village at the gallop. An explosion of sound invaded the peaceful silence, as voices shouted in fear and anger, guns fired, and horses neighed.

Then the savage butchery started. The soldiers slashed with their sabers at the Indians who were running before them. Women were murdered without mercy, and children and babies were run down and trampled. Old men and unarmed warriors were killed and tipis were flamed.

It was a grotesque montage of sound and fury, savagery and color; red blood, white snow, and blue coats.

Wounded Foot ran out of his tent clutching an American flag which had been given to him by the United States Congress when he went to Washington on a peace mission ten years earlier. The flag was Wounded Foot's most prized possession, and he held it up, calling to the soldiers; "American Flag, American Flag!" He was shot at point-blank range, and he sprawled backward in the snow, still tightly clutching the flag.

Matt's first reaction when he woke up was to reach for Tanteo. When he discovered that she wasn't there, he jumped out of bed, then, with the sound of shooting going on around him, he pulled on his pants and boots. Bullets began popping through the skin of the tipi, and one hit the support pole very near him, splintering the pole and sending a small sliver, stinging, into his arm.

Matt had no idea what was going on, or who was doing all the shooting. He knew only that someone had attacked a peaceful village in the

middle of the night. He thought of the lack of
sentries, and he wondered if the Indians would
learn a lesson from this experience. And he wondered about Tanteo. Where was she?

With his pants and boots on, Matt didn't take
the time to look for a shirt. Instead, bare chested,
he stepped out of the tent, carrying his pistol, and
looked toward the sound of battle. He saw a little
child running, and someone on horseback chasing
the child, holding a saber aloft, ready to slash
down on the hapless young victim as soon as he
caught him. Matt raised his pistol and fired, and
the one wielding the saber tumbled from his horse.

By now, several of the Indian warriors had managed to arm themselves, and they stood in a tight
group, firing into the soldiers. The soldiers were
so intent upon shooting and slashing the helpless
ones, that they weren't aware that a defense was
being mounted. A volley of fire from the Indians
brought down three of the soldiers.

"Bugler, sound recall!" Matt heard a voice yell,
and he looked toward the sound to see Fergus
Kelly.

"Kelly," he said aloud. He raised his pistol and
aimed at Kelly, putting Kelly's head just over his
bead sight. All he had to do was squeeze the trigger.

Matt couldn't pull the trigger. With an oath,
he lowered the pistol, and at that moment he heard
recall being sounded. The soldiers broke off their
attack then, and with Kelly at the head, they galloped out of the village, back across the open
ground and into the trees.

"*Huka huka hey!*" several of the Indians around

Matt shouted, and they shook their fists in anger at the retreating soldiers. *"Huka huka hey,"* Matt knew, was a war cry of some obscene expression. He had heard it before, and he knew the anger of the warriors who yelled it, and now he, like the others, shouted the vulgar phrase at the top of his lungs, and he shook his fist as angrily as any of the Indians.

After the anger came the realization of the damage that had been done to them, and after that, came the shock, then, finally, total grief.

Cries of anguish and grief drifted through the camp then as the Inidans began to find the slaughtered bodies of their loved ones. Some of the Indians began weeping aloud, and bashing their heads with rocks, while others walked around with shock and disbelief etched on their faces.

More than two dozen tipis had been burned, and several were still in flames, with the skin burned away, and the burning poles forming glowing cones in the pre-dawn darkness.

Suddenly Matt realized that he had not seen Tanteo since waking, and he started through the camp looking for her.

"Tanteo! Tanteo!" he called. He looked eagerly into the faces of all the Indians, but she was no where to be found. "Have you seen Tanteo?" he asked, but all were too stunned with their own loss to answer him.

Matt saw Mountain Charley, and he ran to him. "Mountain Charley, have you seen Tanteo?"

Mountain Charley was on his knees, and when he looked up, Matt was shocked to see that he was crying! Tears were streaming down his face, disappearing into his bushy, red beard. Below him, on the ground, he saw Sasha's body.

"The bastards!" Mountain Charley sobbed. "The sorry, mangy, low-assed bastards! They've killed my Sasha, Matt. The bastards have killed my Sasha."

"I'm sorry, Mountain Charley," Matt said. He walked over to the big man and put his hand on his shoulder. "I'm so very sorry."

"What will I do without her?" Mountain Charley sobbed. "She was my life."

Matt patted Mountain Charley once or twice, then walked away to resume his search for Tanteo. He passed the hogan which was being used to store the skins, and saw that it, too, had been set afire, and now an entire winter's catch of pelts burned, fouling the air with the stench of burning fur.

Matt had gone from one end of the village to the other without locating Tanteo, and he was about to go back through when he saw one, lone body, about fifty yards beyond the outer-most perimeter of the village. The body was nude, and it was that of a young woman. Matt felt a sinking sensation in the pit of his stomach, and, reluctantly he walked out to it. A spray of red was on the snow around the head, and when he got closer he gasped. It was Tanteo.

Eighty-eight had been killed. Nineteen of that number were children. The Minneconjou held funeral ceremonies all that day and Matt stayed with them, helping to prepare the dead, and to clean up the village. Finally, three days later, with the last body wrapped and placed on the burial platform, Matt prepared to leave the village. He sought out Mountain Charley to tell him good-bye, and to express his sorrow over what had happened.

"Would you like to ride north with me?" Matt asked. "We could keep each other company."

"No," Mountain Charley said. "The truth is, Matt, I don't believe I'm going to be fit company for man or beast for quite a while now. I'm going to have to be alone until I get over this."

"Where will you go? What will you do?"

Mountain Charley sighed. "I don't rightly know. A year's trapping is done for, I know that much." He pointed toward the smoldering ruins of the pelt hogan. "Not only for me, but for these poor devils too." He chuckled, a derisive, sarcastic chuckle. "There are going to be a few fine, rich, white ladies back in Philadelphia, New York and Boston who are going to have to go without their fur muffs and hats I'm afraid. And without the fur to trade for supplies, these people are gonna get mighty hungry. That is, the ones left alive."

"It was a senseless slaughter," Matt said.

"Who the hell was it?" Mountain Charley asked. "Was it really army? Could the army do somethin' like this?"

"It was Fergus Kelly," Matt said.

"Kelly? The soldier-coward? The one married to your Fanny?"

"Yes," Matt said bitterly. "I had him in my sights and I couldn't kill him." He hit his fist into his palm. "I couldn't kill him, Mountain Charley, and I had him right there."

"I could'a killed the son-of-a-bitch," Mountain Charley said ominously. "I could'a killed him with pleasure."

Matt looked at the big man for a moment, then he stuck out his hand. "I hope we run across each other again," he said.

Mountain Charley shook Matt's hand, then watched as Matt climbed onto his horse. "I hope you find Fanny, but not if it means sendin' her back to the bastard who did this."

"I'll find her," Matt said. He clucked at his horse and started the animal north. Then he called back over his shoulder to Mountain Charley who was still standing there, watching him ride away. "But when I do find her, I won't be sending her back!"

Fanny was proud of how quickly and how well she was able to pack the tipi. Four of the long lodge poles were used to construct a travois, and all her belongings were securely wrapped and tied onto the travois. She pulled on her warm, fur-lined boots, wrapped herself in the parka, then climbed onto the animal's back, and she was ready to go by the time the village was ready to move. By sun-up, the entire village was on the march, moving west toward the stand of buffalo Jumping Bear had discovered the day before.

Fanny looked at Jumping Bear. He was riding in front of the column, alongside Ottawa. How erect he rode, how broad his shoulders were. He would be the chief after Ottawa, everyone said so. And she would be his wife . . . . his only wife.

Jumping Bear was pleased with Fanny, she knew

that. Last night, after they made love, he told her again how happy she made him, what pleasure she gave him. It made her feel good to know that she could please him so. And the pleasure wasn't all one sided either, she thought, as she recalled the rapture of the night before. The thought of it warmed her blood, and she welcomed the warmth against the cold, and she wished they could make love right now.

Fanny looked back at the travois, and in her mind, she saw how the travois could be constructed to allow them to lie together back there. They could lie together, under the robes, and they could make love, and no one else in the village would suspect what was going on. She giggled aloud, and felt a renewed heat of sexual excitation as she thought of it. It pleased her to think of such a thing, and she let the thought dwell in her mind as they rode along.   ᕮᏕ

14

THE ENTIRE POST turned out to watch the return
of Captain Kelly and his troops. The women of
soap-suds row stood near their little line of shacks,
dressed in aprons dampened from the washing,
and they studied the saddle-worn soldiers to make
sure their husbands were among those returning.
Mrs. Albertson and the surgeon's wife, the only
remaining officers' wives, stood on the front porch
of the headquarters building as the troops rode
slowly toward the quadrangle where they would be
dismissed by Kelly.

"Oh, look, they were engaged," Mrs. Trotter
said. Mrs. Trotter was the wife of Dr. Trotter.
"See, many of them are bandaged."

"And some are missing," Mrs. Albertson said.

"Right turn, ho!" Kelly called in a loud voice,

and the column of riders turned right, toward the flagpole. The hooves of the horses clopped, the leather squeaked, and the equipment jangled and clanked as the body of mounted men moved into position. When the entire column was in position, Kelly called for them to halt, then he faced them toward the front. He turned his own horse toward the front then, and waited for Colonel Albertson to arrive.

Colonel Albertson, in marked contrast to the trail-grimed soldiers, was sparkling in a fresh, garrison uniform. He clicked to his prancing horse, then rode out to take the report.

"Sir, I have the privilege of reporting the return of Captain Kelly, and the Punitive Expedition," Kelly said, saluting sharply. "Mission accomplished, sir!"

"Thank you, Captain Kelly," Colonel Albertson said, returning the salute. "You may dismiss the men."

"Sergeant Major!" Kelly called, and at that, all the officers in the command peeled out of formation, for Army Drill and Ceremonies do not allow an officer to be in a formation under the charge of an enlisted man. Captain Kelly and the five Lieutenants rode toward the headquarters building, while behind them the Sergeant Major commended the men for their job.

"Captain Kelly," Colonel Albertson called. "Perhaps you would report to me in my office?"

"Of course, sir," Kelly answered, swinging down from his horse. He looked across the quadrangle and saw his orderly approaching, so he gave the reins to the young soldier. "Rub him down good, Jones, and give him an extra ration of oats."

"Yes, sir," Jones said, taking the mount.

Fergus touched the brim of his hat in a greeting to the two ladies as he climbed the steps, then he went into the commandant's office. A map of Wyoming and the Dakotas was on one wall, a manning chart on another. The Regimental flag and the U. S. flag stood in polished holders in each corner.

Colonel Albertson opened his desk drawer and took out a bottle of whiskey and two glasses. He poured whiskey into each of the glasses.

"We aren't supposed to drink while on duty, but I won't tell if you won't, eh, Captain?" he said with a chuckle.

"Mum's the word, sir," Fergus said, taking the proffered glass.

"To an outstanding mission," Colonel Albertson said, holding his glass out.

"Thank you, sir," Fregus replied. He tossed the glass down, feeling the welcome fire of the liquid as it slid past his tongue. "Ahh," he said, when the whiskey was all gone. "That hit the spot, sir."

"That was for need. This is for taste," Albertson said, pouring another glass.

Fergus raised the glass and a beam of sunlight caught a prismatic effect, then sent a burst of color to play against the wall behind Colonel Albertson's desk.

"I read the report the advance courier brought," Albertson said. "It was a brilliant campaign my boy, brilliantly conceived and brilliantly executed.

I would say that splitting your forces like that before the enemy under normal circumstances would be foolhardy, but, genius is sometimes born in unexpected maneuvers."

"I figured that the hour of the attack would afford us the element of surprise," Fergus said. "That would off-set any negative aspects which might be resulting from splitting my forces."

"How were your casualties?"

"We lost three men killed, sir," Fergus said. "The quartermaster has their names."

"You weren't able to recover their bodies?"

"No sir," Fergus said. "By that time, the Indians had re-grouped and it would have meant risking the living to recover the dead."

"I agree with you," Albertson said. "Unless, of course, there may be some question as to whether or not the men were really dead."

"They were dead sir."

Albertson smiled. "Are you sure about that? Are you absolutely sure?"

Fergus was surprised by the Colonel's smile. It seemed strange at a time like this, and he looked at Albertson with an expression of curiosity on his face.

"Yes, sir, I am very sure," he said.

"You were sure once before, remember? In fact, I think those were your very words. You were very sure."

"Colonel, if you will excuse me, sir, I don't know what you are talking about."

"I have some wonderful news for you, Fergus. I have some absolutely marvelous news for you."

"What is it?" Fergus asked.

"Fanny," Albertson said.

"What?" Fergus said weakly. He was so stunned that he didn't even use the term, 'sir', but Colonel Albertson, grinning proudly over the privilege of conveying the news to him, overlooked Kelly's omission.

"It's your wife, Fanny," Albertson said again. "She's alive, Fergus."

Fergus felt his knees turn to water, and his stomach roll sickeningly. He put his hand on the corner of the Colonel's desk to steady himself.

"Here, here, sit down," Colonel Albertson said, sliding a chair toward Fergus. Fergus sat down heavily, then drained the rest of the whiskey.

"How," he started, then he had to cough to clear his throat. "How do you know she is alive?"

"Because we have the Indian who captured her here, in our jail," Colonel Albertson said. "He is called One-Who-Waits. A patrol picked him up more dead than alive, and they brought him in. He tried to bargain with Fanny's life, offering to tell the patrol where she was if they would let him go."

"How do we know he is talking about Fanny?" Fergus asked.

"Hell, it has to be her, man. He described her perfectly. Besides that, he says she was captured last summer during an attack on a wagon train. The Parker party train is the only train to be attacked in over two years. There's one thing I can't figure out, though."

"What is that, sir?" Fergus asked.

"You were so positive she was dead. She must have recovered from a grievous wound. It could be that she doesn't even know who she is, or where she is. That would explain it, I suppose."

"Explain what, sir?"

"Why she hasn't killed herself," Colonel Albertson said. "You know, I can't help but remember the discussion we had in my quarters the very night before the wagon train left. We talked then of the only decent thing for a white woman to do under the circumstances, surely you recall?"

"Yes, sir, I remember it quite well."

"And, as I recall, Fanny was bravely determined to do the right thing should it become necessary. Thus, I can only surmise that the severity of her wound was such that it rendered her senseless for some time. How was she wounded?"

"I beg your pardon, sir?"

"You thought she was dead, you must have seen her wounded. How did it happen?"

"Oh, a uh, war club, sir," Fergus said.

"Yes, that would explain it. I've read reports of people who have suffered severe head wounds, and have lost their mind for a while. That must have happened to Fanny."

"Yes, sir," Fergus said quietly, pouring himself another glass of whiskey without being asked.

"Well, be that as it may, she is still alive, and thus it is now incumbent upon us to go after her."

"Go after her, sir?"

"Yes. Well, we have no choice, do we? Matt Parker has been chasing around out there in the hills for God knows how long now, looking for her while we were laughing at him. Now it turns out that he was right all along, so we can't let him make an ass of the army, can we?"

"No, sir, I suppose not."

"I should hope not," Colonel Albertson went on. He fixed Fergus with a stern glare. "For after all, who would be made the biggest ass, Captain Kelly, if not you?"

"Me, sir?"

"Yes, you. You are the one who thought she was dead. You are the logical one to find her." Suddenly Colonel Albertson smiled again. "But then, look at us, approaching this as if the only thing at stake here was the honor of the United States Army and its officers. Obviously this is a joyous occasion, isn't it? After all, Fanny, your wife, is alive."

"Yes, sir," Fergus said, without enthusiasm. "Fanny is alive. Do we know where she is?"

"No," Colonel Albertson said. "After the prisoner learned we wouldn't bargain with him, he shut up. He hasn't spoken another word. I thought you might be able to get something out of him."

"Yes, sir," Fergus said. He stood up. "I'll go see him right now."

"Fine, fine," Colonel Albertson said. "Perhaps you can join Mrs. Albertson and me for dinner tonight," he added. "I would like to hear more about your victory in the field. Lord, how I wish I could have been there to share the glory with you."

"I would be honored to be there," Fergus said, saluting Colonel Albertson as he took his leave.

Fergus walked across the quadrangle toward the guardhouse. The guardhouse was on the opposite side of the post from the living quarters and the Sutler's store. It was built onto the end of one of the stables, and smelled constantly of barn odors.

There was no floor to the guardhouse, only dried hay to shield against the cold and damp of the ground. It was designed so that it was hot in the summer and cold in the winter, and was, overall, an exceptionally uncomfortable place to be. For an Indian who was used to living outdoors, it was hell on earth.

The guard came to attention as Fergus approached the guardhouse, and he brought his rifle up in a salute.

"I've come to see the prisoner," Fergus said.

"He's a weird one, sir," the guard said. "He just sits there in the middle of the floor all the time, without making a sound."

Fergus looked at the guard, then realized that the Indian might say something he didn't want the guard to hear, so he decided to send him away.

"I'm going to interrogate the prisoner," Fergus went on. "I might have more luck if he thought I was the only one out here. Why don't you go to your barracks for a cup of coffee?"

The guard's face brightened. "Are you certain it's all right, sir?"

"Yes," Fergus said. "I shall take full responsibility for the prisoner."

"Thank you, sir," the guard said. He leaned his rifle against the side of the building. "I want to talk to some of the boys about the mission anyway. How long will you be?"

"Take your time," Fergus said generously.

The guard started across the quadrangle toward the enlisted barracks at a trot, and Fergus watched him for a moment, then he turned and walked up to the barred door of the guardhouse. The smell almost made him gag, and he had to stop for a moment until he could adjust to it. When he looked inside, he saw an Indian sitting in the middle of the floor, cross-legged, with his arms folded across his chest. He seemed to be looking off into space.

"Hey, you, Indian," Fergus called. "One-Who-Waits. Do you know who I am?"

One-Who-Waits looked up. "Yes," he said. "You are Soldier-Who-Is-A-Coward."

"What?" Fergus asked, gasping, and looking around to make sure no one had overheard One-Who-Waits. "What did you call me?"

"You ran from battle," One-Who-Waits said easily. "You were named Soldier-Who-Is-A-Coward. You are the white husband of Real Woman."

"This woman, this Real Woman, where is she now?"

"She shares the blankets of Jumping Bear," One-Who-Waits said. "She is the wife of Ottawa."

"What are you trying to tell me?" Fergus asked. "Are you saying she is actually married to an Indian?"

"Yes."

"And she's living with him? I mean, willingly?"

"No," One-Who-Waits said. "She is wife of Ottawa, but her body belongs to Jumping Bear."

Fergus closed his eyes, and got a mental image of Fanny making love with an Indian. He could see the same expression on her face he had seen when he first discovered that she enjoyed sex. It was disgusting to him, and he clenched his fist tightly. Yes, he could see her living willingly with an Indian. Ironic, he thought, but she was evidently promiscuous, even among the Indians. Why didn't the Indians kill her when he left her? Why didn't she kill herself as any decent woman would have done?

"Soldier-Who-Is-A-Coward," One-Who-Waits said. "Will you hang me?"

"You damned right I'm going to hang you," Fergus said. "Did you think that just because you gave me a little information that I wouldn't hang you?"

"It will be a disgrace to be hanged by a coward," One-Who-Waits said.

"And that's another thing," Fergus said, pointing a shaking finger at the Indian. "I want you to cut that kind of talk out. I don't want anyone to hear you say that."

"You have no wish for the others to know that you ran from battle, and in so doing, killed the little girl?"

"I didn't do that!" Kelly said. "The little girl was already dead!"

"You killed the little girl," One-Who-Waits said. "I will say this from the place where I am to hang."

"No one will believe you."

"Real Woman knows the truth," One-Who-Waits said. "Someday she will say the truth."

"Where is she? Where can I find her?"

One-Who-Waits smiled. "You wish to find her so you can kill her?"

"No, of course not," Fergus said. "She is my wife, why should I want to kill her?"

"She is your wife no longer," One-Who-Waits said. "You wish to kill her, this I know. I will tell you where she is."

"Where?"

"We make deal."

"No deals."

"I will tell others you are a coward," One-Who-Waits said. "If they do not believe me now, soon they will think, and then they will believe."

"You think such a story would even give them cause for thought?" Fergus scoffed. "I just got back from a very successful mission. Colonel Albertson thinks very highly of me."

"Soon everyone will know that the Indians you massacred were Minneconjou, and not Oglala," One-Who-Waits said. "The Minneconjou are traders with the white man. They have many treaties, and they have not made war against the whites in many years. They are a very peaceful people, but they may not be peaceful now."

"I didn't know they were Minneconjou," Fergus said.

"Your guide, Cut Ear, told you they were Minneconjou," One-Who-Waits said easily. "I can tell you where the Oglala village of Ottawa is."

"Why would you do that?" Fergus asked. "Wouldn't you be betraying your own people?"

"I have no people," One-Who-Waits said.

"What do you mean, you have no people? Aren't you Oglala?"

"I was," One-Who-Waits said. "But I became a contraire. But I could not keep this up for long, and I failed. I was in disgrace and I could not go back to the camp."

"And you are willing to tell me where this camp is now?"

"If you will let me go free."

"How do I know I can trust you? You are a man without honor."

One-Who-Waits smiled. "A man without honor, gives his word of honor to a man without honor. Who must trust whom?"

Fergus sighed. "Very well," he said. "Tell me where the Oglala village is, and I will let you go."

"Give me a gun," One-Who-Waits said.

"What? Are you crazy?"

"Give me a gun without bullets," One-Who-Waits said. "Throw the bullets over the wall. I will get them when I leave."

Fergus looked around the quadrangle, then he picked up the guard's rifle. He worked the lever to pump out all the cartridges, then he threw them over the compound wall. He handed the empty rifle through the bars to One-Who-Waits.

"The village is in the valley of the Elk Calf," One-Who-Waits said. "That is five days from here."

"I know where it is," Fergus said. He pulled the latch bar through and opened the door. "Go," he said.

Fergus had no intention of letting One-Who-Waits escape. He intended to let him get about four steps away, then he was going to shoot him dead, and report that he shot him as One-Who-Waits was attempting to escape. He stepped back with a small, smug smile on his face. It would make him feel good to shoot this arrogant Indian, the one who had the audacity to call him a coward.

One-Who-Waits grinned happily at his impending freedom. He took two steps out of the door, then, using his rifle as a club spun around and

brought the rifle butt across the chin of Fergus
Kelly. The sudden move surprised Fergus, and he
went down and out.

"Are you all right, sir?" a voice was saying. Kelly
felt himself being shaken, and he opened his eyes
and looked up. He was lying on the cold, damp
ground, and half a dozen soldiers were around
him, looking down at him anxiously.

"What is it?" Kelly asked. "What happened?"

"The heathen redskin got away, sir," one of the
soldiers said.

"Got away? How?"

"He must have got my rifle," Jones said con-
tritely. "I . . . . I left it leaning against the wall."

"What I don't understand is how he got the
latchbar moved," a sergeant said. He studied the
open door curiously.

"I . . . . I did that," Fergus admitted.

"You did? But, why would you do a thing like
that, sir?"

Fergus sighed. "I was trying to get the location
of the Oglala winter camp. He said he would tell
me if I would let him go."

"So you let him go?" the sergeant said in surprise. "The colonel sure ain't gonna like that."

"What is it I'm not going to like?" Colonel Albertson said, approaching the guardhouse then.
Word of One-Who-Waits escape had spread
through the entire compound.

"I took a calculated risk, Colonel," Fergus said,
rubbing his chin gingerly. "I opened the door in
order to make the Indian think I was letting him

go. He gave the location of the Oglala camp in return. I intended to arrest him immediately, and put him back into the guardhouse, but, Jones had left his rifle leaning against the wall of the guardhouse, and before I knew it, the Indian had it in his hands. He caught me by surprise."

"Jones, did you leave your rifle against the wall of the guardhouse?"

"Yes, sir," Jones said sheepishly. "The Indian's got it now."

"You are confined to the guardhouse for one week," Colonel Albertson said.

"But, Colonel, the Cap'n said I could take a break," Jones protested.

"He didn't say you could give your rifle to a murderin' redskin," the Sergeant said, pushing Jones roughly into the jail. "You could'a got a fine man kilt, that's what you could'a done. If it was up to me, I'd let you take that murderin' redskin's place on the gallows in the mornin'."

A sullen Private Jones was pushed into the guardhouse, and the door was closed and barred behind him.

"Colonel, I could take a patrol out and try to find him," the sergeant offered.

"Don't bother," Colonel Albertson said. "You'd never catch him now."

"I did get some information we can use," Fergus said. "I did find out where the Oglala village is."

"All right, that's more like it," Colonel Albertson said. "And Fanny? What did you find out about Fanny?"

"She's dead," Fergus said. "Just like I said she

was. One-Who-Waits heard that Parker was looking for her, so he thought he could use that to trade with. But he admitted to me that she was killed in the raid on the wagon train."

"I'm sorry, Fergus," Colonel Albertson said, putting his hand on Kelly's shoulder.

"That's all right, sir," Fergus said. "I knew she was dead so I didn't get my hopes up."

"I should have known better anyway," Colonel Albertson said. "Fanny was much too decent a woman to ever allow herself to be taken alive by the Indians."

"I'm sure she was, sir," Fergus said easily.

"So, you've discovered the location of the village. How soon can you be ready to go after them?"

"I can leave tonight, sir."

Colonel Albertson laughed. "Captain, I cannot tell you how much I admire your perseverance and loyalty. But I wouldn't dream of sending you right back out. No, nor the men."

"I'm not asking the men to do anything I won't do, sir."

"I know, but there aren't that many men who can keep up with you. I might even find that difficult. You'll come to my house for a wonderful supper tonight, just as I planned, and tomorrow you and the men will be freshly provisioned and well rested. You can go out again then."

"Thank you, sir," Fergus said.

Colonel Albertson rubbed his hands together with glee. "Yes, sir, this is going to be one winter the Indians will long remember. First the battle of Rocky Butte, and then the battle of . . . . where *is* the camp anyway?"

"Elk Calf," Fergus replied. "It's a valley north of the McGarth Mountains."

"Yes," Albertson said. "Yes, I know where it is." He smiled. "Let the folks at home discuss the battles of Pittsburgh Landing, Gettysburg, Chancellorsville and the others. They'll soon be adding Rocky Butte and Elk Calf to their liturgy. My boy, we've brought glory to the west!" ☙

15

AROUND THE FIRES in the winter camp of the Oglala, the talk was of the soldiers' attack on the village of Wounded Foot. This talk even supplanted the talk of the fine herd of buffalo Jumping Bear had located, and first one and then another would tell stories of people they had known in Wounded Foot's camp who had been killed.

"Do you remember Sasha?" one woman said. "She was Sasha the Healer, because she had great medicine and could heal many wounds and illnesses. She was slain."

"It is too bad she could not heal her own wounds," another replied.

"And Wounded Foot. It is said that he died clutching the cloth which is important to the whites. It is supposed to be big medicine for the whites, but it did not save Wounded Foot."

"Why did the whites do such a thing?"

"Because they wish to kill all Indians. The white man does not obey Wakan. That is why the Indian can never live with the white man."

"But listen. Is not Real Woman a white woman? And does she not live with us?"

"Real Woman was white in the white-before life. In the white-before life, she could not live with us. This is the red-now life, and now she can live with us."

Fanny didn't hear the conversation about her, because it was being carried on simultaneously in several dozen tipis, while she was in her own tipi, around her own fire, with Jumping Bear.

The top flap of her tipi stood up as the smoke drifted through, and the fire warmed the tipi, and gave it a cheery, orange glow, and the meat she was roasting for dinner filled the tipi with a pleasant aroma, and made the stomach growl and the mouth salivate in anticipation.

"There were two white men in the village," Jumping Bear said. "This I have heard."

"Were they living with the Minneconjou, as I live with the Oglala?" Fanny asked.

"No," Jumping Bear said. He walked over to the spitted meat and tried to pull off a small piece, but the meat was hot and he burned his fingers and jerked his hand back.

"Do not go for the meat as a camp dog after scraps," Fanny scolded, though there was a tease in her scold. "Tell me about the white men. If they

did not live with the Minneconjou, why were they
there?"

"Why do you wish to know? Do you wish to
live with the whites again?"

Fanny was turning a sweet potato with two
sticks, and she paused for a moment and looked
into the fire with eyes softly out of focus.

"No," she finally said. "No, I think not. Once
I would have said yes, but . . ."

"But you have become an Indian," Jumping Bear
said. He touched himself on the chest and he
smiled proudly. "And you have known the love of
an Indian warrior."

"There is much to what you say, Jumping Bear,"
Fanny said, and she put her hand on his. "If I
went back now, I would be ostracized for life.
Everywhere I went, people would be angry with
me because I didn't kill myself."

"Kill yourself?" Jumping Bear asked, puzzled by
the statement. He wasn't certain that Fanny had
used the correct words in her newfound mastery
of the language.

"Yes," Fanny said. "You see, the whites believe
that a decent woman would kill herself before she
let herself be touched by an Indian."

Jumping Bear laughed. "Why? Do they think
Indians are bad lovers? Does the white man love
differently from us?"

"Yes," Fanny said.

"How is it different?"

"It just is."

Now Jumping Bear was curious, and he moved
around so he could be in Fanny's line of vision.

"Does the white man make love better or does the Indian make love better?"

"Jumping Bear, what a thing to ask?" Fanny replied, laughing at his question.

"But you can tell," Jumping Bear said. "You have known both."

"I have known only you and my white husband," Fanny said. She never mentioned the rape of One-Who-Waits, and she didn't mention it now. "So how can I compare?"

"You can compare," Jumping Bear said. "One is white and one is Indian."

"I can compare only Jumping Bear with Fergus Kelly."

"Who of us is best?"

"You are awfully anxious, aren't you?" Fanny teased.

"I am best, aren't I?"

Fanny smiled broadly. "Yes," she said. "You are the best."

"Aiiiiyeeeeeee!" Jumping Bear called, and the sound of his yell of pride and victory escaped through the smoke flap and carried over the village, and many heard and wondered what joy could touch this village on such a cold night.

Matt Parker swung down from his horse and looked around the broad, open plain. It was obvious that an Indian encampment of some size had been here, but it was gone now. All that remained to tell of its existence, were a few scraps of hide and bone, one abandoned tipi, and the mark of hundreds of fires.

"Dammit," Matt said to his horse. "Where did they go?"

Matt saw the horse pawing at the ground, and shaking his head, neck and shoulders. His horse blew, and the sound echoed back from the nearby woodline.

"You want to stay here a while, is that it?" Matt said. He sighed. "We might as well. I don't have any idea where to go from here."

Matt took off the saddle and blanket, then slipped on a hobble. The horse raised his foot several times in protest over the hobble, but Matt was persistent.

"I know you don't like it," he said. "But if a wolf or a bear wanders in on us, I don't want you running out on me."

The horse quit protesting and Matt slipped the hobble on, then let him roam around to forage on his own. Matt walked over to look at the abandoned tipi, to see if it could be used for shelter. Even before he reached it, though, he knew why it had been abandoned. The skins had not been properly cured, and they smelled bad. It would be most uncomfortable to spend any time closed up inside.

"Whew," Matt said. "It smells like a charnel house." He turned away and kicked at the ground in disgust. As he kicked, he saw a flash of light under his foot . . . . something bright, like a shiny piece of metal. He was surprised, and he dropped to his knees and began digging through the mud and little bit of remaining snow, until he found it.

It was a gold wedding ring! Could it be Fanny's? He looked closely at it, hoping there would be some sort of engraved inscription which would help him, but there was nothing there.

Matt held it for a moment, staring at it, as if by some divine interpretation he could find an answer, but none came. He pondered the possible meaning of the ring for a moment. Would he want it to be Fanny's, or not? Surely, if it had belonged to Fanny, it wouldn't be here . . . . not if Fanny is still alive. And yet, if she had been killed, wouldn't the Indians have taken the ring for their own? Matt put the ring in his pocket, then started walking around the camp, gathering up wood for a fire. If this was a good enough place for the Indians to camp, it was good enough for him.

"There's no one there," the scout told Captain Kelly.

"What? Are you certain of that? One-Who-Waits was very explicit about it. Elk Calf Valley, he said."

"Well, they was there," the scout said. "They left signs all over the place. But they ain't there now. All that's there now is one solitary hunter."

"A hunter is there? Well why didn't you say so?" Fergus asked. "Let's capture him. Maybe he can give us some information."

"I doubt if he knows anything," the scout said. "But iffen he does, there ain't no need to capture him. Hell, he's a white man. We can just ride into the camp, we won't even spook him."

"A *white* man? Up here, in Elk Calf Valley? But how can that be?"

"If he's worked out some kind of a personal treaty with the Oglala council, he can come 'n go as he pleases. They won't bother him as long as he doesn't bother them."

"Let's ride into the valley and see what this fellow knows," Fergus suggested. He nodded to Lt. Masters, who was second-in-command for the march, and Lt. Masters gave the signal to the column to move forward. The mounted soldiers rode alongside the stream for quite a distance, then the scout pointed out the best place for fording, and they crossed over to the other side. After another mile, they turned away from the stream bed and climbed over a low ridgeline. A pine thicket was on the other side of the ridge line, and beyond the thicket, Elk Calf Valley. One camper was cooking his breakfast, as the troops came out of the thicket and rode toward him at an "under-way gait".

"Damn!" Fergus swore as they approached the campfire. "Do you know who that is?"

"It's Matt Parker," the scout said.

"Did you know it before?"

"No, it was dark. I just saw that it was one white man."

"That son-of-a-bitch has no business out here," Kelly said.

Matt stood as the troops approached. He was drinking coffee and watching them apprehensively.

"What are you doing out here, Parker?" Fergus asked, halting the troop when he reached him.

"I'm just doing a little scouting around," Matt said.

"Scouting around for what?"

"Just scouting," Matt said. "What are you doing up here? I thought you were in Minneconjou country."

"I've got a lead on . . . . how did you know about the Minneconjou?"

"I beg your pardon?" Matt asked innocently.

"How did you know I was in Minneconjou country?" Fergus asked again.

"I don't know," Matt said. "I guess I just heard it somewhere."

Fergus glared at him.

"Cap'n, this'd be a good place to give the men and animals a break," the scout said. "There's plenty of water and wood, and the ground is defensible."

"I don't know," Fergus said. "I'd like to push on."

"Push on to where, sir?" the scout asked easily.

"Why, to the Oglala encampment," Fergus replied.

"Beggin' your pardon, sir, but we don't know where that is," the scout said patiently. "I'm gonna have to go out and look around to see what I can come up with."

"I don't suppose *you* know where the Oglala are?" Fergus asked Matt.

"No," Matt said. He held his hand out, taking in the open area. "They were here," he said.

"Lieutenant, we'll bivouack here for 48 hours," Fergus said, getting down from his horse. "See to the necessary guard details."

"Yes, sir," Masters said, and he relayed the message on to the troops, who began dismounting with exclamations of relief for the rest, and considerable good-natured bantering and laughing.

"Captain Kelly, I'd like to talk to you, alone," Matt asked. "Let's take a walk."

"What's it about?" Fergus asked suspiciously, walking along with him, out of earshot of the others.

"I thought we might share some information," Matt said.

"What information could you have that I would want?" Fergus asked. "And what could I have that I would share with you? After all, you have no right to be out here looking for the Oglala. That is my job, not yours."

"But we are looking for the Oglala for two different reasons, Captain," Matt said easily. "You are looking for them to kill them, and I am looking for them to save Mrs. Kelly."

"First Colonel Albertson, and now you," Fergus said angrily. "Why is everyone else so anxious to save my wife?"

"Why aren't you?" Matt asked.

"Because I know she is dead," Fergus said. "I saw her killed."

Matt took the ring out of his pocket, and showed it to Fergus. "Have you ever seen this?" he asked.

"That's Fanny's ring," Fergus said, then, because he felt he may have said more than he should have, he recanted on his statement. "I mean that looks like her ring," he said.

"Is it, or isn't it?"

"I don't know."

"Kelly, do you expect me to believe that? Are you going to tell me you can't recognize your own wife's ring?"

"Where did you find it?"

"I found it here," Matt said. "Where they were camped."

"You know what that proves to me?" Fergus said smugly. "That proves that she is dead, just as I have been saying, all along."

"No, it doesn't prove she is dead, any more than it proves she is alive," Matt said. "Tell me, Kelly, why are you so anxious for her to be dead?"

"I am not anxious for her to be dead," Fergus said. "How can you even suggest such a thing."

"It's very obvious to me," Matt said. "You are almost hostile to any suggestion that she still be alive."

"It's just that I'm tired of people telling me she is alive when I know she is dead. I *know* she is, because I *saw* her die!"

"And yet, of all the people in the train, hers was the only body we didn't find. And we found her ring here."

"You know the Indians strip the dead of all valuables," Fergus defended.

"None of the other bodies were robbed," Matt said. "What is it, Kelly. Is it that you don't want her to be living with the Indians?"

"I . . . . well . . . . if I don't, there is a good reason for it," Fergus said. "After all, they are savages, and everyone knows how they treat women and children."

"They don't hack them to pieces with a saber," Matt said.

Captain Kelly's eyes narrowed. "What are you talking about?"

"Nothing," Matt said.

"It's for her own good that I hope she is dead,"

Fergus went on. "No decent woman should have to go through the indignity Indians subject their captives."

"Is that really the reason?" Matt asked. "Or is it because she saw something which you don't want known."

"I have no idea what you are talking about," Fergus said.

"Tell me, Captain, have you ever heard the name 'Soldier-Who-Is-A-Coward'?"

"*Where did you hear that?*" Fergus asked, turning nearly white with anger.

"Oh, then you *have* heard the name?"

"No, I've never heard the name," Fergus said. "I don't know what you are talking about."

"It's too bad you never heard the name," Matt went on. "Because it's the name the Indians have given you."

"What? What do you mean? Anyway, what do I care? They are nothing but ignorant savages, no one pays any attention to them anyway."

"I know," Matt said. "Even when an old chief wraps himself in an American flag and cries that he is your friend, you pay no attention to him, do you?"

"I don't know what you are talking about," Fergus said.

"I'm talking about Wounded Foot, Captain Kelly," Matt said. "And I'm talking about the slaughter of innocent men, women and children, by the Army. By you, Kelly. By you and the men under your command."

"You've been listening to the wrong kind of stories," Fergus said. "It wasn't like what you've

heard, you would have had to be there to understand what really . . . ."

"I *was* there," Matt said coldly.

The two men had been walking along the bank
of the stream, and now Kelly stopped and looked
at him. "What?" he said weakly. "What do you
mean, you were there?"

"Wounded Foot's village was a trading village,"
Matt said. "It was where all the trappers brought
their furs. In fact, Wounded Foot had a contract
with a major fur company back east. They were
a peaceful people, Kelly, until you came along and
slaughtered them."

"Where were you?"

"I was sleeping in the village," Matt said. "When
I heard the killing begin, I ran outside. I saw it,
Kelly. I saw everything with my own eyes. I saw
babies, not yet able to walk, being clubbed to
death as if it were some kind of macabre game.
I saw women and children shot and slashed, and
I saw unarmed men murdered. I also saw Wounded
Foot, wrapped in the American flag, being shot
down in cold blood. Oh, yes, Captain Kelly, I *do*
know what it was like, because I was there."

"It was a matter of military necessity," Fergus
said. "You aren't aware of the overall picture."

"There is one picture in my mind that I shall
never forget," Matt said. "It's the picture of you
in my gun sights. I let you live, Kelly, though God
only knows why. If I had known about Sasha and
Tanteo then, I wouldn't have. And if I ever get
you in my sights again, I won't."

"See here," Kelly said. "Are you threatening me,

sir? Are you threatening a United States Officer in the pursuit of his duties?"

"I'm not making a threat, Captain. I'm making a promise. If I ever see you in similar circumstances, I will kill you. Now, from here, I'm going west. I suggest you go north."

"Why should I?" Fergus asked.

"Because you might live longer that way," Matt said easily. With that, Matt turned and started back to where he had made camp. Already several dozen campfires had started, and the soldiers were getting themselves set up to spend the next two days, right here. Matt started packing his own things as soon as he returned.

"Mr. Parker, you're welcome to stay with us a spell," Lt. Masters said.

"No," Matt said. "No, thank you." He looked toward Fergus Kelly, who was walking toward him now. "I think it would be healthier for a few of us, if we parted company here. You fellas go your way, and I'll go mine."

"Is it true you are looking for Mrs. Kelly?" Masters asked.

"It's true."

"Do you think you'll find her?"

"I *know* I'll find her," Matt said.

"I wish you good luck, then," Masters said.

"Lt. Masters!" Kelly called.

"Yes, sir?"

"Lt. Masters, provide a two man, armed escort, to accompany Mr. Parker to the other side of the ridge line."

"Sir, the men are pretty tired," Masters said. "I

don't think there is any danger which could befall Mr. Parker just between here and the ridge line."

"You miss my point," Kelly said with a sardonic smile. "We aren't just escorting Mr. Parker, we are throwing him out. Parker, if you return to this valley while we are here, my men will have orders to shoot you on sight."

Matt smiled, and threw his saddle onto the back of his horse, cinched it down, then climbed on. He looked down at Kelly.

"You might find it a little more difficult than you thought," Matt said. "You see, unlike sleeping women and children . . . . *I* would shoot back."

Matt tipped his hat, then slowly rode out of the camp, feeling a burning in the small of his back as he waited for someone to shoot him.

Mercifully, he was allowed to leave the valley unmolested. ◂§

16

In the early spring, One-Who-Waits took a new name. His new name was Bloody Knife. It was a fine, terrible sounding name, and it came to him in a vision while he was in the Sweat Lodge. The vision told him to return to his people and select a few who would be warriors, and then to go to the village of the Minneconjou and there, also recruit warriors!

Such a thing had never been done before. The Minneconjou and the Oglala were brothers, and sometimes they made camp together, and surely if the Crow or the White Man had attacked a camp of the Minneconjou and the Oglala they would have fought together, but never had a small, mobile raiding party been composed of individual warriors from both tribes.

Bloody Knife's new name had come to him in a vision in the sweat lodge, therefore all who heard him make the proclamation accepted it, for a vision was a message from *Wakan* and it couldn't be questioned.

"Why do they accept him now?" Fanny asked. "He struts around the camp as if he were a great chief. Only last month he feared to come before the camp because he had failed on his vow of a contraire."

"He has had a vision," Jumping Bear explained patiently. "Do you not understand that a vision is a sacred thing? He is no longer bound by the vow."

"How do we know he's had a vision?" Fanny asked. "He could just be saying that."

"No," Jumping Bear said. "Maybe when you have lived long enough in your red-now life, you will forget some of the ways of your white-before life. You do not understand that a vision is a sacred thing that no man would lie about. A vision is as sacred as the medicine bag he carries."

As Jumping Bear spoke, he, un-consciously, fingered the medicine bag he wore around his own neck. Fanny had once, teasingly, asked him what was in it, and when she had reached for it, Jumping Bear displayed the only anger she had ever seen him show toward her. She had learned then, without understanding, how dear the small, leather pouch was to all the warriors.

"Jumping Bear, because you are a good, honest man, you see goodness and honesty in everyone. You even see good in your cousin, One-Who-Waits.

But I tell you that there are some things I learned in my white-before life which would serve Indians well. And that is that some people may appear to have honor when they have none."

Jumping Bear laughed.

"Why do you laugh?" Fanny asked, irritated by his behavior.

"Because you, a woman, think you can tell me, a warrior, about life."

"You think you are so smart," Fanny said. "But believe me, Jumping Bear, you have much to learn!"

The discussion was developing into the first argument Fanny and Jumping Bear had ever had. Fanny didn't delude herself into thinking that their relationship had been so idyllic that no previous argument had occurred. She knew that quite the opposite was true. There had been no argument because until now there had been no real communication between them, other than the most basic exchanges. There had been moments of tenderness, yes, and physical pleasure too. But there had never been an ideological exchange before this conversation.

"I have learned much," Jumping Bear said, smiling at her anger.

"What have you learned?"

Jumping Bear reached for her. "I have learned the way to make you feel much pleasure."

"No!" Fanny said, turning out of his grasp. Jumping Bear looked at her with an expression of surprise on his face. She had never denied him before. "You have something else to learn," she added.

"What more must I learn?"

"You must learn that there is more in a relationship than shared buffalo robes."

Jumping Bear's look of surprise turned to confusion, and then to sullen anger. He stared at Fanny for a long moment, then, abruptly, he stood. "I am going to scout the herd," he said.

"Will you be back before night?"

"No," Jumping Bear said sullenly, and he pushed his way angrily through the tipi opening.

Fanny watched him leave the tipi without calling out to him. At another time, perhaps, she would have called out to him, apologized to him if that were necessary to maintain peace between them. But Fanny was having great difficulty in maintaining peace between them, now, because she couldn't maintain peace within herself. And Fanny had no peace within herself, because she had just discovered that she was going to have Jumping Bear's baby.

Fanny had often dreamed of having a baby. When she was at Fort Laramie and Fergus was out on one of his frequent, long patrols, she had thought of how nice it would be to have a baby to occupy her time. But the realization that she was going to have a baby now brought her no joy at all. She did not want Jumping Bear's baby. She was filled with a tremendous sense of guilt over her feelings, but she couldn't help it. It was as if having the baby would forever trap her in this life, and though she had more or less accepted the fact that she may have to live among the Indians from now on, there continued to burn deep down inside the spark of hope that someday, somehow, she might return to her own people. When the baby was born, even that spark would be extinguished, for Fanny realized that she would never be able to return to her own people with an Indian baby.

When Jumping Bear left the tipi, he saw several warriors standing near Ottawa's lodge in the center circle, listening to a speech given by Bloody Knife.

"Listen," the one who was once One-Who-Waits said. "I have seen a vision of my many victories. I have seen the white soldiers killed by warriors from the Oglala, and warriors from the Minneconjou. And in this vision, I, Bloody Knife, have led the warriors."

"But why should we fight the white men now?" one of the warriors asked. "Did we not strike at the soldiers when they desecrated our holy ground? Did that not teach them a lesson? What reason is there to fight now?"

"Are the Minneconjou not our brothers?" Bloody Knife asked. "Have we no love for our brothers that we can allow the white crime against them to go unpunished?"

"Why not let the Minneconjou avenge the crimes which were done against them?" another asked.

"The Minneconjou will avenge the crimes against them," Bloody Knife said. "But they will be fighting side by side with the Oglala, their brothers under my command. Now, I tell you that the vision spoke of much glory for Bloody Knife. Come, if you wish to share in this glory. Come, and visit the camp of the Minneconjou with me, and together we will ride against the white man to a great victory!"

Bloody Knife shouted his last declaration, and the Indians cheered, then someone broke into song, and as he sang, he danced, and the others danced behind him.

> Listen, we are warriors.
> The God Dogs, our horses,
> Run swiftly
> Between our legs.
> The arrow and the lance
> Fly true in their path.
> The blood of the toka, our enemy,
> Stains the ground
> Beneath the hooves of the
> God Dogs.
> We will have glory.
> We will count many coups.
> Listen, we are warriors.

Those who would be warriors joined the dancing men, and the one who danced with the lightest step and sang with the loudest voice was Running Rabbit.

"Cap'n, the messenger's comin' in," the Sergeant Major reported to Fergus Kelly. Though he had originally intended to stay only a few days, Fergus was now in his fourth week of encampment on the site of the old village of Ottawa's band. Every day he had sent scouting parties out to try to lo-

cate the new encampment, and every day they
had returned, having had no luck at all. When
the supplies the soldiers brought with them started
running thin, Fergus sent a messenger back to
Fort Laramie to ask Colonel Albertson what he
should do next. It was the return of that messenger
his sergeant reported to him.

Fergus was sitting on a fallen log, trying to fight
the damp chill of early spring by warming himself before a fire. He had a command tent, but he
was unable to burn a fire inside the tipi because
the smoke would make the tent uninhabitable.
Also, there was the danger of a fire. Therefore,
when Fergus wished to get warm, he would have to
come outside and stand or sit near the fire.

Cut Ear and the other Indian scouts of the expedition suffered no such problem. They had dis-
dained the use of the army issue tent, preferring
instead their own tipis. The four or five tipis which
had been pitched by the Indian scouts were far
superior, and easily the most comfortable places in
the camp. Several of the soldiers singly, or in small
groups, made frequent visits to the scouts' tipis, but
Fergus discouraged it, because he believed such
visits were an admission of white man's engineer-
ing inferiority to the Indian.

"Bring the messenger to me," Fergus ordered. He
held his hands out over the fire and shifted his
feet. Surely, no one fighting in the war back east
was suffering as much discomfort as were he and
his troops. Yet the *Harper's Weeklys* which still
came to his Fort Laramie quarters, addressed to
his wife, made much of the hardships and priva-
tions of the troops in the war. Fergus had searched

all the magazines diligently, but he had not found one word about the army fighting the Indians, either in the Northwest, or the Southwest territories.

The messenger saluted Fergus as he reported to him, then gratefully accepted the offer of a cup of coffee from one of the men.

"What did Colonel Albertson say?" Fergus asked.

The messenger held the coffee with eager fingers wrapped around the cup, enjoying the warmth the coffee brought to his hands.

"Beggin' your pardon, sir, but Colonel Albertson asked why you bothered to send a messenger to him in the first place?" the messenger reported. "He said you are the field commander and it is your decision to make."

"Damn," Fergus swore. "What is the purpose of a commander, if not to offer advice when it is asked for? Now the fault will be mine, no matter what happens with this expedition. If I continue the search and place my command in jeopardy because of depleted supplies, then I am in error. If I abandon the search, only to let the savages get away, then I am again in error. It would appear as if I am caught upon the horns of a dilemma."

"Perhaps not, Captain," Lieutenant Masters suggested.

"What?" Fergus replied. "What do you mean?"

"Perhaps there is a way we can do both," Lieutenant Masters said. "If I may make a suggestion?"

"By all means, Lieutenant, please do," Fergus said.

"Suppose you return with the main body of men," Masters proposed. "Leave but one company of men with me. I can continue the search, and as our numbers are smaller, we can take enough supplies from the existing provisions to last us much longer. As you will be returning to the Fort, you will need fewer supplies. If I find the Oglala Village, I will send word immediately."

"Yes," Fergus said, smiling at the suggestion. "Yes, Lieutenant Masters, that is an excellent suggestion."

"Why, thank you, sir," Masters said, beaming proudly at Captain Kelly's praise.

"But it is I who will remain in the field," Fergus went on. "While you return with the main body of men to the fort."

"But Captain, Kelly, that would place me at the head of four companies. Are you sure you wish to trust me with such a sizeable command?"

Fergus knew that Lieutenant Masters was merely trying to reverse the decision as to who stayed in the field, and who returned to the fort. If Lieutenant Masters stayed in the field and actually located the camp, he would attack of his own initiative, thus leaving Fergus out of it entirely. Fergus did not intend to let that happen, so he reiterated his stand.

"Nonsense, Lieutenant, I have every confidence in your ability to take the men back to the post. Hold them in readiness there for my summons. You will be in on the kill when we locate these devils. That I can promise you."

"As you wish, sir," Masters said, disappointed by the turn of events. "How soon should I start back?"

"You should start back immediately," Fergus said.

"In fact, let us all break camp now, you to return to the fort and I, with one company, to continue on the hunt."

Fergus was smiling broadly now. Lieutenant Masters' idea had been a brilliant one, and Fergus would put it into effect immediately and enthusiastically. In fact, Fergus was so enthusiastic over the plan that already he was beginning to think of it as his own idea. By this time tomorrow, he wouldn't even remember that Lieutenant Masters had come up with it in the first place.

Bloody Knife's scouts had reported to him that the soldiers who were camping at the sight of the Oglala summer village, had now split into two groups. One group was starting back, in the direction of Fort Laramie, while the other group, a much smaller group, continued West, along the river.

"It is a trick," Two Buffalo said. "Once before the white soldiers divided their force when they attacked the village of Wounded Foot."

Two Buffalo was a Minneconjou, one of the many who had joined Bloody Knife. He had been in the village on the morning of the attack, and his father and mother and sister and his sister's baby were all killed. The girl he was to marry was also killed, and Two Buffalo had cried, and made a vow that he would cut himself once each day until he had taken a white scalp for each of the ones he had lost in the raid which the Minneconjou now called 'The fight of the lying-down death', because so many had been killed while lying in their beds sleeping. His body was now covered with self-inflicted scars.

"I think it is not a trick," Running Rabbit said.

"You are but a boy. You have never been in a battle, and you cannot know all the tricks of the white men," Two Buffalo said.

"It is not a trick," Running Rabbit insisted. Running Rabbit had been with the scouts when they discovered that the white men were dividing into two groups.

"Why do you say this?" Bloody Knife asked.

"Because the soldiers who return to the fort have few pack horses, while those who stay have many. If the soldiers who return to the fort were going to turn and come back, they would have as many pack horses as the others."

"He is right," one of the other scouts said. "I saw this with my eyes, but I did not see it with my reason until the young one said this."

"Then we will attack the small group," Bloody Knife said. He looked at Running Rabbit. "You have done well."

Running Rabbit beamed proudly at this recognition. Although he still did not like Bloody Knife, Bloody Knife was the leader of this war party, and to be recognized by him would mean much when the stories of this battle were told back in camp.

Bloody Knife pointed to the river. "We will wait for the soldiers where the river goes through the Room of Devils. There we will attack."

The Room of Devils was a high, narrow canyon. There was a constant, moaning sound in the canyon, due to the organ-pipe like formation of the rocks, and it was from that sound that the canyon had been given its name. Once the soldiers were inside the canyon, escape would be impossible. Bloody Knife could hide his braves in the rocks alongside the river and trap the soldiers between the river and the canyon wall.

"Yes," Two Buffalo agreed. "The room of Devils is a good place to make the attack. When the white soldiers are killed, the demons will be there to claim their souls."

Bloody Knife turned to the warriors and explained his plan to them. They shouted enthusiastically, because they realized that the opportunity was great for them to kill many soldiers, and they followed eagerly as Bloody Knife led them to the place where they would wait for the attack.

The Indians were in position for more than half an hour before the white soldiers came. On the flat plains, boxed in by canyon walls, sound travelled far, and the soldiers, who had no idea that they may be in any sort of danger, took no pains to deaden the sound. Cups and mess skillets, canteens and sabers, harness and hardware clanged and banged and rattled. The army was making as much noise during its approach as they would make had they been accompanied by a marching band.

Running Rabbit heard the army approaching, and, even though it was cold and he was lying in wet mud, he felt hot in the flush of excitement which was upon him. He would count many coups this day, and when he returned to the village all would see the feathered lance he would carry, each feather tipped in red to denote the counting of coup.

Suddenly Running Rabbit got an idea! He would count coups against a soldier who was still alive! If he could ride up to him and touch him with his coups stick while the soldier was still alive, then he would be able to claim the highest honor any warrior can claim! Counting coups against a dead enemy was honor enough, but, once dead, the enemy represented no danger. To count coups against a enemy while he lives would be the cause for stories and songs to be celebrated around many campfires, and, surely, it would be entered in the sash of the winter count.

The winter count was the history book of the tribe. Symbols were painted on a long, winding cloth for each winter, in order to designate certain significant events of that winter as a year of remembrance. Though the white men called this year 1865, the Indian had no such numerical system. This year was simply, 'this year', and it would not have a name until the winter count was complete, then it would be remembered for the most important event of the year. Last year was 'The year of the white buffalo calf' because one of the hunters had seen a white buffalo calf during a hunt. Running Rabbit had been born in the year the white men called 1850, but when he was asked, he told his tribal brothers he was born in 'The Year of the spreading fever' for many in the village were sick that year, and in fact, both of Running Rabbit's parents died with the fever. Now, Running Rabbit thought, as he lay behind the rocks and listened to the noise of the approaching soldiers, this winter could well be known as 'The year of Running Rabbit's Live Coups', and he will be remembered forever among his people.

The soldiers rode into the mouth of the canyon with their officer to the front. Almost immediately the officer's identification traveled through the Indians. "It is Soldier-Who-Is-A-Coward! It is the one who attacked the village of Wounded Foot!"

"Do not kill Soldier-Who-Is-A-Coward!" Bloody Knife ordered. "He is for me to kill!"

"But I have sworn vengeance upon him," Two Buffalo said.

"You have sworn vengeance upon the white soldiers," Bloody Knife said. "Kill as many as you wish. But Soldier-Who-Is-A-Coward belongs to me."

Two Buffalo, whose chief purpose was to kill at least as many soldiers as were members of his family killed by soldiers, agreed, reluctantly. He cared not which soldier's blood he spilled, as long as he spilled the blood. He, like Running Rabbit and the others, waited, as the soldiers approached.

17

WHEN CAPTAIN KELLY's command was committed to the canyon, and inside the ambush zone, Bloody Knife jumped onto a rock and let out a terrible war cry. His cry was joined by that of dozens of others, and then a fusilade of bullets and arrows were launched toward the soldiers.

"Oh, my God, my God!" Fergus shouted. Fergus reined his horse to a halt. "We're being attacked. Dismount, and take cover!"

"No!" his sergeant shouted, countermanding the order. "Cap'n, you've got to try and ride on through the canyon! It's our only chance! We are surrounded!"

"No!" Fergus said. "No, we'll all be killed if we stay mounted. We must take cover!"

The sergeant who had attempted to change Captain Kelly's mind was struck then, and he tumbled from his saddle, coughing blood. Without his influence, Fergus Kelly was left to issue unchallenged his ill-conceived commands, and he made the same basic mistake he had made when his wagon train escort party was attacked. He dismounted, thus depriving his soldiers of their only chance, their mobility.

Once dismounted the soldiers lost all cohesion as a fighting force, and they began to mill about in panic, shooting at shadows, and screaming in terror as the Indians leaped from boulder to boulder to cut them down with war clubs and lances.

Running Rabbit headed straight for Soldier-Who-Is-A-Coward. Since Bloody Knife had given orders that the officer's life was to be taken by no one but him, Fergus Kelly was an ideal subject for his live coups.

Running Rabbit leaped from a rock and landed right on Fergus Kelly's chest, knocking him down. Kelly saw the Indian on him. The Indian's face was painted in grotesque color, and his lips were peeled back in a hideous smile. His war club raised to bash in his brains. Fergus screamed.

"You scream like a woman," Running Rabbit said in perfect English. "You bring dishonor to she who was your wife. The one you called Fanny."

"What?" Kelly asked, shocked by the Indian's remarks. "Did you say Fanny?"

"In her white-before-life she was known as Fanny. Now she is called Real Woman. Once she was your wife, but no more."

"You're lying," Fergus said. "My wife is dead!"

"It is you who will soon be dead," Running Rabbit said. He smiled again. "But not by my hand." He touched his coups stick to Fergus's head. "I claim coups."

After Running Rabbit claimed coups he stood up and gave a shout of victory. When he looked around he saw that the battle was nearly over. There were a few soldiers still holding out behind a cluster of boulders near the river, but only Kelly remained alive of those who had not made it to cover.

Running Rabbit had claimed coups on Fergus, but he had not harmed him. More important, he had not disarmed him, and though Running Rabbit considered Kelly to be the vanquished foe, Fergus was still armed, terrified, humiliated, and filled with hate. Fergus rose to his feet behind Running Rabbit, raised his pistol, and fired a ball into Running Rabbit's head killing the young Indian instantly.

Two Buffalo saw Running Rabbit killed and he reached out and grabbed the pistol from Fergus, then raised his war club to kill him.

"Wait!" Bloody Knife shouted. "I have claimed him for myself."

Two Buffalo lowered his war club, which was now red and gory with the blood and visceral remains of those he had already killed.

"I care not who kills him," Two Buffalo said. "Only that he be killed."

Bloody Knife raised his war club then, and started toward Fergus Kelly.

"Wait, for God's sake, wait!" Fergus said, holding out his hand in supplication. "I saved your life, remember? You owe me!" Fergus dropped to his knees and began crying, "I saved your life, I let you go," he said.

Bloody Knife stood over him with his war club poised for a long moment, then he lowered it.

"Turn your soldiers over to us, and I will spare your life," he finally said.

"What? You mean if I surrender, you will spare us?"

"Not all of you," Bloody Knife said. "I will kill them. Only you will be spared."

Fergus was still on his knees, but he looked up at Bloody Knife with an expression of wild hope in his eyes. "You mean . . . . if I surrender my men to you, you will let me go? I can go free?"

"Yes," Bloody Knife said.

"I have only to surrender my men to you?"

"So that I can kill them," Bloody Knife said.

"But . . . . but they are going to be killed anyway," Fergus said, more to himself than to Bloody Knife. "This way, at least, one of us would live. They should be happy that their lives won't be given in vain. I'll have to lie to them, to get them to come out."

"Lies come easy for white men," Bloody Knife said.

"I'll call them," Fergus said. He stood up and cleared his throat. "Men!" he called. "Men, hear me. I've talked with Bloody Knife. If we all surrender now, he will let us return to the Fort."

"How do we know we can trust 'im, cap'n?" one of the men behind the rock called.

"What do we have to lose?" Fergus replied. "If

you fight any longer, you will surely be killed. We are badly outnumbered."

"Yeah, but we'll take a few more of these sons-of-bitches with us," the spokesman said.

"Now, listen to me," Fergus called. "I'm *ordering* you to surrender."

"Cap'n, right now, you ain't got the authority to do that," the voice replied laconically.

"Please, men," Fergus said, now with some degree of desperation. "This is our only chance. I'm begging you, give yourselves up! We'll all be killed if you don't."

"Give us a moment to talk it over," the voice behind the rock said.

Bloody Knife took a lance from one of the near-by Indians, and he placed the point of it against Fergus Kelly's neck.

"If they come out, you go free," he said. "If they fight, you die."

Fergus felt the point of the lance against his neck, pressed hard enough to prick the skin and to cause a small trickle of blood to run down. Any harder, Fergus knew, and the trickle would be replaced by a gushing, warm, torrent of blood.

Fergus waited for an interminable length of time, then the spokesman called out again.

"Alright, cap'n, we're comin' out," he said, and he and the others tossed their weapons over the rocks. A moment later, six soldiers stepped out, holding their hands high in the air. Those six men were all that remained of the fifty troopers who had ridden in with Fergus Kelly.

The Indians let out a loud cheer of victory, and

they started dancing around the white men, closing them in a tighter and tighter circle. The soldiers knotted together and looked at the dancing circle with obvious fear etched on their faces.

"Bring a horse for Soldier-Who-Is-A-Coward," Bloody Knife said, and one of the Indians brought a mount to Fergus.

"You go now," Bloody Knife said. "I have paid you for my life. If we meet again, I will kill you."

"Where's our horses?" one of the six men called.

"Yeah," another put in. "Cap'n Kelly, what about our mounts?"

Fergus, who was now mounted, looked down at the six men. "I'm sorry," he said. "This was the only way."

"What? You sold us out, you son-of-a-bitch!"

"What could I do?" Fergus asked helplessly. "They would have killed me."

"Damn your hide!" One of the six men shouted, and he started toward Fergus, but before he had taken three steps he was shot with an arrow. He gasped, made a futile effort to pull the arrow out, then he fell, quivered a few times, and died.

"I'm sorry," Fergus said again. He slapped his ankles against the side of the horse and the horse burst into a gallop. Within moments he was out of range of the Indians, riding hard for Fort Laramie.

"I'll get that son-of-a-bitch for that if it's the last thing I ever do," one of the soldiers said.

Another laughed, a bitter laugh. "Where are you going to do it, in Fiddler's Green?"

"Fiddler's Green?" the youngest of the five remaining troopers asked. "Where is Fiddler's Green?"

"You're about to find out, son," the oldest of the men said. "It's a place all soldiers go when they die. It's a cool, shaded, green, where the drinkin's free, and all the soldiers who ever heard a bugle call are waitin' for judgment day."

The soldiers were bound with rawhide thongs. Then the Indians formed two long lines, facing each other, holding arrows in their hand. The Indians looked expectantly toward the five, hapless soldiers.

"What's happening?" the youngest soldier asked.

"The in'juns is about to play a little game," one of the troopers said. "I've seen it before . . . . that is, I've seen the victum. You have to run down the line and each one of them gets a chance to stick an arrow in you. You're runnin' fast, 'n they're tryin' to do it by hand, so the arrows don't go deep. But they don't have to go too deep, 'cause by the time you reach the other end there's twenty or thirty arrows stickin' out of you. You'll be dead enough, I reckon."

The youngest trooper closed his eyes and looked away.

"What the hell?" the soldier who had explained the grisly game said. "Someone has to be first. Tell you fella's what, I'll go find us a nice shade tree to sit under at that Fiddler's Green place O'Grady was a'tellin' us about."

The soldier started down between the two lines of Indians.

"Stick it in deep, you heathen bastards!" he shouted. "Damn you! Damn you one and all!"

The soldier's curses and shouts turned from anger to pain, and finally to one, last, agonizing scream. He fell, less than three quarters of the way through the line. As soon as he fell the Indians converged on him, kicking, stabbing, and clubbing. Within moments his body was a bloody mess.

"Oh, Jeez, lookit that," one of the remaining four said.

"I envy him," another said. "It's over for him. And it's about to be over for me." This was the soldier who had sworn to 'get' Fergus Kelly, and now he, like the man before him, started through the line of Indians, shouting his curses as loudly as before. He was finally felled at about the same place as the one before him, and he, too, was mutilated by the Indians.

None of the three remaining offered to run the gauntlet, so two Indians grabbed one and forced him into the line. He had no choice but to run, and he didn't make it half way before he, too, was dead.

Now there remained only the oldest soldier, Corporal O'Grady, and the youngest, Private Babcock.

"Lad, I'll go before or after ye', whichever way ye' wish," Corporal O'Grady offered.

"I . . . I'll go first," Babcock said, but as he started to leave, one of the Indians who had been watching, let out a sharp command. The Indians grew quiet and looked toward him. It was Bloody Knife.

"Let these two live," Bloody Knife said. He looked at the two troopers, and he smiled, evilly at them. "Return to the fort," he said. "Tell the others of the great victory I, Bloody Knife, won

here today. And tell them of the dishonor of Soldier-Who-Is-A-Coward."

"If you mean Cap'n Kelly, I'll damn sure do
that," O'Grady said.

Bloody Knife spoke to one of the Indians, and
that Indian walked over to cut the bonds on the
two troopers. Another Indian brought them a couple of horses.

"Tell the others I am the enemy of all white
men," Bloody Knife said to the two soldiers.

O'Grady and Babcock climbed onto the horses,
still not sure they were being set free, then, when
it sunk in to them, they kicked their horses in the
side, riding out as quickly as did Captain Kelly.
Behind them lay the bodies of 47 troopers. Behind
them also, the singing, shouting laughter of fewer
than thirty Indians. Captain Kelly had not been
beaten by superior numbers, but by superior tactics.

Fergus Kelly rode hard. When night fell, the
moon was bright, and he could see nearly as clearly
as if it were day, so he pressed his horse on. Once
or twice, when it became apparent even to him
that his horse was laboring with exhaustion, he
stopped long enough to let the animal breathe.
Then before his horse had a chance to recover,
he would climb on and urge him forward again.

During each stop he searched the distant horizon, and he listened to detect any possibility of
being followed. So far, as far as he could tell, he
was safe. The heathens had kept their word.

Fergus worried about what he would tell Colonel Albertson. How could he report back to him as the only survivor a *second* time? On the other hand, when he had feared a reprimand from Colonel Albertson the time before, he had been promoted to Captain and nominated for the Medal of Honor. He didn't receive the Medal of Honor, but he had been nominated.

Slowly, and with the fear of imminent death now safely removed, Kelly began to go over in his mind, just how he would make out the report. And the more he thought of it, the less concerned he became about what Colonel Albertson's reaction would be. If he had been regarded as a hero before, then surely he would be regarded as such now. Perhaps he would even be promoted again.

Major Kelly. Major Fergus Kelly. Yes, that had a most appealing ring to it.

"Damnit!" O'Grady swore. "Babcock, laddie, m'horse has gone lame."

"Lame?" Babcock said in a frightened tone of voice. "No, he can't be lame. We've got to get out of here!"

"We're far enough away, let's stop for a moment," O'Grady said, and they pulled up, then got down from their heavily breathing animals. "The poor beasts need a blow anyway," O'Grady added.

Babcock looked back in the direction from which they had just come, searching diligently for any sign of their being followed. While Babcock was searching the horizon, O'Grady was gently running his hand along the legs of his horse.

"Oh damn me," he said softly. "Lookie here lad, what I've found."

Babcock looked at O'Grady's horse and then gasped. For there, sticking about half an inch out of the horses left flank, was the ugly, jagged remains of a broken arrow shaft. New, red blood was streaming down over old, coagulated blood. It was obvious that the wound had been bleeding for some time.

"Oh, what a cruelty I've done the poor creature," O'Grady said, "ridin' him while he was pumpin' his own life's blood out. 'Tis a wonder he's yet on his feet."

"Can you get it out?" Babcock asked.

Now that the horse had stopped running, the great heart it had called upon seemed to desert it, and it took a few staggering steps, then fell. It lay on the ground, breathing with a wheezing sound.

"Oh, damn!" O'Grady said. "The wolves'll be on the creature sure, 'n I've no pistol to shoot him with."

"Come on," Babcock said anxiously. "Come on, let's go. The horse is going to die, you know it."

"Aye, that I do know, lad. But this horse carried me outta that heathen camp, 'n if he's goin' ter die, I aim to stand by and see that it's a peaceful death, and not one that's tormented by the wolves."

"Corporal O'Grady, we *can't* stay here, don't you understand? The Indians, they'll,"

"They'll not be comin' after us, lad," O'Grady said easily.

"What makes you think so?"

"The devils are wantin' us to do their work for them."

"Their work?" Babcock asked, confused by O'Grady's statement.

"They are wantin' us to tell the others about Cap'n Kelly's cowardice."

"Well then they're going to get their wish," Babcock said. "Because I intend to climb to the roof of the Sutler's Store and shout it at the top of my lungs."

"No," O'Grady said.

"What? Corporal O'Grady, what are you talking about? What do you mean, no?"

"Why should we give those heathen bastards the satisfaction o' seein' us turn on one o' our own, just to satisfy some devilish design o' theirs?"

"I don't consider Captain Kelly one of our own," Babcock said resolutely. "I consider him a coward, unfit to wear the uniform of the United States Army."

"Cap'n Kelly ain't the point, boy," O'Grady said. "But you've done put your finger on what is the point. And that be the uniform. Whether the cap'n's disgraced hisself or not is one thing, but the uniform he's wearin' can never be disgraced."

"Yes it can," Babcock insisted. "Captain Kelly disgraced it."

"No," O'Grady said. "Kelly ain't fit to wear it, but the uniform, the symbol of the American Army Officer, is still there. And I'll be damned if I help a bunch o' savages show disrespect to it. Don't you see, lad? If we do this thing, if we carry this story into the fort, then we are no better than

Kelly. Kelly bought his life with the lives o' his men. But we'd be buyin' our lives, with the honor of the whole U.S. Army, 'n I can't do that."

"You're really serious about this, aren't you?" Babcock asked.

"Yes."

"Why? What's the army ever done for you?"

"It's fed me, and clothed me, and housed me," O'Grady said. "But it's been more'n that, and you know it. The army's my wife 'n children, my brothers, 'n yes, my mother 'n father too. I came over from Ireland at the age o' fourteen, 'n 'twas only the U.S. Army that seemed to tell me 'twas glad they were to see me. I've been in the Army now, man and boy, for thirty years, 'n I'll stay 'till I'm ready for the old soldiers' home, or 'till I get a pass to Fiddlers' Green."

"I, I see what you mean," Babcock said. He sighed. "But it doesn't seem right to let the son-of-a-bitch get away with it. He'll probably be treated like a hero, when he should be taken out and shot."

O'Grady chuckled.

"What is it?" Babcock asked. "What do you think is so funny?"

"I want to see the expression on Cap'n Kelly's face when you'n me come ridin' into the Fort," O'Grady said.

"Yeah," Babcock said, laughing along with O'Grady. "I would say he's going to be most uncomfortable."

"We won't say a thing," O'Grady said. "We'll just play it real easy, like, 'n it'll drive him plumb loco, wonderin' when we're goin' to spill the beans."

"Corporal O'Grady, I have to give you credit," Babcock said. "Not even the Indians themselves could have devised a more exquisite form of torture." ঙ্গ

18

WORD OF Bloody Knife's great victory reached back to the camp by advanced messenger, and the camp was already celebrating before the main body of warriors arrived. Fanny saw no call for celebration, because she knew so many of the soldiers from Fort Laramie that she was certain many of her friends had been killed in the battle. Therefore she stayed in her tipi, refusing to join the celebration.

"Here," Jumping Bear said, offering her a pot of black smudge paint. "Put some of this on your face."

"Why?" Fanny asked. "Isn't that for mourning? Will it not make it more obvious to everyone if I mourn the death of so many who were my friends?"

"There is one Oglala you can mourn," Jumping Bear said sadly.

"Surely not. For to mourn a warrior who does not belong to you would bring disgrace to those who live," Fanny said, showing that she had managed a fine grasp of the customs of her new people.

"You can mourn one who had no family," Jumping Bear said sadly.

"Who would that . . . . Jumping Bear, no! Running Rabbit?"

"Yes," Jumping Bear said.

Fanny thought of the young Indian boy who had done so much to make her transition into her new life bearable. Tears sprang quickly to her eyes. "Why was he with them? He was just a boy."

"He called himself a warrior," Jumping Bear said.

"In fact, why did they make war at all?" Fanny went on. "Will this foolishness never end?"

"There will always be wars until either the white man or the red man is gone," Jumping Bear said.

"Then the red man is doomed," Fanny said. "For there are more white men than there are blades of grass."

"Mourn then, not just for Running Rabbit, but for all the Indian people," Jumping Bear said. He reached out and touched Fanny lightly on her stomach. "Mourn for he whom you carry in your belly, for he is Indian."

Fanny gasped. She had not yet told Jumping Bear that she believed she was pregnant. In fact, she had told no one. How did he know?

Jumping Bear smiled at her surprise, then he left

the tipi to join with the others. He did not feel
like celebrating, because he felt the death of Running Rabbit very keenly. Also he knew that Real
Woman must have lost many friends in the battle.
But if he did not join in the celebration, others
would think he was jealous of Bloody Knife's victory, and he did not wish to give that impression.
Therefore he visited the paint pot of victory, and
smudged his face, then joined in the dancing and
singing, and listened to the words of the warriors
as they told of their victory and their punishment
of the prisoners.

"Listen," one of the warriors called proudly.
"Hear my new song."

The other singers stopped so that only the warrior's words would be heard. His song was sung
in a two note chant, with a rhythm which was
fine for dancing, so, even as he sang the dance
continued.

> "We heard the soldiers coming,
> And we waited behind the rocks,
> Our blood ran hot
> And our hearts were strong.
> Soldier-Who-Is-A-Coward died
> Many deaths and his Spirit
> Wanders with the living.
> The grass will grow green in
> The moon of making-fat, because
> It has fed off the blood of the
> Toka."

"So, you let Soldier-Who-Is-A-Coward live?"
Jumping Bear asked Bloody Knife. Bloody Knife

was drinking some of the whiskey which had been taken from the dead soldiers.

Bloody Knife took the bottle down and wiped his lips with the back of his hand. He smiled at Jumping Bear. "He lives to tell the others of my glory."

"Why would he tell of your glory and thus show his own dishonor?"

Bloody Knife laughed. "Because after the game of the arrows in which we killed three prisoners, we let the last two go. They will tell, for they saw the dishonor of Soldier-Who-Is-A-Coward."

There were others close enough to hear the conversation now and they laughed as they recalled the game of the arrows. They shouted to Jumping Bear that he should have been with them, rather than staying warm in the buffalo robes of Real Woman. It was a challenge which stung Jumping Bear, for he could see that his leadership was eroding.

Jumping Bear and Bloody Knife, as grandsons of Ottawa, were in position to assume the leadership of the entire village some day. Jumping Bear had shown the earlier signs of leadership. He had been the swiftest runner, the best rider, and the surest hunter. He had distinguished himself in battle with the Crow many times, but he had never fought against the white men. Bloody Knife had now fought two battles with the whites, and he had won both. This had not gone unnoticed by the others of the tribe, and in truth, it had not gone unnoticed by Jumping Bear. And yet, he had no desire to make war against the whites merely to enhance his own glory.

Jumping Bear realized that he might soon be forced into a battle with the whites whether he wished it or not. If Soldier-Who-Is-A-Coward yet lives, he may lead an attack against Ottawa's village while they sleep, as he did against the village of Wounded Foot. If that happened, many, many Oglala would be killed. Jumping Bear was concerned about that possibility. He was so concerned that he left the celebration to seek out Ottawa. He and Ottawa would have to find some warriors who would volunteer to sleep by day and stay awake by night so that the camp could be guarded, even as the soldier forts are guarded at night.

Bloody Knife had drunk much of the liquor and he felt the fire burning inside him. He was intoxicated, but not by the whiskey. He was intoxicated by the exuberance of his own greatness. He listened to the songs which were sung in his honor, and he heard the praises to his name, and he knew that it would be Bloody Knife, and not Jumping Bear, who would some day be chief.

Bloody Knife saw Jumping Bear going into the lodge of Ottawa. At first it angered him. Jumping Bear should have remained at the celebration to praise him. He left because he could not face the fact that Bloody Knife was now the more popular leader of the two. But the anger didn't last too long, because Bloody Knife suddenly realized that there was opportunity in Jumping Bear's absence.

Bloody Knife looked toward the tipi Jumping Bear shared with Real Woman. Real Woman was still inside the tipi. She had not come out to sing one song of praise, and Bloody Knife was angered by that.

Bloody Knife had also, long carried an anger against Real Woman for spurning him in favor of Ottawa. She had gone to the council to plead that she be allowed to take Ottawa as her husband, and then, once the council granted its approval, she left Ottawa for Jumping Bear! That had been a blow to Bloody Knife's pride and it was compounded by the fact that she now lived openly with Jumping Bear.

As Bloody Knife thought of his anger with Real Woman, he remembered the night of her capture. That night he had shown her the strength of his *cezin*. He had taken her as she lay tied to the ground.

Bloody Knife felt a *cezin* anew, and he rubbed his bulging penis through the loin cloth, and he thought of what it had been like on that night. The thought made his blood even hotter and he knew that he would know no peace until he was with her again. He looked toward the lodge of Ottawa, and saw that Jumping Bear was still inside. Bloody Knife smiled, rubbed himself again, and started toward the tipi of Real Woman.

Inside the tipi, Fanny heard the celebrating continue. She was busying herself with a small dress. She had started the dress a few days earlier, when she was certain that she was pregnant but she had kept it hidden from Jumping Bear. Now that he knew about it, there would no longer be a need to keep it hidden.

As Fanny worked on the dress, holding the tiny garment in her hand, she began to feel a sense of joy over the baby. And why not? As a mother, didn't she have the right to welcome a baby? What if the baby were Indian, hadn't she undergone a ceremony to become Indian? Besides, no woman could deny her own baby, and even as the child grew within Fanny, she found herself growing anxious for the day she could actually hold it and love it.

Behind Fanny the tipi flap opened, and someone came into the tent.

"Look, Jumping Bear," Fanny said without turning around. "See the dress I am making for the baby?"

There was no answer, and Fanny turned to see why, then she gasped, and put her hand to her mouth. Bloody Knife was standing just inside the tipi. His painted face was underlit by the orange glow of the tipi fire, and the fire and shadow gave him the look of a demon. He stared down at her, menacingly.

"One-Who-Waits," Fanny said, then she realized what a mistake she had made, for to call him that was to recall his earlier shame. "I mean Bloody Knife," she corrected. She was frightened, but she tried not to show her fright. She looked behind him, hoping that Jumping Bear was with him.

Bloody Knife smiled, but rather than making his face more pleasing, the grin seemed to pull his firelit features into an even more hideous countenance.

"Why have you not come to celebrate my victory?" Bloody Knife asked.

"I . . . . I am in mourning," Fanny explained.

"You mourn for the white devils who were killed?"

"I mourn for Running Rabbit," Fanny said. "And for the white soldiers. I knew many of them in my white-before life."

"Running Rabbit was a fool," Bloody Knife said. "He tried to make a live coups, to take the glory that was mine."

"Why are you so concerned with glory?" Fanny asked. "Do you think everyone else is?"

"You belong to me," Bloody Knife suddenly said.

"What?" Fanny gasped. "What are you talking about?"

"You belong to me," Bloody Knife said again, and he touched himself on the chest. "It was Bloody Knife who captured you. You should be in my tipi, cooking my meals, and warming my bed."

"It was *not* Bloody Knife who captured me, it was One-Who-Waits," Fanny said, hoping to reason with him. "And One-Who-Waits is no more."

Suddenly, and without warning, Bloody Knife swung the back of his hand across Fanny's face, sending her sprawling. She was so surprised by his action that she didn't even cry out.

"Now, I will show you what it is like to be taken by a warrior," Bloody Knife grunted. "You have known only an old man, and a timid hunter."

Fanny looked up just as Bloody Knife came down over her, and she saw the reflected light of the flames in his eyes. The light gave his eyes a demonic glow of lust. Fanny opened her mouth to scream, but a wicked blow from Bloody Knife's fist cut her scream short. She tasted blood, and realized that her lip was cut. Then she felt herself being gagged, as Bloody Knife used the baby dress she was making to stifle any further screams, by stuffing it in her mouth.

Fanny tried to scream, even around the gag, but it was useless. Then she let her body go limp. Bloody Knife, thinking that she was giving in to him, grinned, and relaxed his grip. That was the opening Fanny was seeking, and she rolled over and tried to get up.

Bloody Knife perceived then what she was doing, and he gave her a wicked kick in the stomach, knocking her back down.

Fanny had never felt such pain! The kick in her stomach absolutely paralyzed her, and after the initial shock of pain, she was numb from her shoulders down. She had no feeling at all, and was only barely aware of her legs being spread wide by Bloody Knife.

Suddenly, through the numbing haze of near unconsciousness, Fanny saw another man in the tipi, and her heart leaped with joy! It was Jumping Bear!

Jumping Bear bellowed in rage, and he grabbed Bloody Knife by the hair of his head, jerked him up, then threw him outside the tipi. He followed outside, and as a stunned Bloody Knife was trying to get up, Jumping Bear brought the back of his hand across his face, knocking him down again.

"You are dog which eats its own vomit," Jumping Bear cursed. "You are a worm, crawling in human dung!"

Every time Bloody Knife tried to get up, Jumping Bear would knock him down again, uttering an oath as he did so.

The celebration which had continued unabated even as Bloody Knife was in Fanny's tipi, had stopped abruptly, and now all had gathered in a large circle to watch.

"Fight me!" Bloody Knife finally called. "Give me a weapon so that we may fight!"

Jumping Bear was standing beside a warrior who had been carrying a lance during his dancing, so Jumping Bear grabbed the warrior's lance and threw it at Bloody Knife's feet. It stuck in the ground. Bloody Knife pulled it out, then turned it toward Jumping Bear.

Jumping Bear had made a major mistake! He had armed Bloody Knife before he, himself was armed, and now, as he started to arm himself, Bloody Knife made a thrust at him, cutting him off.

"Unfair," someone called. "Let him arm himself!"

But Bloody Knife paid no attention to the shouts. Instead, he continued to thrust the lance toward Jumping Bear, who could do nothing now but dance out of the way of each thrust.

"Tonight you will see me lie with your woman," Bloody Knife said. "Your severed head will be hanging from the lodgepole, and I will prop your eyes open so that you will see everything!" He made another jab with the lance, and Jumping Bear avoided it as he had the others.

Fanny had come to the outside of the tipi now, holding her stomach against the pain which was now deep inside, and she saw what was happening.

She felt a tightness in her chest as she realized that Bloody Knife was armed, and thus had the advantage over Jumping Bear.

But then the situation changed! Bloody Knife made a lunge which Jumping Bear managed to avoid, and as Bloody Knife was trying to recover, Jumping Bear cuffed him on the back of the head sending him sprawling, face down, in the dirt. Bloody Knife dropped the lance and Jumping Bear picked it up, then, as Bloody Knife turned over onto his back, Jumping Bear put the point of the lance at Bloody Knife's throat.

"Kill him!" someone shouted. "You have bested him fairly!"

Bloody Knife looked up at Jumping Bear with hate and defiance in his eyes. "Kill me," he said. "I will wait for you in the other world."

Jumping Bear held the lance for a moment, then he pulled the point away. "No," he said. "You are the grandson of our grandfather. I have no wish to kill you." He dropped the lance, then started toward Fanny, to see how she was.

As Fanny watched Jumping Bear approach her, she was filled with pride, because he had defended her honor. Now, perhaps the glory Bloody Knife had so ardently sought would dissipate and he would be less a threat, not only to her, but to peace between the Indians and the whites.

Then, with horrifying suddenness, the point of the spear burst out of Jumping Bear's chest! Blood squirted from around the shaft, and Jumping Bear, surprised, put both hands up to feel it, then he fell forward.

"Jumping Bear!" Fanny cried out in shock and

horror. She looked up and saw Bloody Knife on his feet. Bloody Knife had picked up the spear Jumping Bear had dropped beside him, and hurled it at Jumping Bear's back. So great was Bloody Knife's anger induced strength, that the lance penetrated all the way through Jumping Bear's body, going in the back and coming out the chest in front.

"Seize him!" Ottawa shouted, for he had been drawn from his lodge by the fight. Ottawa pointed toward Bloody Knife, and two nearby Indians started toward Bloody Knife to obey Ottawa's command.

"No!" Bloody Knife said, knocking the two Indians away. He took a couple of hesitant steps backward, looking into the faces of those who, only a short time before were paying him honor, but now were ready to kill him. "He deserved to die!" Bloody Knife said. "She was my woman! She was my woman!"

Bloody Knife turned and ran toward the remuda. He leaped onto the back of the first horse, grabbed the line of another, spooked the remaining horses, and rode quickly, into the night.

"Get the horses!" Ottawa commanded. "Get the horses, then ride him down and bring him to me!"

The Indians, many of whom were drunk from the liquor, ran, stumbling and bumbling into the night, trying to catch the skittish horses. None of them were successful, and Bloody Knife made good his escape.

* * *

Fanny stood with the others the next morning as Jumping Bear's body was raised onto the burial platform right alongside the platform with the body of Running Rabbit. How beautiful the moving ceremony was. How eloquent were the words spoken by Jumping Bear's friends, and by the elders of the village. And though there was no priest, or representative of her own religion, Fanny, quietly, prayed for the soul of the two Indians who had meant so much to her.

Fanny also prayed for the baby which would never be, for Bloody Knife's cruel blow to her stomach had terminated her pregnancy.

"Hear these names," Ottawa called. "These are the honored names of those who are in the spirit world, and they shall be spoken no more in this life. Running Rabbit, and Jumping Bear."

As the villagers returned to the village, Kettle Woman, who was comforting Fanny, told her that the council had expelled Bloody Knife for life. Never, she said, would he be able to return to the village of the Oglala.

"Do you wish to come to our lodge to sleep?" Kettle Woman asked, and even Willow Branch and Morning Flower were solicitous of her because they no longer considered her a rival for position with Ottawa.

"Your offer fills my heart," Fanny replied. "But tonight, I will sleep in the tipi I made for him." She was careful not to say the name. "His spirit is still there and I will be there too."

Jumping Bear's remaining belongings were disposed of during the day, and many stopped by to express their grief, and to leave gifts of food, or clothing. Not once did anyone mention Jumping Bear's name.

Finally night fell, and Fanny went to bed, thankful that the long day of mourning was over. She felt a little numb over everything, and she wondered what her future would be now. Perhaps she could persuade Ottawa to let her return to the white world. But the question she asked herself just before she fell asleep, was if she would really want to. Could she really face Soldier-Who-Is-A-Coward again?

Soldier-Who-Is-A-Coward. Fanny chuckled. She had thought of Fergus in that way, rather than by his own name.

Fanny heard a sound. She wasn't sure how long she had been asleep. In fact, it was a moment before she even realized she had been asleep, and now, she floated back to consciousness only with effort.

She lay there in the quiet darkness, listening for a long time, to see if the sound returned. It was the stirring of the camp dogs she had heard, she decided. That, and nothing more.

The sleeping blankets were warm, and her senses were still groggy from sleep, and from the emotional activities of the long day, and soon Fanny drifted off again.

Fanny was awake less than a minute later, and this time she was wide awake, with her eyes open and her heart pounding in fear! But as soon as she perceived the danger, she was gagged, and

before she could cry out, she saw Bloody Knife
kneeling over her, smiling evilly down at her.

"You are my woman!" Bloody Knife said. "You
are coming with me!"

Fanny tried to call out against the gag, but she
managed only a small, whimpering noise. Soon,
even that was muffled, as she felt herself being
bound up in a buffalo rug, wrapped from head
to toe so that she was unable to see, as well as
unable to cry out. Bloody Knife tied rawhide thongs
around the buffalo rug, then bound her tightly, so
that she was a completely helpless prisoner.

Fanny was scooped up, and carried out of the
tipi. She felt herself thrown across the back of a
horse, then Bloody Knife climbed onto the horse
with her. He slapped his legs against the side of
the animal, and Fanny, belly down over the horse,
was carried away into the night.   ঙচ

19

FANNY HAD BEEN Bloody Knife's captive for ten days now. During that ten days, they had seen no one else. Bloody Knife kept away from main trails and waterways to make certain they were undetected. They may as well have been on the moon, so alone were they.

Bloody Knife knew that his life would be worthless, whether he was captured by the Indians or the whites, so he moved from campsite to campsite, and never stayed in any one site longer than a single night. They traveled without a tipi, and had only the robe in which Fanny had been wrapped, to warm them against the cool spring nights.

Bloody Knife had used her sexually, many times since her capture. Fanny no longer tried to fight him off, not because he had won her over, but because she realized that fighting was futile, and it was much easier to bear up under it until it was over. She had developed the art of making herself go numb, completely closing her mind to the degradation she was suffering.

Sometimes when they travelled, Bloody Knife allowed her to ride on the horse with him, but more often than not, she was forced to trail behind, on foot, at the end of a long tether, with her hands tied behind.

Fanny had grown much stronger during her time with the Indians. She had hauled wood and erected tipis, and skinned game and that had a tremendously beneficial effect to her endurance. It was only because of that strength that she was able to survive the ordeal, and even so, she was tried to her utmost capacity.

Fanny was allowed to eat, but only after Bloody Knife had eaten. She was always very careful to break the bones and suck the marrow, in order to utilize as much as she could from the food she did get. On the night of the tenth day, as she was sitting quietly, waiting for him to finish a game bird, agonizing because it was so small that she knew there would be little left, Bloody Knife told her to get some water.

"Aren't you afraid I will run away?" she asked.

Bloody Knife pulled the meat off a bone, then smiled at her. "You will not run," he said, matter-of-factly.

"How do you know?"

"I have the horse," he said. "I can find you. And you are hungry, and cannot run for long. And if you run, I will beat you when I catch you. No, I think you will not run. Get the water."

Fanny picked up the buffalo stomach flask, and started down toward the stream. With the spring thaw, the ice was gone from the streams, but they were still running cold from the snow which remained in the higher elevations. The water was so cold that if one were to throw themself in it their breath would be taken away, and they would drown quickly.

"*Oh, dear, no church, not even the Roman Church, would consider such a thing suicide,*" Mrs. Albertson had said, that night in her parlor.

Now, the thought of suicide, spoken of only as a point of philosophical interest so long ago, began to look attractive to Fanny. For the first time since her capture, she considered suicide as a serious alternative.

Fanny walked down to the stream, but, instead of filling the flask, she looked at the swift, flowing water. She walked closer to the edge, then she closed her eyes and prepared to jump.

"Don't do it, Fanny!" a voice called from the darkness.

Fanny gasped, and turned around with a start. There, standing just behind a rock, she saw Matt Parker!

"Matt, it's you!" Fanny ran to him, throwing her arms around him in unrestrained joy.

"Shhh. How many are there?"

"There's just one," Fanny said. "There's just Bloody Knife. Oh, Matt, thank God you've come. Get me out of here. Get me away from him, please!"

"Yuza!" Bloody Knife called, using the name

which meant slave-wife. "Yuza, why do you take so long? Bring the water now. I am thirsty!"

"What's he saying?" Matt asked.

"He wants me to take him some water."

"Call him down here," Matt said.

Reluctantly, Fanny left Matt's arms, then stepped back toward the edge of the water.

"Bloody Knife, please come, I need you," she called.

"What is it?" Bloody Knife answered, irritably.

"Please come," Fanny said. "Something is wrong with the flask. I cannot get it to hold water."

"Perhaps if I beat you you will learn how to use the flask," Bloody Knife said. "Shall I come and beat you?"

"Please come help me," Fanny said. "I cannot do this."

Bloody Knife swore at her, then stood up and started down toward the river. As he passed the rock, Matt called out to him.

"Bloody Knife, look over here, you heathen bastard!"

Bloody Knife turned quickly toward the sound of the voice, and, even as he turned, a knife appeared in his hand.

Matt pulled his own knife out and the two of them faced each other, each crouched in a fighting stance. Their right arms were held out with the blade of their knives projecting from their hands and the points moving slowly. They were like the tongues of snakes, facing each other in a dance of death.

"No, Matt, don't fight him that way," Fanny said. "Shoot him."

"There are Indian war parties all around here," Matt said. "I've been avoiding them for the last three days. A shot would bring them."

"They are looking for Bloody Knife. They won't harm us," Fanny said.

Matt smiled at Bloody Knife. "So, you've even got your own people after you now, have you?"

"Matt, shoot him," Fanny called again, but when Matt tried to reach for his pistol, Bloody Knife slashed at his hand, bringing on a sudden stream of bright, red blood.

"Try to shoot me," Bloody Knife said, grinning evilly. "I will kill you before you can do it."

"He's got a point there," Matt told Fanny. "I really don't have time to mess around with him."

Matt danced in then, lightly for a big man, and he raised his injured left hand toward Bloody Knife's face to mask his action. He feinted with his knife hand, then when he saw Bloody Knife react the way he wanted, he stepped in and jabbed quickly, sending the blade of his knife into Bloody Knife's diaphragm, just under the ribs.

Bloody Knife made a small, gasping sound, and he stood there in the moonlight for a long, long, second. The knife slipped out of his hand, and he looked toward Fanny with an expression of surprise on his face. "Now, I can rest," he said. He smiled, then, finally he began to fall, expelling a long, life-surrendering sigh as he did.

"Do you have a horse?" Matt asked, putting his knife away.

"Yes," Fanny said. "That is, Bloody Knife has one." She looked for a long moment at the one who had been her enemy, and for some inexplicable reason, she felt a small sadness.

Matt was wrapping his hand with a handkerchief. "Get it," he said. "He sure won't be needing it."

The next morning, Fanny sat up quickly and looked around. For a moment she had to think of where she was, then, when she saw Matt Parker bent over a campfire, she knew.

"I've already made biscuits," Matt said. "And I'm cookin' up a little camp stew, using beans and dried deer meat. I hope that suits you. Oh, and there's coffee here."

"Coffee?" Fanny said. "Oh, do you know how long it's been since I've had coffee?"

Matt smiled and poured a cup, then he brought it and a pan of his 'camp stew', along with a couple of biscuits over to her.

"I remember when you brought me my supper once," he said.

Fanny was so hungry it was all she could to to keep from wolfing down the food. "That seems so long ago," she said. "And it seems almost as if it happened to someone else."

Matt brought his own breakfast over and settled down beside her. "I've been looking for you ever since that time," he said. "I've searched the Snake, I've been all the way up to Wind River Canyon, the Tetons, Yellowstone, I've been everyhwere."

"I was beginning to think that I was going to spend the rest of my life with the Indians," Fanny said.

"I heard you were married to Ottawa," Matt said. "How'd you wind up with Bloody Knife?"

Fanny looked at the ground in quick shame. "You heard I was married to Ottawa?"

"Yes."

"How did you hear that?"

"I heard it from Wounded Foot. I was in the Minneconjou village when the cavalry hit them."

"You were one of the two white men!" Fanny said.

"Yes. The other was a fella by the name of Mountain Charley. Have you ever heard of him?"

"Yes, I've heard the Indians speak of him," Fanny said. "They say he hasn't been seen since the day of the lying down death."

"The lying down death?"

"That's what the Indians call the fight at Wounded Foot's village," Fanny explained.

"Their name is quite descriptive," Matt said. He poured the last dregs of his coffee onto the fire. "It wasn't a fight, it was a massacre. The cavalry attacked early in the morning while everyone was asleep. They murdered everyone, indiscriminately; old men, young women, children, even babies." Matt looked at Fanny. "Your husband led the attack."

"I know," Fanny said quietly. "Soldier-Who-Is-A-Coward."

"You've heard the name too?"

"It is the only name the Indians use when talking about him. Did he tell you I was still alive?"

Matt laughed a short, bitter laugh. "Are you kidding? He insists that he saw you killed. He said he saw you and the little girl, Mary, cut down by an Indian's war club."

"Fergus killed Mary himself," Fanny said.

"What?"

"He was running away, fleeing from the battle. I tried to get him to take Mary and he ran her down. She was killed by his horse."

"That son-of-a-bitch," Matt swore.

"Did you hear of the fight in Devils' Room?"

"No," Matt said.

"Fergus was leading one company of men when Bloody Knife ambushed them. Bloody Knife killed many and a few were trapped. Fergus was taken prisoner, and he traded the lives of his remaining soldiers, for his own life."

"Fanny, surely, you don't want to go back to him, do you?"

"No," Fanny said. She looked down toward the ground, and tears came to her eyes. "I don't know what I want to do now," she said. "Everything is so confusing. I just don't understand anything, anymore."

Matt put his hand gently on her neck. "Don't cry and force yourself to understand anything yet," he said. "You've been through one hell of an ordeal. You need rest."

It was the first tenderness Fanny had been shown since Jumping Bear, and she reached up and held Matt's hand in hers for a moment. She felt Matt tense, then he stood up and took a few steps away, looking out over the valley where they were camped.

"We'll camp here for a while," Matt said. "The

buffalo are south of us, so I don't think we'll have any problems with the Indians. You just rest."

Fanny was a little hurt by the fact that Matt had pulled away from her. Then, she realized that what people said must be true. After all, if she had been with an Indian, she must somehow be 'tainted'.

"Yes," Fanny said quietly. "I'll rest." She sighed, and looked out over the valley.

The trees in the valley were full of flowers, while the valley itself was a profusion of color as wild flowers filled the air with their sweet perfume. Behind them a brook splashed and bubbled as it wended its way through the valley. It was as beautiful as any park.

"I'm going to check that glen of trees down there," Matt said. "I saw deer sign. We could use a little fresh meat."

"Yes," Fanny said. "That would be good." Fanny spoke the words quietly, without looking at Matt, and Matt turned back toward her.

"What's wrong?"

"Why do you ask what's wrong?"

"I don't know, you don't seem very happy to be free."

"Should I be?"

Matt sighed. "Look here, Fanny, what are you trying to tell me? Are you trying to say that you *want* to go back to the Indians?"

"Don't you think I should?"

"If I thought you should, would I have spent the last year looking for you?"

Tears began to roll down Fanny's face. "Now that you've found me, are you sorry?"

"Sorry? Of course, I'm not sorry. Why would you ask such a thing?"

"Because I'm tainted," Fanny said.

"Tainted? Fanny, girl, for the life of me, I don't know what the hell you are talking about."

"Yes, you do know," Fanny said. "Do you think I didn't feel it when you tightened up a minute ago? I put my hand on yours and you pulled it away."

"For God's sake, girl, is *that* what this is all about?" Matt asked. He moved to her quickly and put his arms around her. "I . . . . I just didn't want to rush things, that's all. I didn't want to frighten you. Fanny, if I can't prove my love for you by looking for you for one solid year, how can I ever prove it?"

Now a year of fear, sorrow, anxiety and uncertainty all came to the surface at the same time, and Fanny began to cry. She cried huge tears, for herself and her ordeal, for Mary, and the other passengers of the wagon train, for the soldiers, and, yes, for Jumping Bear and Running Rabbit. And all the while she cried, Matt cushioned her head on his shoulder, comforting her.

Fanny wasn't certain when the comforting changed to wanting, and when the closeness became need, but when they lay down full length, body against body, kissing, it felt right and natural to her, and for that moment all which had gone before had never existed. There was no time of travail with the Indians, and there was no Fergus Kelly. There was only Matt and Fanny, together in this garden of paradise.

As Fanny thought such thoughts, Matt moved

his sure and exciting hands over her body, easily slipping the deerskin dress up over her head so that she was nude before him. Quickly, he slipped out of his own clothes, then came to her.

Matt moved his fingers across Fanny's smooth body, over the curves, and across the breasts, stopping at the nipples, so small and tight after the velvety firm feel of her skin.

Fanny delighted not only in the touch of him, but in the smells; sun-warmed skin, fragrant flowers, pungent earth, even her own musk. She pulled Matt to her, using him to purge away the evil brutalizing she had suffered under Bloody Knife.

Matt kissed her with lips of fire, and Fanny tasted his tongue, drawing it hungrily into her own mouth. Then, when he took her with a deep, sensory-laden thrust, she raised to meet him, pushing against him to take the pleasure of it, and share the joy of it. Her body was like the tall, prairie grass, waving before the restless winds, moving in undulating waves and promising more.

Then, like the crack of lightning and the peal of thunder, a pleasure broke over her, as intense as a ripping summer storm, greater still than any sensation she had ever felt before.

Fanny didn't try to control her reaction to the orgasm. She let the sounds of joy and the moans of pleasure escape from her lips, and she threw her arms around Matt, pulling him to her, trying to accept all of him into her womb. Then the lightning struck again, twice, three times, and finally a fourth which was greater than all the others, and it stayed with her for several dizzying seconds, so intense that she felt as if she would pass out from the sheer joy of it. She arched her body again, bridging against him, holding him in her as she felt him join her in the maelstrom of pleasure.

Finally they both collapsed back into the grass, and lay in each other's arms, feeling at one with each other, and at one with the vast panorama of nature which had been stage for their act of love.

"I love you, Fanny," Matt said quietly and sincerely. "I've loved you from the moment I first saw you, back in Fort Laramie. I've chased you for one year, and I'll never let you go again. Never."

Fanny felt his body next to hers, still warm from the fires they had kindled, and she thought of what he had said. One year ago, when she had been Fergus Kelly's wife, she had wanted to do this, but if she had done it she would have been so consumed with guilt that she would have suffered from it for the rest of her life.

She didn't feel that way now. Her experience with the Indians had given her the ability to go right to the truth of things, and she knew that a feeling of guilt now would be an exercise in hypocrisy.

Did she love Matt Parker? She didn't really know. Certainly no one had ever made her feel the way he just had, and certainly no one had ever been a more welcome sight than he had been. And there had been many times over the past year when she had thought of him, and remembered the stolen kiss and the pleasure of her fantasies about him. She wasn't ready yet to say that physical pleasure, and gratitude were enough to make her believe she was in love with him, but neither would she let a little thing like the fact that she was still married to Fergus Kelly stand in her way if love should come. If Matt would have her, she would go with him from this day forward.

20

"THEY ARE back there, sir," the Sergeant Major said. "They are both lying on their bunks."

The Sergeant Major was speaking to Colonel Albertson, who had just stepped inside the unlisted barracks.

Colonel Albertson looked down the long row of empty bunks and saw the two men he was looking for, lying in their bunks at the end of the row. In contrast to the Colonel and the Sergeant Major, both of whom were dressed in their finest uniforms, the two men were wearing only their duty uniforms.

Colonel Albertson cleared his throat, then walked down to stand at the foot of the bunks. The two men saw him, then jumped up, coming to attention.

"Well, at least you have enough sense to come to attention when I approach you," Colonel Albertson said angrily.

"You are an officer, sir," Corporal O'Grady said. "You have our respect."

"Well, that's good to know," Colonel Albertson said. "That's truly good to know. Now, would you mind telling me just what in the hell is going on here?"

"What do you mean, sir?" Corporal O'Grady asked.

"What do I mean?" Colonel Albertson replied, exploding with the question. He pointed toward the quadrangle. "Don't you realize that the entire garrison is in formation out there, waiting for the Medal of Honor to be presented to Major Fergus Kelly? There has never been a Medal of Honor given in this theater of operations before, and it is an honor to us all."

" 'Tis a load of shit, sir," Corporal O'Grady said.

"What? What did you say?" Colonel Albertson gasped, nearly choking.

"He means it's all a sham, Colonel," Babcock put in quickly. "And we want no part of it. Perhaps the Colonel would like to hear the whole story?"

Colonel Albertson glared at the two soldiers for a long moment, then he looked back toward the Sergeant Major, and he sighed. "Sergeant Major, suppose you step outside for a while, and let me talk to these two men?"

"You sure you don't want me to stay, sir? I can guarantee you that I'll get them straightened out . . . . if I have to put them in the guardhouse for six months apiece."

"No, that's quite all right," Colonel Albertson said. "Please, just wait in the sallyport for a while."

"Very well, sir," the Sergeant Major said, and he saluted, then left the barracks, so that only Colonel Albertson and the two men were left in the long room full of empty bunks.

"All right," Colonel Albertson said, after the Sergeant Major had left. "We are all alone. Suppose you two tell me just what the problem is here?"

The two men looked at each other, then O'Grady spoke. "We don't want to take part in this ceremony, Colonel. We don't believe it's right."

"I see," Colonel Albertson said. "Is it because you feel that you should deserve the medal as well? Because if it is, let me say that, upon Captain . . . . excuse me, I mean upon *Major* Kelly's recommendation, I put both of you in for the same award."

"Kelly put us in for it, did he?" O'Grady asked.

"Yes he did," Colonel Albertson said. "He spoke most highly of your bravery and your dedication to duty. I'm only sorry that the War Department didn't see it the same way Major Kelly and I saw it, but at least we tried. And this is how you show your gratitude?"

"Colonel, iffen this formation was for us, I'd'a done more than just stay in here. I'd'a probl'y lit outta here," O'Grady said scornfully.

"I'm afraid I don't understand."

"It's just that we aren't like Soldier-Who-Is-A-Coward," Babcock said. "We won't take something we didn't earn."

"Soldier-Who-Is-A-Coward? What are you talking about?"

"That's the name the Indians have for Major Kelly, sir," Babcock said.

"Why, why, that's preposterous! Why would the Indians give Fergus Kelly such a name? He has shown his bravery time, and time again."

"Colonel, I'm going to tell you what really happened at the battle of Devil's Room," Babcock said. "I wanted to tell you before, but Corporal O'Grady had too much respect for the army, and he wouldn't let me tell it. Now we have too much respect *not* to tell the true story."

"Sit down," Colonel Albertson said, and as the men sat on their bunks, he sat on a nearby trunk. "I want you to explain to me, if you can, what this is all about."

The soldiers who were standing in formation out in the quadrangle had all been given the command of 'at ease', and they shifted their weight restlessly from foot to foot. Despite the fact that they weren't standing at attention, the long wait was beginning to take its toll, because the relentless sun beat down upon them as they stood row after row in their hot, dress blue uniforms, and sweat was running in rivulets down their backs. One by one the men began passing out, sometimes groaning, sometimes falling silently, while a team of first aid men hurried through the formation picking up those who had fallen out, carrying them back to let them lie in the shade of the wall. It would have been a good way of getting out of the formation, except for the fact that anyone who passed out had to pull two weeks of extra duty.

The question that was running through the ranks, whispered because the men weren't supposed to speak at the position of at ease, was "Why haven't we started? What's holding us up?"

Though the formation had been called to honor Major Fergus Kelly, no one was more uneasy at this moment, than Fergus Kelly himself. He was standing in front of the assembled formation of men, just under the shadow of the flagpole. He was supposed to have received his medal thirty minutes ago, but, as yet, the Colonel hadn't showed up. What is the problem? he wondered. Has something gone wrong?

It was not only the soldiers who were assembled, but the entire garrison, to include wives, laundresses, assigned scouts and civilians, and even several visitors. In fact, there were nearly as many civilians present for the ceremony, as there were soldiers.

One of the civilians was a big, bear of a man, with a full, bushy, red beard, and long scraggly red hair. He was dressed in buckskins and buffalo robes, and he smelled of the trail. Most who happened near him, were giving him a wide berth, staying upwind of him when possible.

"Lieutenant Masters," Fergus called, when the waiting was beginning to become unbearable.

"Yes, sir?"

"Find out what the problem is," Fergus ordered. He smiled, as if he were concerned about the men, and not worried about the ceremony itself. "We can't keep the troops in the sun forever, can we?"

"No, sir," Masters said.

Fergus watched the Lieutenant walk across the

quadrangle, then he turned his head back toward the men. He was looking at them, but he wasn't seeing them. At least, he wasn't seeing all of them. He was seeing again, the two men who had appeared at the gates of the Fort the day after the Indians had let him go. Corporal O'Grady and Private Babcock had arrived the next day, doubled up on one horse.

Kelly had been terrified by their arrival, and had even considered running away. But, oddly, the men never said a word. Not one word! Once, he had tried to talk to them, to see what they wanted, but they acted as if they didn't understand what he was talking about. The fact that they knew of his shame, acted on Kelly as if he were sitting on a bomb, with a slow-burning fuse. It was going to explode someday, he knew that. It was merely a question of when.

Now Kelly searched the ranks, looking for the two men. They had both been reassigned, due to the fact that their entire company had been wiped out in the battle, and that made it difficult to find them. Where were they?

As Kelly searched the ranks for O'Grady and Babcock, he saw Masters returning. "Yes, what is the problem?" Kelly asked.

"It's O'Grady and Babcock," Masters said.

"O'Grady and Babcock? What . . . . what about them?" Fergus asked, his voice rising in fear. No wonder he couldn't find them in the ranks.

"I don't know. The Sergeant Major says they refused to attend the ceremony. Colonel Albertson is in talking with them now."

"What's he talking to them about?" Fergus asked

anxiously. "Why won't they come to the formation?"

"I don't know," Masters said. "Perhaps it has something to do with the fact that they were put in separate companies. You know how sensitive the enlisted men are to something like that."

"Yes, perhaps so," Fergus said.

Masters turned and started to walk away, but before he had gone more than a few steps he stopped and looked back.

"By the way, Major, I just heard that there is a trapper here who is telling a rather unbelievable story about Matt Parker. Have you heard it?"

"A story about Matt Parker? I wouldn't be surprised about anything one might tell about that man. What is it?"

"It concerns your wife," Masters said. "The trapper claims that Fanny is still alive, and she is living with Matt Parker." Masters laughed. "Now, isn't that the most ridiculous thing you've ever heard?"

"Yes," Fergus said. "Who is this trapper, anyway? And what's he doing here? This isn't the season for trading."

"I don't know anything about him. The story is he is looking for a soldier, someone the Indians call Soldier-Who-Is-A-Coward."

"What?" Fergus asked, gasping and turning white. "Who did you say he is looking for?"

"Someone called Soldier-Who-Is-A-Coward." Masters laughed. "How would you like to be hung with a name like that?"

"That trapper shouldn't be allowed in here," Fergus said. "Have him run off."

"Why? He isn't doing any harm, is he? Besides, Colonel Albertson wanted to open the post to everyone today. He's as proud of your medal as if he were getting it himself."

"But a man like that, calling soldiers cowards, he's bad for the troop morale," Fergus said nervously. "Take two men and escort him out of the fort."

"If you say so," Lieutenant Masters said. "Oh, oh, too late now. Here comes the Sergeant Major. I guess we are about ready to get started."

"Good," Fergus said. "Good, we've waited long enough to . . . . why is the Colonel going into the headquarters building? Why isn't he coming over here for the award ceremony?"

"I don't know," Masters said. "Maybe the Sergeant Major will know."

The Sergeant Major came up to the two officers, stopped, then saluted. "Major Kelly, the Colonel wishes to speak with you in his office, sir. Lieutenant Masters, the Colonel sends his regards sir, and asks you to dismiss the formation."

"Dismiss the formation? But what about the awards ceremony?" Lieutenant Masters asked.

"I don't know anything about that, sir," the Sergeant Major said. "Perhaps he'll tell the Major."

Fergus barely heard the last exchange. All he heard was the fact that the Colonel wanted to see him in his office. Why? And why had the medal not been given?

They had talked! There was no doubt about it now, O'Grady and Babcock had talked, no doubt telling the Colonel all sorts of lies! The same kind

of lies the trapper was telling when he said that
Fanny had been found and was living with Matt
Parker.

"Sir? Sir, didn't you hear me? The Colonel wants
to see you," the sergeant Major said again.

"Oh, I'm sorry," Fergus said. "I'll go at once
to see what he wants."

Fergus started across the quadrangle toward the
Colonel's office, but half way there he stopped,
and looked toward the enlisted men's barracks.
They were in there, laughing and joking, and enjoying the damage their lies had done. How did
they survive the Indians, anyway? Why weren't
they dead like the others were? It would have been
much better if they had died.

Perhaps he could take care of that now, he
thought. Perhaps he could correct the mistake the
Indians made when they let the two men live.
Bloody Knife had gone back on his word! He said
he would kill the others. Didn't he realize what
trouble this caused?

Fergus turned, and headed not for the commandant's building, but for the enlisted barracks,
where Babcock and O'Grady waited. As he walked
toward the barracks he unfastened the flap which
held his pistol down, and loosened it in his hol-
ster. He would show them. He would show them
that he wouldn't stand for their lies!

Fergus stepped up onto the porch, and as he
did so, he heard the sound of laughter inside. They
were laughing at him! Well, he would see who
had the last laugh! He pushed the door open, drawing his pistol as he stepped through the door.

"Babcock, O'Grady!" he called, and the two men looked toward him. Both saw his pistol, and their expressions reflected their fright.

"What are you going to do, Major?" O'Grady asked.

Fergus smiled, an evil little smile.

"I'm going to kill you," he said. "I'm going to kill both of you." He took deliberate aim, and cocked the pistol.

"You can't get away with it!" Babcock said. "The Colonel knows everything now. He'll know what happened!"

"It'll be my word against yours," Fergus said. "Only you'll be dead, so my word will have more weight."

"How are you going to explain what happened?" Babcock asked. "How are you going to explain killing us?"

"It's simple. I'll tell the Colonel I came to talk to you, to try and get you to confess to your lies and you threatened my life. I had no alternative but to shoot you."

"But we aren't even armed!"

"There are two of you," Fergus said. "There is an ax on the wall behind you. It will be found near your bodies."

"Turn around, Soldier-Who-Is-A-Coward," an ominous voice suddenly said from behind Fergus. "Turn around, you son-of-a-bitch. I want you to look into the face of the man who is going to kill you."

Fergus grew white, and he let the gun lower just a quarter of an inch. "Who is it?" he asked. "Who are you?"

"My name is Charles Gwaltney," the voice said. "Mountain Charley to most people. Now you know who I am, turn around so you can see what I look like. When you go to hell I want my face to be the last thing you see."

Fergus's lips started quivering. "But why? Why do you want to kill me?"

"Because you killed Sasha."

"Sasha? I've never even heard of someone named Sasha. I don't even know who you are talking about."

"That makes it worse, you bastard. You killed her and you didn't even care enough to find out who she was. Now turn around or I'll shoot you in the back!"

"No, I, I won't turn around," Fergus said. "I'm going to put my gun down, now, and if you shoot me, it'll be murder. These men . . . . they'll be witnesses."

"What say you 'n me take a stroll over to the Suttler's Store?" O'Grady said to Babcock, as if it were no more than a casual Sunday afternoon.

"We might as well," Babcock said. "There's nothing going on around here."

"No!" Fergus shouted. "You must stay! Can't you see? He's trying to . . . ," suddenly Fergus whirled around. He was faster than Mountain Charley would have thought, and he caught Mountain Charley by surprise, so he managed to squeeze off a shot. The bullet hit Mountain Charley in the shoulder, but Mountain Charley returned fire with his rifle, filling the end of the barracks with a flash of fire and a cloud of smoke. When the smoke rolled away, Mountain Charley was leaning against the door jamb, holding his shoulder. Blood spilled between his fingers and ran down his sleeve.

Sprawled on the floor in front of Mountain Charley, belly up, with a large, gaping hole in the middle of his chest, lay Major Fergus Kelly. His eyes were still wide open, but the expression of fear was gone now. All expression was gone, because his features had already taken on the sombre countenance of death.

"What is it? What happened?" someone shouted, and moments later dozens of soldiers were crowding into the barracks, drawn there by the sound of the shots.

"Arrest that man!" one of the Sergeants called, pointing to Mountain Charley.

"No!" O'Grady called out. "No, he saved our lives."

"What? What do you mean he saved your lives? He killed Major Kelly."

"Let him go," Colonel Albertson's voice said then, and, seeing the commander, someone called attention so that everyone grew quiet. Colonel Albertson stepped inside and looked down at Fergus Kelly's sprawled body. "Sergeant, get a burial detail together. We'll bury him today."

"Today, sir?" the Sergeant asked, surprised at the quick disposition of the body.

"Yes. The quicker our post is rid of this man, the better off we'll be."

"But I don't understand, sir," the Sergeant said. "I thought he was going to get the Medal of Honor."

"That's all changed," Colonel Albertson said. He walked over to Mountain Charley. "It doesn't look